QUICK ON THE DRAW

Recent Titles by Susan Moody

MISSELTHWAITE
FALLING ANGEL
RETURN TO THE SECRET GARDEN
LOSING NICOLA *
DANCING IN THE DARK *
LOOSE ENDS *
A FINAL RECKONING *

The Alex Quick Series

QUICK AND THE DEAD *
QUICK OFF THE MARK *

* available from Severn House

QUICK ON THE DRAW

Susan Moody

This first world edition published 2018
in Great Britain and the USA by
SEVERN HOUSE PUBLISHERS LTD of
Eardley House, 4 Uxbridge Street, London W8 7SY.
Trade paperback edition first published
in Great Britain and the USA 2018 by
SEVERN HOUSE PUBLISHERS LTD.

British Library Cataloguing in Publication Data
A CIP catalogue record for this title is available from the British Library.

ISBN-13: 978-0-7278-8731-3 (cased)
ISBN-13: 978-1-84751-845-3 (trade paper)
ISBN-13: 978-1-78010-905-3 (e-book)

All Severn House titles are printed on acid-free paper.

Severn House Publishers support the Forest Stewardship Council™ [FSC™],
the leading international forest certification organisation.
All our titles that are printed on FSC certified paper carry the FSC logo.

Typeset by Palimpsest Book Production Ltd.,
Falkirk, Stirlingshire, Scotland.
Printed and bound in Great Britain by
TJ International, Padstow, Cornwall.

ONE

Sandro Grainger is probably the most beautiful human being I've ever met. Or ever expect to. Sitting opposite him in the upmarket Kensington restaurant he'd chosen for this meeting, I felt as though I was lunching with a flesh-and-blood Botticelli angel. Plentiful blond-tipped brown hair pushed carelessly back from his face, skin the colour and consistency of beige satin, chocolate-brown eyes surrounded by thick gold eyelashes, a full Pre-Raphaelite mouth. Magnificent. And not in the least bit effeminate. A perfect blend of his parents: Dominic's classic Anglo-Saxon good looks mingled with Maddalena's dark Mediterranean beauty.

I'd met them many times, since Maddalena was a cousin of my Italian brother-in-law, Carlo. I'd even spent holiday time at their villa on Corfu, along with Carlo and his wife, my sister, Meghan. The Graingers were legendarily rich. As well as Corfu, there was the house in Rome, the house in London and an apartment in New York. Plus vast tracts of southern England.

As for Sandro, I'd known him for years, first as an adorable toddler, then as a beguiling and – mercifully – pimple-free adolescent, and then as an almost-adult in his early twenties. We went back a long way, but sadly only on an occasional and casual basis. I wasn't quite old enough to be his mother, unless I'd been knocked up by some perv. So it came as something of a surprise when he'd telephoned and asked me out for lunch. Flattered? Not really. Obviously he wanted something.

I swallowed the last morsel of my chocolate cheesecake, wiped my mouth with my starched linen napkin and leaned back in my chair. 'OK, Sandro,' I said. 'Nitty-gritty time. So spill.'

His eyes slid away from mine. 'Uh . . .' he said.

'Your company is delightful,' I said. 'And I've very much

enjoyed our extremely good lunch. But I can't kid myself that a twenty-five-year-old guy such as yourself would seek out a woman of my age if he didn't have some kind of an agenda. Am I right?'

He squirmed. 'Uh . . .'

'So level with me.'

He fiddled with his water glass, then with the salt cellar in front of him. Picked up his dessert fork and put it down again. 'Thing is, Alex . . .' He fell silent.

'Yes?' I encouraged.

'Look, I know . . .' Another silence. He rootled in a pocket, brought out a small Swiss Army knife, put it back. I got the impression that he was not at ease.

'Which is more than I do,' I said.

'Uh . . .' He cleared his throat. 'You used to be a police officer.'

'This is true.'

'So you must be something of a detective.'

I smiled. 'And you want me to do some detecting on your behalf?'

His face relaxed. He gave a half-laugh. 'Ex*act*ly.' He gazed round the room like someone whose troubles were finally over.

'This is fascinating stuff, Sandro. But could you give me some further details?'

He thought about it, then sighed. 'Yeah. I guess I have to.'

'Otherwise there's not a whole lot I can do.'

'I quite see that.' More nervous fiddling with salt and pepper. More twisting of the water glass.

'Sandro!' I placed my hand on top of his. 'For goodness' sake, tell me what the problem is.'

'OK.' He nodded fiercely to himself. 'So, earlier this year, I was staying in my Uncle Cesare's place in Venice, while he and my aunt were attending some high-level meetings in Geneva. He is the Marchese Cesare Antonio de Farnese de Peron, to give him his full title, and has this rather grand apartment in one of the *palazzi* along the Grand Canal. And I decided to hold a dinner party, you know, a real grown-up dinner party, to celebrate my birthday. Catered, private chef, black tie and all. My generation tends to go round in ripped jeans all the time, so I thought it would be fun to dress up a bit.' His eyes were wide with earnest sincerity, while I thought that many of his generation probably weren't able to afford much more than jeans, ripped or otherwise.

'Sounds great. How many people did you invite?'

'Just ten. Well, nine really, since I was one of them.' He laughed nervously. 'Was going to be eight, but at the last moment Tony – my girlfriend's brother – decided to come after all.'

'And all went well? Nobody threw *pasta con vongole* at the priceless tapestries, or drew a moustache on the Contessa's portrait?'

'Of course not!' He seemed shocked. 'My friends are all very . . . *beneducato*. Well-bred. They know how to behave.'

'Even well-brought-up young people can go off the rails.'

'Of course. Anyway, the next day I had cleaners in to make sure the apartment was immaculate before my aunt and uncle came back. Naturally I'd asked my uncle's permission to hold the party, because if there's one thing I don't want to do, it's to get into Cesare's bad books. He can be . . . fierce.' Sandro shuddered dramatically. 'I mean *fierce*!'

'So what do you need me for?'

'Well . . .' Sandro hesitated. 'I still can't quite believe this, but I was walking down New Bond Street the other day and I noticed a ring in the window of a pawnshop. It looked exactly like a ring that has been in my uncle's family for generations – an heirloom supposed to have been given to one of my aunt's ancestors by some doge or other way back when, as a mark of his esteem or something. And then, when I looked closer, I could see that in fact it didn't just *look* like my uncle's ring, it *was* my uncle's ring – or my aunt's, to be more precise. Right there, in a *pawn*shop!'

His privileged young voice displayed scorn and disbelief at the very notion. Did he have any idea of the hand-to-mouth existence led by some sectors of society? How much reliance some people placed on pawnbrokers? Or, for that matter, what a respectable history the pawnshop possessed? Didn't sound like it.

I cleared my throat. 'Sandro, let me give you a little

background here. Pawnshops are not all about furtive criminals slinking in to try and fence stolen property. Nor are they men pawning the family teapot in order to get drunk before staggering home to some sordid slum in order to beat up their wife and kids. In fact, in the United States, they're often referred to as deluxe collateral lenders. They're patronized by all sections of society, people looking for short-term loans, from high-end rollers and doctors, to lawyers and even bankers, believe it or not. And the collateral these punters offer can be as upmarket as wine collections, or fine art, or cars. Even uncut diamonds. And for your further information, Isabella of Spain used a pawnshop to finance Christopher Columbus's expedition, and whichever French king it was pawned the royal jewels to raise money for the war against Henry the Fifth. There's even a famous pawnshop which was in fact a charity.'

'How come you know so much about it?'

'I had to do a research project when I was at uni,' I said.

'Well, what about *this* . . .' He choked slightly with indignation. 'A couple of days after I saw the ring, I was in an art gallery, looking for a gift for my mother, and there on the wall was a small Botticelli, a young man, head and shoulders, with a pastoral scene visible through the window behind him. Very delicate, very lovely.' He coughed. 'I couldn't believe my eyes. I went in – and again, it was my uncle's!'

'You're sure?'

'Well, to be honest, it was probably painted by an apprentice, rather than the master himself, but you'd have to be an expert to spot it. Anyway, it was definitely hanging in the *salotto* of my uncle's *appartamento* the night of my dinner party, because somebody said something about how much it looked like me.'

'So what did you do?'

'Well, naturally there was no choice. I had to buy it from the owner of the gallery. Like I did the ring from the pawnshop, earlier. And then I flew to Venice and managed to replace both objects before Uncle Cesare could return from his fundraising meetings and find them gone.'

'Problem solved, then,' I said.

'Not quite. First of all, it cost me a whole heap of money. Then I want to know who was responsible for stealing the two objects from Cesare's place – I mean, it more or less has to be one of my friends, don't you think?'

I couldn't resist saying, 'In spite of them being so well-brought-up?'

He shrugged me off. 'As you said, people can do silly things. But not as silly as stealing my uncle's prized possessions.'

'Just off the top of your head, which of them would you suspect?'

'I don't know.' For a moment, he gazed into the middle distance. He picked at one of the half-dozen charity wristbands on his arm – cotton weaving, beaded bands, plaited leather, crude plastic, some with words printed on them. Help for Heroes. Men's Health Awareness.

'I like the jewellery,' I said, nodding at them. 'What the well-dressed man about town is wearing these days.'

He flushed. 'One of Suzy's clients produces them, so she's always giving me samples to wear, in order to promote them.'

'Love indeed.'

'Whatevs.' He paused. 'But it's not just the thefts . . .'

'What else?' I asked, repressing the urge to sigh.

'The problem is, Alessandra, I also urgently need to find out if anything else was taken. Because if it was, and I'm not aware, then when my uncle finds out, I shall be in very serious trouble.'

'And how exactly do you think I can help?' The way he said my name was toe-curlingly sexy.

'I don't know. Maybe you could go and talk to them,' he suggested.

'And ask them if by any chance they stole a faux-Botticelli or a doge's ring? Or any other valuable trinket of that sort? Come on, Sandro, as far as they're concerned, I'm a total stranger. I can't just turn up and start interrogating them.'

'But you're with the police.'

'Used to be. Not any more. Besides, I don't think I'm qualified for this kind of job. Sounds to me as though you need to engage a private detective of some kind. There are plenty of them around. Look in the Yellow Pages. Or I can recommend—'

'Alessandra, you *must* do this for me. I can't have any fuss

made. Think of the scandal it would cause if anyone found
out, the shame and dishonour it would bring to my family, to
my *mamma*. It would be intolerable. I need absolute discretion.
And then . . .' He picked up his wine glass and swallowed
its contents. 'I have Sicilian blood running through my veins.
And as it says in the Bible, *la vendetta è mia*. Vengeance is
mine. When I say vengeance,' he added hastily, 'I don't mean
swords at midnight, or ground glass in the coffee. I just want
the person responsible to suffer. Well, not suffer, exactly, but
certainly to be punished in some way.'

'I always thought vengeance was the Lord's and *He* was
the one who would repay.'

Sandro waved his hands about. 'That is beside the point.'

'Would the Lord see it that way?'

'And quite apart from anything else' – Sandro wagged a
finger at me – 'to steal from your host is an appalling abuse
of hospitality.'

He sounded much as his grandfather, an Italian aristocrat
renowned for his crustiness, might have done, rather than a
guy in his twenties.

'And how am I to meet these people? Let alone begin
cross-examining them?'

'I thought of that. I shall have a small gathering in my
flat. To celebrate my mother's birthday. Invite all of them
– plus a few others. Including my aunt and uncle, of course.
Plus some people of your age.'

'Oh, *thank* you, Sandro,' I said humbly.

'Obviously also my parents and maybe a few of my
colleagues from my office. And maybe your brother – he
knows my parents. Would that work?'

'It might.'

'I'll set it up as soon as possible and let you know.'

'Won't your friends find it a bit odd, that you're having
another party so soon?'

He shook his head. 'I don't think so. I entertain a lot. And
they know that I prefer to eat at home rather than in a restaurant. Though it'll be a buffet rather than a formal sit-down
dinner. Meanwhile . . .' He reached into the inside breast
pocket of his suit and brought out a piece of A4 paper folded

into four. 'I thought you might need some more information, so here are the coordinates of the people who were at my dinner party in Venice.'

He poured out the last of the wine while I unfolded the page he'd handed me and looked at what he'd written. A list of names, basically. 'So expand, Sandro,' I said.

'Well, for a start, all of them have one parent who is Italian and one who is English. Like me. So they're all equally at home in either country. And they're all kind of interconnected. For instance, I went to school with Harry and Jack Jago. Fabio Wisdom is a great friend of Katy Pasqualin – their mothers are cousins. And Katy herself is one of my Aunt Allegra's nieces, so is a sort of cousin to me as well.'

'And what does Katy do?'

'She's the manager of an art gallery in Kensington.'

In other words, one of those as-soon-as-my-boyfriend-proposes-I'm-outta-here sort of jobs. I could just imagine her, all designer scarves and big ethnic necklaces made of lava and seal tusks, with expensive patent leather shoes on her elegant feet.

'She's also a bit of a championship swimmer,' continued Sandro, surprising me. 'And Fabio is a fashion designer in Milan. He's just set up his own evening gown label. Then there's Laura, who's a model. Not in the Claudia Schiffer or Cara Delevingne class yet, but on the way there. She's done quite a few shows for Fabio.'

'And . . . uh . . .' I looked down at the list in my hand. 'Bianca Mondori?'

'She works in the City. Like I do.'

'What about your girlfriend?'

'Suzy?'

I scanned the sheet of paper. 'Suzy Hartley Haywood.' I knew the name because she was always in the trash mags: seen in a nightclub with Prince Harry, holidaying in a minuscule bikini in Malibu, flaunting her luscious attributes as she falls out of her dress (as the tabloids have it) at some glitzy function or other. Despite my best efforts, I could feel my lips purse. Miss Hartley Haywood didn't sound like high quality daughter-in-law material.

'She's with a PR company,' Sandro said.

'Makes sense.'

'And her brother, Tony, works with his parents at their stud farm near Cheltenham.'

'What do Harry and Jack do?'

'They're twins. They farm. Or maybe you could call it more of a large allotment than an actual farm.' He grinned at me, showing the kind of beautiful white teeth it takes thousands of pounds to achieve. 'No, that's not fair. It's like a cottage industry, really, very small, which is how they want to keep it. They're not far from the Hartley Haywoods, as a matter of fact. They're into healthy eating, growing organic kind of stuff. Honey and fresh herbs, dodgy-looking vegetables, genuine free-range eggs, peat-raised cabbages. That sort of thing. Vegetable boxes, it's called. It's all the rage. You subscribe to their website for a year, and they deliver a big box of seasonal fresh stuff to you once or twice a week or fortnight. As often as you like.'

'Sounds like a good idea.'

'I'll say. They're making a packet.'

'Your friends sound like a busy lot.'

'They are.' Sandro's face drooped. 'I just can't believe that these thefts have anything to do with any of them.'

'If you absolutely had to name one of them in particular, or think one of them is more capable of this theft than the others, who would it be?'

'If I absolutely had to . . .' He paused, then shook his head. 'I can't. I've known them most of my life. I'd have said they were all absolutely trustworthy.'

'But if it was life or death . . .'

'I suppose I'd . . .' He dragged the words out reluctantly. 'Tony Hartley Haywood. Suzy's brother. But only because there was some trouble at his tennis club, years ago . . . He was accused of stealing somebody's engagement ring. It turned up again, but people said that was only because he got scared he'd be found out, so he dropped it in the girl's sports bag where it was bound to be found. Tony can be a bit of a . . .' He failed to complete the sentence, but I got the drift anyway.

'Hmm . . . What about the cleaners in Venice, who came

in the day after your dinner party? Or one of the catering staff?'

'I don't think it could have been the caterers because we were all still around long after they'd packed up and gone. As for the cleaners, I imagine they'd have been too scared to steal anything, with my uncle's *governante* – housekeeper – right there, keeping a beady eye on them. Besides, I already checked, and all the staff who came that morning have been with the company for years. My family has used them many, many times before. And why steal something on that particular day, with all of us still hanging around, when they've had so many other opportunities?'

'So you think it boils down to being one of your guests?'

Sandro nodded, looking absolutely miserable. 'It almost has to be.'

'Does the fact that you discovered the two artefacts – the ring and the painting – in London point to anyone in particular?'

'Not necessarily. All my friends live or work both here and in Italy. As I said, I went to school with the guys, and the girls are the daughters of my parents' friends – as well as being part of my crowd, I mean.' He ran his hands through his beautiful hair. 'It's an absolute nightmare.'

'I can see it's not an ideal situation. Have you told any of them about any of this?'

'I wasn't going to, but Katy kind of hinted at something she'd noticed while they were all in Venice. The worst thing of all is that Suzy was one of the guests. Suppose it's her? What on earth would I do?'

'Dump her?'

'But I *love* her,' he said.

Ah, the artlessness of youth, I thought. I patted his hand in Great-Aunty mode. 'I'm sure we can sort this out, one way or another. Meanwhile, right now I've got to get to another appointment, so I'll have to leave very soon.'

'Will you help me? You knowing my parents and all?'

I sighed. 'I'll try. But I really can't see how much assistance I can offer. So I warn you, I absolutely can't promise anything.'

'Thank you, *cara* Alessandra!' He beamed at me, as though all his troubles were over. I wished I felt as much confidence.

TWO

'Remind me why we came here,' I said.

'It's supposed to be the in-est place in town,' said my companion, though he sounded doubtful, as if he might have made a mistake and come to the wrong pub. He looked away from me as he said it.

I squirmed a bit on the tiny barstool I was sitting on, set up next to a high Frisbee-sized table on a stick which barely had room to hold our glasses and a small bowl of mixed nuts.

'That would be as in the most "in", would it?' I gave the phrase an ironic little twist, and hoped my lips didn't have one too.

The guy wasn't digging the sarcasm. He stared round the room, attention on almost anyone else but me. Just as well, or he'd have picked up my mood by now. Been aware of the atmosphere on my side of the table. The place was heaving with posers and pseuds, City-types for the most part. Hedge-fund managers, financial consultants, bankers, eyeing up the competition, scoping out the potential, white linen or blue-striped cotton shirts unbuttoned at the neck with silk ties trailing from pockets just to assure their panting public that they had one. Diamond studs in earlobes, faces gleaming with moisturiser. More Louis Vuitton wallets than you could shake a stick at. One or two were even wearing funky designer sunglasses. Oh, please. Sunnies, at this time of night, in this dimly lit bar? But perhaps I was being uncharitable and they all had chronic eye problems. None of them seemed to be in the slightest bit worried about the results of the recent refer-endum and the dire financial prognostications issuing daily from government sources.

Boredom had set in maybe twenty minutes ago. Or was it weeks? Possibly longer. I was losing the will to live. But I was hanging on in there because my companion – Darren Carver, an affected and fairly dislikeable wannabe who was hoping to make a name for himself as 'artistic', without actually putting in the man-hours in learning how to draw, paint, sculpt or blow bubbles – was the editor of a trendy new art magazine, thanks to the modest pile of money he'd recently inherited from a devoted aunt/godmother/cousin. I wasn't sure which. He had specifically invited me up to London to discuss an article – or with luck, a series of them – on painting in Venice in general, and contemporary art in particular.

Why me? Maybe because I'd recently been a guest contributor on *I Know What I Like*, a blog written by a friend which had become something of a must-read for the arterati. Or maybe because he thought that since I wasn't based in London, he'd get me cheaper. If so, he was in for a nasty shock.

I'm not a sucker. Maybe once, but not any more. I'd joined the police fast-track programme from a vague desire to do good, fallen for and married Jack Martin, a fellow copper. I was blissfully in love, I'd reached the rank of detective inspector at an early age and, to crown it all, I discovered I was pregnant. I also discovered Jack 'Love Rat' Martin had been having an affair with a manicurist from the local beauty parlour more or less from the day of our wedding. In fact, thinking back, it had probably begun on the *day* of our wedding. I would have forgiven him, but when I told him I was expecting our child, he said he wasn't ready for fatherhood, wasn't sure he ever would be, and wasn't even ready to be a husband. And then he took off for the beauty parlour lady – with whom he'd subsequently had several children. The possibility of running into him at the station was so unbearable that I felt I had no choice but to resign from the force. Needing something to take my mind off the disaster my life had turned into, and given my fine arts degree, I started compiling a portfolio of famous paintings and drawings of babies and children and writing text to place alongside each one. It was intended for my coming child. And then came an even worse disaster. A miscarriage! I didn't think I'd ever get over it. But to my surprise, *Baby, Baby* was picked up by a small publisher (who'd heard of it from a friend of a friend) in time for the Christmas market. It proved a big hit, and led me into a whole new life. Nonetheless, I'd lost any faith I might once have had in the human race, and had grown a skin of cynicism and mistrust to hide my pain. So I didn't let people push me around.

I wondered if anyone glancing at us thought we were an item. God, I hoped not. I tried to picture it. Darren and me? Impossible. In fact, I couldn't see him as an item with anyone, except possibly the face he saw in his bathroom mirror. At least he didn't have a soul patch and a shaved head, like several of the other loud, laughing nerds in the room. Not that that made him any more congenial than them. Or was I growing more and more like a maiden aunt from the provinces, unwilling to accept that life ebbed and flowed, and soul patches were just part of the trend? A television set fixed high up on a wall was an irritating distraction. It was almost impossible to avoid looking at the flicker of it, though we were far enough away from it for me not to be sure what sport was being played.

My rugby-playing friend, Sam Willoughby, ambled into my thoughts. I tried to picture Sam with a soul patch . . . what an excruciating image. Sam was a lot of wonderful things, but trendy wasn't one of them. Which is how I liked it. He was currently visiting his brother Harry and family in New Zealand, *'Where men are men and sheep are scared, ha ha!'* as my father always chortled whenever the country came up in conversation, erroneously supposing himself not only witty but original.

The bar was jammed almost solid. As far as I could see, I looked to be the only woman in there, unless you counted the two sitting at a small table up against the window, holding hands and gazing deeply into each other's eyes. Silk shirts, good trousers, short wedge-cut hair . . . Actually, hang on, now I looked closer, they were men too.

'Ludovico de Luigi,' Darren said, still not meeting my gaze. 'Giorgione. Guardi. Bellini. Botticelli. My God, Alex, Venice is crawling with them. Awesome. And there are some totally amazing galleries there. I'd like you to give me an overview of those, too.'

'Obviously you're talking more than one article, in that case,' I said, hoping I sounded efficient and in control. 'That is if you want to cover any of them adequately, let alone discuss individual artists.'

'Which of course I do. And you're just the woman to do it.' He didn't sound at all convinced.

I took out my diary and flipped through it. 'Give me a rough estimate of when you'd want the first one. I've no idea what your lead time is, of course . . .' Not too long, I hoped, and I'd certainly be asking for most of my money upfront. I knew from sad experience that art magazines were as ephemeral as smoke.

'Shall we say two months?'

Oh, man! Not for two months, and that was only for the first one? Darren Douchebag was obviously either a gifted optimist, or less loaded than I'd realized.

'Let's not,' I said. 'And how many pieces do you want? To even begin to do justice to the subject, I'd need at least six.'

'Six?' He looked at me properly for the first time. '*Six?* That's a big ask. And we're a quarterly.' An apprehensive light gleamed briefly at the back of his eyes, which I now saw were a green-brown colour, like the north-facing side of a tree trunk. Sweat pinpricked his upper lip. 'That's way into next year.'

'Four pieces, then. I do have a reputation to consider—'

'Which is why we contacted you in the first place.' His lips parted in what I think was intended as a friendly smile. I really wished they hadn't.

'And I'd hate to deliver work which was substandard in any way,' I went on, steely as a crowbar, using my professionally brisk voice. It usually worked with dithering editors.

Come on, come on, I muttered internally, *give me the damn contract so I can leave and go home*. I wondered how long his funds were going to last. Perhaps he did too, which would explain the sweat. The diamond stud in his ear winked apprehensively.

He ostentatiously stuck out his arm, bent it at the elbow and brought his wrist close to his face. 'Hey, will you look at the time,' he said. 'Gotta bounce in ten.'

Gotta bounce . . . I reminded myself that he had a West Coast wife and three half-West Coast children. And that I would probably manage to pressure him into giving me a commission within the next seven minutes. To understand all is to forgive all.

In the end, it took another fifteen minutes before I was able to slide my butt off my uncomfortable perch and head for the door. But at least I had a secure, if grudging, verbal contract for three articles, with the possibility of more if there were no unexpected glitches. Such as him running out of cash (not that he put it like that). This meant that I was going to have to spend a few days in Venice at the very least. So I'd better start looking for other assignments to run concurrently with his, since paying my own expenses meant I would have to kill two birds, if not three, to make it worthwhile. Nonetheless, all in all, a successful evening – or it would have been if, as I was leaving, I hadn't caught sight of myself in one of the huge gilt mirrors which lined the bar. I was definitely putting on weight. And my hair needed pruning. Living down in the sticks, it was really easy to get careless about such things.

I'd come up to London by train, since it was much easier than driving up, throbbing my way through the traffic and then trying to find parking. Now, seated facing the engine, as London drifted away from me, I was chuffed enough to be able to tune out the shrieking kid at the end of the carriage. Not so the irritating woman across the aisle, who seemed to think the train was her office and was conducting her business affairs in a loud voice on her phone, oblivious to the glares that I and my fellow passengers were shooting at her.

Arriving back at my station – Longbury – I could smell the sea and the heady promise of summer in the air: wallflowers and chicken tikka. Up on the hill top, on the far side of town, perched the university buildings, lit up like a cruise ship anchored off shore. Someone somewhere nearby was eating or had just eaten fish and chips from the Golden Mackerel, leaving an atmospheric trail of hot fat and vinegar. The pubs were full of a more genuine crowd of customer than those in the West End, give or take the ones in leather jeggings or ripped jeans teamed with white T-shirts. A couple of guys were wearing dinner jackets and laughing with two girls in sequinned cocktail frocks. Big night at the Students' Union, I guessed.

I had the weekend ahead of me. Remembering my reflection

in the mirrors of the London pub, I promised myself that tomorrow I would go for a long, calorie-reducing run along the cliffs. Meanwhile, I'd throw away what was left of that lemon cake I'd bought in a misguided moment. Make a big salad and leave the gin bottle firmly in the door of the fridge. Drink only water from now on. I imagined myself svelte and lithe, an almost impossible task. Not that I was anywhere near obese.

Coming up the stairs to my flat, I could hear the phone ringing. I managed to catch it before it went to voicemail.

'Dinner. Next Tuesday. Flat's free,' said the voice in my ear.

'Thank you, Herry,' I said. But the receiver had already been replaced. My brother Hereward is notorious for the brevity of his communications – verbal, that is. There were no written ones. As I decoded the message, I took it to mean that I was bidden to dine with him next Tuesday and was welcome to stay the night in the basement which he and his wife, Lena, had converted into a flat. Tastefully, of course. The two of them were nothing if not tasteful. He earned a huge income doing something I'd never quite understood, while she had been a Swedish furniture designer before her marriage and subsequent move to London.

Briefly I considered calling him back, asking if I could bring a friend, but the question would throw them both into a panic. Besides, it would be too cruel to upset the numbers in what I knew would be a carefully calibrated table arrangement. In any case, who would I bring, with my close friend, Sam, off in the Antipodes? It wasn't that I didn't know anyone else who was male, just that I didn't know them intimately enough to subject them to the cut-glass intricacies of the social life Hereward and Lena lived in Chelsea.

I poured myself a healthy glass of water, took a swallow and threw the rest into the sink. Enough already with the health kick! I opened the door of the fridge and hoicked out the gin bottle along with the vermouth next to it. I never add ice to my martinis, for fear of diluting them; instead, I keep the ingredients in the fridge, on a high state of alert for when occasion called. I considered this an occasion.

There were three messages on the phone. Glass in hand, I listened to them. One was from Major Norman Horrocks, saying that if I were to walk down to his place, he had something interesting to show me. The next was a recorded voice saying something about PPI, which I instantly deleted. The third was some query from my publisher, which I'd deal with in the morning.

I sucked up more of my ice-cold martini. Oh, jeez, it was good. I tried to kid myself it was medicinal, but in fact it was celebratory. With a nice commission in my pocket, all I had to do now was figure out how to cover the cost of flying across to Venice and putting myself up there for three or four days, because if one thing had been made clear during my conversation with Darren Carver, it was that he had no intention of footing the bill – though, after some firm pressure on my part, he had rather sulkily conceded that he might be able to make a *small* contribution towards my expenses. All in all, an extremely satisfactory state of affairs.

Venice . . . I replenished my glass, took some relevant books off my shelves and curled up on the sofa with them. I hadn't been to Venice for several years. The last time was with the Love Rat, my former husband. How happy I'd been back then. How innocent. How ignorant.

THREE

Mid-morning the following day, I walked along the lower road out of town, heading towards the Major's house. I cut through the woods and took the path which would end up in Honeypot Lane, leaving me just a few yards down from the only houses in the narrow road: a semi-detached pair of brick-and-flint cottages which stood like conjoined twins halfway along. *Rattray* and *Metcalfe*. In the fields on the opposite side of the lane, tractors were busy muck-spreading up and down the plough. Birds chirped in the hedges. Cows moved languidly, their jaws working as though their mouths were full of Wrigley's spearmint gum.

As I walked up the flagged path towards the Major's kitchen door, I couldn't help noticing that the lopsided bush which stood to one side had been altered in some way. Last time I was here it had been just an untidy growth. Obviously he'd been at it with his shears since then. Knowing his ill-advised penchant for topiary, I wondered what member of the animal kingdom it was meant to represent. I was guessing some kind of small mammal which had been severely damaged either during its emergence from the womb or by being caught in a trap. A three-legged guinea pig, maybe. Or possibly a tail-less weasel.

I could hear frenzied barking from the house as the dog Marlowe – so named because of his former owner's fondness for crime fiction – registered my arrival. Marlowe was about the size and shape of a toothbrush, more like a runaway moustache than anything else, and came up no further than my instep. The noise he produced was completely disproportionate to his diminutive size.

At the end of the long garden rose the canal embankment, where trees shifted in the slight wind. I could smell elder and wallflowers, a whiff of manure underlaid with diesel fumes from the tractors out on the fields.

I rapped on the open door and called out as I stepped inside the kitchen. I found the Major in a tweed-green cashmere sweater and cavalry twill trousers. A cravat pimpled with fox heads filled the space between the two edges of his open-necked shirt.

'Good morning, my dear,' he said. 'Heard you coming – or rather, Marlowe did. I've just put the kettle on. How lovely to see you.'

He loaded up a tray with mugs, a milk jug and an old-fashioned brown teapot, together with a plate of his homemade chocolate chip cookies, and carried it all into his surprisingly unmilitary sitting room.

Having chomped down three cookies in short order, I said, 'Have you ever considered setting up a cookie company? You make the best biscuits I've ever tasted.'

'I can't say I've—'

'People love homemade biscuits. I bet you'd make a fortune.'

'But think of the work involved. I'd be baking night and day. Never have time for a pint in the pub. And all the rules and regulations I'd have to take into account. Health and safety and such. And the equipment I'd need. Let alone publicizing the company. Doesn't bear thinking about.'

'You could give batches of them as presents, and if anyone wanted to give a monetary gift back . . .'

'Sounds a bit amateur to me. No, it's a wonderful idea, but I think not.'

After some further desultory chat, I said, 'All right, Major. What was it you wanted to show me?'

'Finish your tea, wash your hands, then put on a pair of these . . .' The Major produced a pair of blue plastic gloves, the disposable sort that colorectal doctors put on before doing some embarrassingly intimate probing. I, too, had used them when I was still on the force. Not to explore anyone's personal spaces, but in order not to tamper with evidence.

'This is all very mysterious,' I said.

'You just wait, m'dear.' He tapped the side of his nose and then, as though the sight of the disposable gloves had for some reason reminded him, said, 'By the way, I saw that husband of yours the other day.'

'Doing what . . . directing traffic?' I asked, caustic as lemon juice and not trying to hide it. I had thought that I was truly over DCI Jack Martin. That my broken heart had mended and even my anger had dissipated. Not so. The truth was that I was still pretty damn bitter about the defection of my former husband to the willing arms of a masseuse or poodle-parlour lady, something of that sort. 'I thought he'd moved to Wales.'

'He may well have done, but there he was, large as life, walking along the High Street.'

'Alone?' Not that I cared one way or another.

'Well, no.' The Major was looking like someone who very much wished they had never begun this conversational thread. 'He was with a . . . um . . . not to put too fine a point on it . . . he was with a—'

'Woman,' I said.

'Precisely.'

'He did remarry, you know.'

'Yes, indeed. I just got the impression that it probably wasn't to this . . . uh . . . if I'm completely honest . . . floozy.'

Good old Jack, I thought, without any reminiscent affection. Still up to his old tricks. Unable to keep his dick in his trousers. Some people never learn.

'Anyway, now you've finished your cuppa, let's have a look at what I wanted you to see.' The Major got up and went towards the next room, with me following. My stomach felt like a pickled walnut, all sour and twisted. What was Jack the Love Rat doing parading himself in Longbury? It was bad enough that he'd walked out on me more than three years ago, leaving me pregnant, and had gone off with someone else, the creep. Someone with whom he'd been having an affair the entire length of our three-year marriage. What I hated him for most was not the infidelity but the fact that once I found out, the knowledge had soured all the happy memories I had had of our time together. The *bastard*. And of course, when I lost our baby, although he knew about it, there was no sympathetic message from him, no hint of concern for me, let alone the loss of the child I'd been carrying. *His* child. The absolute *sod*. The other woman was more than welcome to the faithless son of a bitch.

While I was thinking these venomous and fruitless thoughts, the Major was faffing about at the small oak gate-legged table in his dining room. He stood back, gesturing like a conjuror's assistant. 'So,' he said. 'What do you think of these, then?'

I looked at the two drawings in front of me. And looked again. My immediate thought was Wow! My second thought was *Wow!*

'Can those possibly be what I think they are?' I said. I bent closer. Surely I was staring at two pen-and-wash sketches by Tiepolo. I squinted at them again, carefully held them up to the light and sniffed them. Without speaking, the Major handed me a large round magnifying glass on a handle and I bent closer, moving the glass around until I had covered the entire surface of them. 'I'm not an expert by any means,' I said at last, straightening up and jamming my fists into the small of my back. 'But those look authentic to me.'

And copies or genuine, at least one of them was easily recognizable as belonging to Tiepolo's Pulcinella series. That would be Giovanni Domenico, not his father Lorenzo or younger brother Battista. The conical hat, the ruffed and buttoned clown suit, the grotesque mask, the hunched back, bulging midriff and misshapen nose were clear trademarks. I tried to remember how many of these drawings he had produced: over a hundred, I seemed to recall from my days as a student.

The other drawing, on grey paper, showed the head and shoulders of an old man, bearded and balding, his face in profile, with – as so often with Tiepolo – his back to the viewer. I was stunned. The artist had taken two chalks, a white and the famous red, or *sanguine*, and filled the space using no more than a few delicate strokes. Beautiful. I wanted more of them than just these two.

The Major had remained silent while I studied the pages spread out on the table. 'So . . .' he said eventually.

'Where did you get them?' I demanded. 'Whose are they?'

'Well . . .' He coughed gently. Wiped an imaginary biscuit crumb from his moustache. Said, 'Actually, I suppose they're mine, really. Within the letter of the law, that is.'

'But how? If they're genuine, they must be worth a good

deal of money.' Though much more exciting than that was the possibility that I was looking at work which the eighteenth-century master himself had executed. That *his* fingers had moved across this paper, *his* hand had traced these figures.

He sighed. 'Doesn't bear thinking about, really.'

'Major, where did you get them?' I emphasized each word.

'They must originally have belonged to Nell Roscoe. As you know, she left me her house next door and all its contents. Including the dog Marlowe, of course.'

At the sound of his name, Marlowe started prancing about and yapping.

'*And?*'

'Well, I've just begun to clear poor Nell's place, which obviously entails going through her things, d'you see? Looking at the contents of the cupboards, setting aside the more obviously valuable stuff. And then yesterday, I started taking down some of the paintings she had on the wall. And blow me if the string on the back of one of them didn't break, probably hadn't been moved since she first put it up, smashed on to the floor, glass all over the show, splinters of wood everywhere, and now there's three pictures lying there instead of one. An oil depicting a thatched farmhouse with cornfields and sheep and so forth, painted by the art mistress at the girls' high school, as I happen to know since Nell showed it to me when she first acquired it. Plus, to my astonishment, these two. Nell must have hidden them behind the oil painting for safe-keeping.'

'How amazing!'

'I'll say. I could see at once they must be something special.'

'Of course, you're going to have them valued.'

'Yes, but I wanted you to look at them first.'

'I appreciate your faith in me, Major. But you need to take them up to one of the big auction houses and ask them for an opinion.'

'I realized that. But I'm not too keen on the thought of traipsing all the way up to London only to end up looking like an ignorant old fool in front of some whippersnapper fresh out of art school in a cheap suit. In fact . . .' He looked at me with a pitiful expression. 'I was wondering if you would take them up for me. I can't be doing with the big city nowadays.'

I considered. 'I'm going to London next week,' I said, 'but I do feel that as the owner of the drawings, it would be much better for you to go up yourself.'

I was conscious of a thrill which was obviously not shared by the Major. The two sketches must be worth quite a bit. Hard to see just how they could have been transferred from Italy to this small country cottage in the south-east of England. After all, they must be art museum pieces. Which made me wonder if I was entirely wrong in believing them to be authentic. I bent over the two sheets once more. They certainly appeared to be genuine. I turned them over, noticed the small smudge of blue in the left-hand corner of the one featuring a ruffed clown – paint? ink? – and once more studied the two images.

'Have you examined any more of Mrs Roscoe's pictures?' I asked. Maybe the former high school headmistress had other treasures hidden behind the everyday stuff she had displayed.

'Only a few. Haven't found anything else so far.'

'I wonder where she got these.'

'Just what I thought. Though truth to tell, I don't know much about art, but I know I don't like this one.' He slapped a hand down on the Pulcinella. 'Nothing more than a clown in a weird mask prancing about in his pyjamas. I ask you.'

'I suppose that's one way of putting it.' Whatever your views on their artistic merit, they must be pretty valuable, and the late Nell Roscoe must have been aware of that or she wouldn't have hidden them. 'As well as the clown, there's this wonderful head of an old man. You have to admit it's pretty stunning.'

'I suppose so,' he said grudgingly.

'I wonder how they got here,' I said.

He shrugged. 'I should imagine that she picked them up on that holiday she went on, to Italy, back in the spring. Poor old Nell – the heart attack occurred soon after she got back.'

'She might not have acquired them in Italy, of course.'

'Very true.'

'Major, there's no way she could have stolen them, is there?'

The Major looked at me. I looked back. We both shook our

heads. Nell Roscoe and stolen property did not belong in the same sentence. Not even on the same page.

'Did she have any other valuables?'

'Not much. Some silver. Bits of jewellery . . . a couple of decent diamond brooches, two or three nice rings, some good pearls – you know, the kind of thing that women of her generation liked to wear.' He put a blue plastic-gloved hand on the table, where it lay like some rare sea creature dredged from the depths of the ocean. 'Not that I'm an expert on that sort of thing. Give me a firearm and I'd be much more useful.'

I could see his army days gathering behind his eyes, that increasingly distant epoch when Major Norman Horrocks still meant something, had significance, was somebody. A chill skittered briefly along the back of my neck. Was that what growing older was all about – losing one's sense of self-worth? Realizing that one's time in the sun was over?

I wanted to put my arms round the Major's broad chest, but reckoned he would be completely flummoxed if I did. 'I can't really see Mrs Roscoe collecting guns,' I said.

At our ankles, Marlowe bounced about, barking and fussing about at the mention of his late mistress.

'As a matter of fact, you'd be surprised.' The Major walked over to a sideboard and fished about in its recesses before bringing out a heavy black pistol. 'Look at this. It was in her bedside drawer, believe it or not.'

'Is it real?'

'I should say so. *And* loaded, when I found it.'

'Good heavens! I wonder why.'

'Well, that's just it. If these drawings are as valuable as you think, is it possible that someone knew – or suspected – that she had them? Which might explain why she hid them. Maybe the poor old girl was afraid that someone was aware of them, and likely to break in, force her to reveal them, tie her up and torture her until she revealed their . . . um . . . whereabouts.' He shook his head. 'Doesn't bear thinking about.'

'Who could she possibly suspect? Who was likely to be aware that an elderly retired teacher might possess what are undoubtedly works of art? Did she ever say how they came into her possession? I'd love to know.' I had a sudden, vivid mental image of a distressed former pupil knocking at the door late at night, terrified features concealed beneath a rain-slicked hood, begging her former headmistress to help her, staring wildly about her to check whether she'd been followed by whoever it was she was fleeing. 'Take them!' she might have said, in this unlikely scenario. 'Keep them hidden until I get back! And, if I don't, they're yours to keep.' Then hurrying off into the storm, never to return.

Not privy to my lurid imaginings, the Major wrinkled his forehead. 'Talking about it, it's coming back to me. I seem to remember that she *did* pick them up in Venice, but I can't be sure. My memory these days . . . I vaguely recall her telling me that she and her friend the art mistress went into this antiquarian bookshop – Fiona something or other. Or was she called Philippa?'

'Was who?'

'The art mistress. I was very fond of her, and we enjoyed many an alcoholic beverage together – this is Nell I'm talking about now – but she was always extremely sparing of any personal information.' Shared shepherd's pies danced briefly behind his eyes.

I jerked him back to the here and now. 'This bookshop . . .'

He laughed. 'She said it was about the same size as a coffin. Young man in there, apparently. Minding the shop while his father ran to the bank. Nell picks these drawings out of a folder, pays what he asked and away the two ladies go. She didn't show them to me at the time, but she told me all about it.'

'What about that cousin of hers who . . . um . . . died?' I asked. 'Did she have any idea that Mrs Roscoe might have stumbled on a real treasure?'

'Very much doubt it, my dear.'

We were silent for a moment, both of us probably remembering Lilian, the late cousin, who had horribly killed herself in the most painful way possible by drinking Drano.

'What about the husband?' I asked.

'Nell disliked him intensely. I'd rather keep him out of it, if you don't mind, especially as I can't see that he could possibly have anything to do with it.' The Major dusted his hands together.

'Understood.'

'Heigh-ho,' the Major said eventually. 'Let's go into the garden, and I'll show you my latest offering in the bush-clipping line.'

'Do I get a prize for guessing what it is?'

'It ought to be perfectly obvious, m'dear.' His face fell. 'But I know it's not. I wonder if anyone locally offers evening classes in topiary.'

FOUR

The walls of my brother's Chelsea dining room were a dark olive green, handsomely accentuated by white-painted wood and elaborate plasterwork. White drapes splashed with what looked to me like giant artichokes hung at the two floor-to-ceiling windows. Everything was most exquisite, from the two crystal chandeliers suspended above the table to the few small but precious paintings on the walls, including half a dozen charming originals from Carl Larsson's *Lilla Hyttnäs* series.

Hereward and Lena, my sister-in-law, like everything just so, and on the few occasions they have visited me in my own home, have had a hard time concealing their disgust at what they call my 'clutter'. But I'm grateful for the family tie whenever I go to theirs, because otherwise I doubt if I would have had the opportunity to socialize with the august and esoteric people who are their friends, most of whom seem to be heavily creative. Authors, playwrights, theatre directors, artists, musicians – the company is always distinguished. That night, for instance, there was a brace of novelists, an ambassador, an opera singer and her husband, two renowned TV journalists, a couple of other odd bods. And me!

The table was as sumptuously set as those in any palace, chateau or *palazzo* you cared to name. The heaviest of silver cutlery. The finest of Orrefors glass. The thinnest of white porcelain bordered with a gold Grecian key pattern. I longed to tell Lena I'd just read in the style pages of the paper that very morning that proper dinner services were out and collections of oddly matched china were in. But why be needlessly cruel? In any case, neither she nor Hereward would have believed me. Or, for that matter, cared what hoi polloi had to say.

I was seated beside one of the odd bods, a stocky man called Renzo, who turned out to be an art dealer with premises in

London and Rome. He had thick black hair on the back of his hands and quite a bit more on his head, alert, dark eyes and a body obviously worked on by a personal trainer and probably a masseur as well. Or, more likely, a masseuse. It was a pity that the body only came up to my shoulder. He was dressed in the kind of very English clothes that only someone who wasn't English would wear. Added to that, even the most doting of Italian mommas couldn't truthfully have called him anything but plumb ugly. Until he smiled. It was the difference between light and shade, between summer and winter.

As was usual at this kind of dinner party, he and I established each other's credentials, found mutual acquaintances in the art scene, exchanged anecdotes and information designed to demonstrate how well we fit into and even shared the same setting. He spoke unaccented and almost flawless English, suggesting a sojourn at some high-class English educational institution. The general dining-table conversation covered the threat of so-called Isis, climate change, the EU referendum in England and Donald Trump. Most of the company was firmly for staying in the EU. Our collective opinion of Trump was unanimous.

I'd never understood exactly what beetling brows were until that evening. Renzo's large black ones looked like two hairy insects pulling in opposite directions to get as far away from each other as possible. He turned them on me, having momentarily concentrated on the wine just poured into his glass (the third one, the first two having been removed after being used for earlier wines) by efficient staff. I watched him, thinking that everybody was well aware that the English did not on the whole know much about wine, but that on the other hand, the previous stuff produced during the meal had been pretty damn good. He took a small sip of the new offering, swilled it about a bit and then swallowed it before nodding appreciatively.

'So,' he said. 'Alexandra Quick . . . Where do we go from here?'

One of those questions it's impossible to answer, so I didn't try.

'I have read articles by you, have I not?'

'You may well have done – probably have,' I said. 'If, that is, you subscribe to some of the better-quality art journals.' Why be modest when boasting might get you somewhere?

'Ah!' He smote his forehead theatrically. 'Yes, it comes back to me. *Ripe for the Picking.*'

'That's right.' He referred to a compilation of text and paintings depicting fruit and vegetables which I had put together with my former friend and esteemed colleague, Dr Helena Drummond. I wished her persona did not so often rise from the grave to consort with me. It was bad enough that she was dead without having her doing the Banquo's ghost thing at unforeseen moments. Though perhaps I should have expected it, given that I continued to work in the same field as the two of us had done so happily together before she was murdered.

'Yes, very enjoyable,' Renzo said. 'A splendid concept, if I may say so. Bringing art to the masses. I have myself bought a couple of your books as gifts for my dear mamma. So tell me what other irons you currently have in the fire.'

'I've been working on a new compilation,' I said. '*Eat, Drink and Be Merry*. And I've been commissioned by *Nirvana* magazine to write some pieces on Venetian painters, past and present.'

'How very interesting. For which I would be willing to wager that you'll be paid peanuts, no expenses included.'

I laughed. 'You obviously know the market.'

The eyebrows did their beetle thing again. 'And when would you be travelling to Italy?'

'I haven't quite decided. Fairly soon, though.'

He began discreetly to slap at his person until he brought out a wallet of leather so fine you could have spread it on toast and had it for breakfast. He extracted an engraved card and handed it to me. 'Please keep in touch, Alexandra. I shall be in Venice soon myself, and would be delighted to take you out for dinner. I might even have an interesting proposition to make to you.' He flashed that smile at me and I could feel myself wanting to slaver, though I managed to hold it back.

'That would be wond— good,' I said, remembering to sound businesslike rather than slobberingly grateful.

'Also, I maintain an apartment on the Grand Canal, a

particularly interesting apartment in that it contains a *stanza segreto*, a secret room.'

'Like in Pompeii, do you mean? Full of esoteric paintings?'

'I'm afraid mine is more ordinary than that. But interesting, nonetheless. A room of glass. Well worth a visit, especially for an art lover such as yourself.'

'I'd love to see it.' I meant it. 'Glass . . . do you mean mosaics? Mirrors?'

'It is lined in glass fashioned by a famous Murano glass worker of the seventeenth century and judged by those who have seen it to be one of the finest hidden treasures in Venice.' He sighed. 'So much of my beautiful birthplace is, thank God, unknown to the outside world. Unseen by the tourists who are without any concept of art or beauty, afflicting our city like a plague of cockroaches and making our lives a misery.'

'That's a bit harsh, isn't it?'

'Probably.' He smiled his ineffable smile.

'Why else would they be coming to Venice if not to admire and appreciate?'

'You have a point. And of course they bring revenue to the place, though given the rampant corruption among our leaders, not enough of it gets spent on the necessary substructures that any city needs, especially one like ours which is slowly sinking beneath the waves, however hard we try to stop it.'

This seemed a good time to change the subject. Make an enquiry or two on the Major's behalf, though by now he might well have taken Mrs Roscoe's putative Tiepolos up to be examined and assessed by experts. 'Tell me,' I said. 'How many of those Pulcinella drawings did Tiepolo produce? I can never remember whether it's one hundred and three, or one hundred and four.'

'Nobody is absolutely certain,' Renzo said. 'Some say one thing, some say another. And of course, there has always been talk surrounding them, suggestions that there may well be others which were lost or stolen over the years.'

'I'm fascinated to hear you say that.'

'And why would that be?'

I tried desperately to keep my mouth shut but didn't succeed.

I told myself later that it wasn't really my fault; if it came
down to a face-off between the eyebrows and me, they were
going to win every time. 'Because someone I know has just
inherited what appear to be two original sketches.'

'Are you serious?' He shifted in his chair to look directly
at me.

'Absolutely.'

'But this is astounding. You have actually seen them?'

'Yes. He called me in for my opinion.'

'And what was it, your opinion?'

'That they are indeed genuine Tiepolos. Giambattista that
is, not his father or brother.'

He nonchalantly broke a water biscuit in half. Did I just
imagine it, or did I detect a hint of the rancid odour of a
hunting predator? His nails were cut short and matt varnished.
'And how would an ordinary mortal such as myself get a
glance at these possible works of art?'

'That's not for me to say.' Too late, I remembered this man
was an art dealer and therefore likely to be someone with an
eagle eye to the main chance. 'After all, they don't belong to
me, and I shouldn't really have mentioned them to you.'

One of his hairy fingers gently touched the back of my hand.
'You can rely on me not to break your confidence,' he said.

Like hell I can, I thought. 'I hope so,' I said. 'It was really
most imprudent of me to mention them.'

'Don't worry, my lips are sealed. In my business, absolute
discretion is vital.' He lifted his glass. 'Blame your brother's
excellent wine for unlocking your own professional caution.'
Tipping his glass to his mouth, he said softly, 'To Tiepolo!'

It was about time to turn, in the traditional manner, to the
people on our other sides. Before I could do so, he added,
'In Italy, we would describe the colour of your hair as
Titian-red. It was the colour Tiepolo preferred on his models
in so much of his work.'

My turn to smile. 'So I've often been told.' We looked
each other directly in the eye. Exchanged beams of mutual
admiration. Adopted expressions intimating fruitful further
discussions in the not-too-distant future. Clearly indicated
that neither of us was a pushover.

I turned to my other neighbour and shifted slightly. He was called Jock McSomething, a long-time friend of my brother's whom I'd first met years ago when Herry was up at Cambridge. 'I thought you emigrated to Australia,' I said.

'I did.'

'So what happened?'

'Love,' he said.

I remembered belatedly that he was a Scot and, in keeping with his heritage, a man of few words. Most of them dour. 'Here? Or there?'

'There.'

'Unrequited?'

'Unfortunately.'

'What are you doing now?' There were probably three too many superfluous words in the sentence.

'Farming.'

'What sort?'

'Dairy.'

'Right.'

There wasn't a huge amount to say after that.

Renzo caught up with me later as the party began to break up. 'May I know when you are likely to be in Venice?' he asked.

'As I said, fairly soon.'

'The point is, Alexandra, as I said, I maintain an apartment in Venice – a legitimate business expense, of course – and I would be honoured if you would care to take advantage of it.'

'How very kind of you,' I said. I can do gracious, if pressed. Not that I felt pressed here. Quite the opposite. And after my minimal conversation with Jock McSomething, my vocal chords were grateful for an airing.

'If you let me know, I can alert the staff,' he said. 'And I would be particularly happy were our visits to coincide.'

'How kind.' I didn't bother to offer payment. However firmly I proposed, I could guarantee that there was no way this guy would allow me to pay for my accommodation, though he was quite likely to expect some kind of payback in return.

He seized my hand, bent slightly and raised it to his lips.

'*Arrivederci*, Miss Quick. I look forward with impatience to our next meeting.'

'*Well!*' Hereward said later that evening, after the last guests had gone. He, Lena and I sat with our shoes kicked off and tiny glasses of Grand Marnier in our hands.

'Well what?' I raised my eyebrows as nonchalantly as I could, knowing exactly what he was talking about. Brothers, eh?

'You and Renzo Vitali. The two of you appeared to be getting along like a house on fire.'

'He seems like a nice guy.'

'He's a lot more than that. Belongs to one of the wealthiest families in Italy. Is a renowned expert on a number of matters.'

'Recently widowed; three children,' added my sister-in-law.

'What's that got to do with anything?' I asked.

'Just saying.'

'You could do a lot worse,' Hereward pronounced, looking judicious.

'What in the name of fortune do you mean?' I spoke a trifle belligerently.

'Fortune is just about the word.'

'You're not by any chance trying to pair the two of us up, are you?'

'A match made in heaven,' murmured Lena. She rested both hands on her enormous belly.

'But he only comes up to my knee.'

'Alexandra, you are always so absurd.' Lena smiled gently. I distinctly saw a hand or foot pushing at her stomach, like a bird desperate to escape from its maternal nest and be hatched.

'A delivery in the morning,' declared my brother. 'What do you bet, Lena, *min älskling*?'

'Absolutely. One hundred per cent certain.'

'Red? Or white?'

'White, to start with, I should imagine.'

'You're almost certainly correct.'

The two of them sat across from me, cosied up together, looking much-married and unbearably smug. I rose to my feet and said with dignity, 'I have no idea what the two of you are talking about, but if nobody has any objection, I'm off to bed. Thank you both for a splendid evening.'

They smiled with such insufferable expressions of self-satisfaction that I wanted to smack their heads together. I went into the hall and opened the interior door which led down to the basement flat, shouted, 'Good night!' and descended the stairs.

Red what? White what?

I found out the following morning. A giant basket of white roses arrived from the most exclusive florist in Knightsbridge, addressed to Signorina Alexandra Quick. From Renzo, of course.

'You have them – there's no way I'm carting that lot down to Longbury,' I told Lena. OK, I can do gracious if I have to, but I'm a whole lot better at ungracious. 'What was the silly man thinking?'

'The silly man was thinking that you're pretty hot stuff,' said my brother. 'Poor deluded idiot. Little does he know.'

'We could have them sent down to you,' said Lena. 'If we hurry, one of the specialist services could even get them to you by this afternoon.'

'Ridiculous,' I scoffed. 'What a waste of time and money.' But they were beautiful roses, tight-budded, creamy at the base, the petals tipped with pink, the leaves and stems healthily green. I was really reluctant to abandon them. So it was arranged that they'd be sent down to Longbury by some kind of messenger service.

The basket was already standing outside my door when I got back, looking none the worse for wear. I brought them into my flat and dumped them on the table in the kitchen. I'd redistribute them later if I could find enough vases . . . it seemed a pity to have just one display when I could have several.

The light on the telephone was blinking, indicating a message. It was from Major Horrocks again. 'Would you believe it? The auctioneers haven't finished their authentication, but they think they're genuine,' he said gloomily. I felt a rush of guilt at my indiscretion the previous evening. 'Call me and I'll take you out for lunch to celebrate.'

No need to ask what 'they're' were. I called him back immediately. 'You don't sound in a very celebratory mood.'

'Truth to tell, m'dear, I'm not.'

'Tell me all about it.'

I felt more and more uncomfortable about having told Renzo Vitali about them. Oh dear. At least I hadn't said who the owner of the paintings was. And Renzo had assured me of his absolute discretion, which probably didn't amount to a hill of beans.

Later, I walked along the seafront and turned left into the High Street. I'd arranged to meet the Major at the Fox and Hounds and found him to be more cheerful, but still somewhat depressed. Turned out he was worried about what to do if the drawings were definitively identified as being by the Venetian artist.

'I keep asking myself what Nell Roscoe would have wanted me to do,' he said.

'I think first and foremost, she'd want you to be happy, especially considering that you were good friends for so long, and that you're now the primary carer for Marlowe.' I leaned my elbows on the table. 'What would *you* like to do? If it works out well, you'll have enough cash to do anything you wanted, more or less.'

'A restaurant,' he said wistfully. 'Often toyed with the idea, d'you see? Perhaps in France. Checked tablecloths. Candles stuck into wine bottles. Smells of lavender and garlic.' He looked around him at our fellow lunchers. 'Or even here, in Longbury. Or a teashop.'

'Great idea. Or even that cookie company I mentioned the other day. You're so good with the biscuits and cakes, Major. You'd be able to afford all the equipment and help that you'd need. People would come from miles around for one of your cream teas.'

He smiled. 'Tell you what . . . I've been thinking I could turn Nell's house into a small restaurant, use the garden for teas in the summer.'

Hadn't Sam Willoughby – who so far on his Antipodean adventure hadn't sent me a single email – mentioned doing something of the sort when he'd finally taken over Edward

Vine's wine shop and expanded Willoughby's Books? 'You should get together with Sam Willoughby,' I said. 'When he gets back from New Zealand. *If.*'

'That's a good idea. He sent me an email the other day, now that I've got a computer. Maybe I could discuss the proposition long-distance with him.'

'Good thinking,' I said, as a feverish kind of pumping, green-coloured throb set itself up somewhere close to my ribs.

I had the definite feeling, as I walked home later, that someone was either watching or following me. It would look too eccentric to keep on whirling round to check behind me, so I sat down every now and then on one of the benches facing the sea and cast a quick eye around. I saw nothing in the least suspicious. A couple of old girls tottering along arm in arm, a young woman pushing a pram with massive thighs clad in unflattering black tights and an almost non-existent skirt, neither of which did her any favours, a man some distance back in an unbecoming beret with a supermarket carrier bag, several little kids on bikes or scooters enjoying the sunshine with their parents. Not exactly threatening. A couple of cyclists went by. A passing dog relieved itself copiously on a fennel plant at the edge of the shingle.

I eyed the man in the beret more closely. If you were trying to be inconspicuous, how easy it would be to carry several hats in a bag and keep changing them. So he could easily dive behind a beach hut and come out the other side as a man in a baseball cap. Or a watch cap. Or a woolly hat with a bobble on top. Add a stick-on moustache or a pair of sunglasses. Or a white stick. Perfect disguise. It would take all of thirty seconds. Nobody would look at him twice.

The man in the beret eventually reached my bench and passed on, trailed by a black-and-white spaniel. A dog was too much of a giveaway, whatever hat its owner was wearing. I was getting paranoid. Yet I couldn't shake the notion that someone, somewhere, was following me. Or watching me. I didn't much like the feeling, but on the other hand, I don't generally pay much attention to hunches and presentiments.

I carried on to my flat, climbed the stairs instead of taking the lift, and paused outside my front door.

There was that feeling again! I paused with my key in the lock. What was I going to find behind my door? I hesitated. Then thought, *Fuck it*. Get on with it, Quick. Apart from a body oozing blood all over my precious antique Kashan rug (a wedding present from my grandmamma, Lady Stanhope de Cuik), how bad could it be? Pretty bad, actually. My computer gone, for instance. All the notes for my next publication trashed. Much worse than a body could be.

Tentatively I turned the key and pushed slowly at the door. Walked into the hall. Surveyed the terrain. Breathed out a long-held breath. A light blinked on the telephone, but my rug was unsullied. My computer stood on the desk, beside it my open files of notes. What lay beyond, in the other rooms? My bedroom, for instance? Would I be able to sleep in a bed on which I had discovered a body?

'Hullo?' I shouted. The sort of foolish call a Damsel-in-Jeopardy might make approaching a deserted boathouse at midnight. Not Alex Quick, ex-copper, though. Pulling myself together, I marched through the rest of the flat, looking for telltale signs of intrusion, theft or murder. Nothing. I looked into closets, under beds, behind doors. Zilch.

So much for premonitions.

If my friend Sam Willoughby had been in town, I could have called him to come and have a nightcap with me.

But he was off in New Zealand. And not contacting me, close friends though we were supposed to be. Too busy gallivanting around instead with a beautiful Antipodean.

And jolly good luck to him was all I could say.

FIVE

Sandro Grainger lived in the kind of London apartment
that a good number of people would have prostituted
themselves for. The rooms smelled of fresh flowers, newly
polished furniture and trust funds. Quite unsuitable for a
twenty-five-year-old, in my Great-Aunt opinion. How was he
ever going to face the slings and arrows if he started out on
life's journey from a residence as palatial as this one? But
then, how many of either was this privileged scion of a rich
and noble family ever likely to encounter?

There were two long tables set, covered in white linen, one
with bottles and glasses, the other with plates and cutlery and
a pretty generous array of mouth-watering food.

My parents were there, chatting away to Sandro's. Maddalena
was a cousin of my sister's Italian husband, and had been
introduced to Dominic through them. Dom was not only enor-
mously rich, but I seemed to remember that he also farmed
in an eccentric sort of way: alpacas, was it? Or ostriches?
Something slightly offbeat.

All four of them were gazing up at an Escher which I
presumed was a print rather than an original – though there
was no reason why I should make such an assumption, given
the amount of money in the Grainger family – while my father,
Edred, made expansive gestures of a mathematical kind.
Maddalena seemed a little bemused by my father's exchanges,
which were apt to veer away from any conversational paths
already being pursued and soar off into fantasies which no
one but my mother, Mary, was (occasionally) able to follow.

Sandro's little gathering seemed have metamorphosed into
a largish party. There were quite a few pretty girls with long,
straight blonde hair hanging down on either side of their faces
and perfect white teeth. Too perfect, in my opinion. I find the
current trend for washday-white teeth looks unnatural and
therefore off-putting. Obviously some of these girls must be

the friends who were at Sandro's dinner party in Venice. The same with some delightful young men possessed of both charm and good manners. *Beneducato*, indeed. And much too young for me, unfortunately, but a great pleasure to come across, nonetheless. Among the older generation, there were three or four of those terrifyingly chic women with artfully greying hair you could bounce rocks off, and husbands you instinctively wanted to.

Sandro was on the other side of the room, talking to my brother, but when he saw me he excused himself and came straight over. 'I'll introduce you in a random sort of way,' he said. 'So nobody suspects why you're here.'

'I can't see why they'd suspect anything at all,' I said. 'I wasn't planning to slap a deerstalker on my head or start taking people's fingerprints.'

'Of course not.' He produced an indulgent smile.

'Do they even know you discovered the doge's ring or the little Botticelli?'

He writhed a bit. 'Actually, I did tell Katy. She seemed to be the one least likely to be the thief.'

My eyebrows lifted. 'But not Suzy?'

'Um . . . not yet.'

'Why's that?' It looked as though he didn't trust her. Not a good basis for a relationship.

'Because I realized, after speaking to Katy, that it might be more – what's the word? – diplomatic not to mention it to anyone else. By the way, my Uncle Cesare is in town and insisted on joining us tonight. When you meet him, you may realize why I am so worried about *objets* going missing from his *appartamento*.'

'OK.'

'Now, I must introduce you to some of the principal players in my little drama.' He took my arm and led me – in a random way, of course – round the room. I met nearly all of the suspects. As I had guessed, three of the long-haired girls were respectively Suzy, Katy and Bianca. The fourth, Laura, was quite different, a raven-tressed, olive-skinned beauty with a surly mouth and unfriendly style. Heavy brows, shaped like wings, flared above her black eyes. We've all seen those unpleasant-looking, emaciated models at fashion shows from New York to Rome and back again: Laura fitted right in. She stalked grimly round the room, the epitome of every sullen female in mad shoes and clothes no one in their right minds would ever wear, let alone pay good money for, striding down international catwalks with zombie make-up and cheek-bones you could slice cucumbers with. Whereas Laura wore black, the other three were in floaty floral dresses and expensive sandals with ribbons tied round their ankles instead of straps. They looked like clones. I could scarcely tell them apart. They exuded a kind of collective innocence which I guessed stemmed from never having had a life trauma to contend with. Not yet, at least. I wondered how any of them would react if a stone was chucked into the orderly pool of their existence.

We chatted about this and that. Laura deigned to join us but didn't speak, preferring to gaze aloofly towards the far end of the room. At an appropriate moment, I asked how they'd enjoyed Sandro's last party, in Venice. No significant glances were exchanged. No one flushed a guilty red or tried to avoid my disingenuous gaze. They were enthusiastic.

'My favourite city!'

'Wish *I* had an uncle living there.'

'Lucky Sandro.'

'The Doge's Palace – all that gilt plaster and those painted ceilings.'

'*Gorg*eous!'

The young men were all determinedly courteous, kindly taking time to talk to the older people in the room, including my parents, laughing at Edred's excruciating jokes and asking intelligent questions of Mary. I didn't take to Suzy Hartley Haywood's brother, Tony, however. I could quite see why Sandro, albeit reluctantly, had nominated him as someone who might have stolen the Marchese's family treasures. Grossly unfair, probably, but that's what happens when a man won't look you in the eye. Also one whose upper lip is raised in a perpetual slight sneer. Shiftiness is an unattractive trait, and this guy had it in spades. Even so, despite these disadvantages, there was no denying that Tony Hartley Haywood was extremely good looking. I wondered how many hearts he'd broken over the years.

'I don't think I've ever met an ex-copper before,' he said, after Sandro's introduction. Smirking in a careless sort of way, I might add.

'I bet you've met some serving ones,' I said.

He stared at me with hostility. Or, rather, not at me so much as at parts of me. Mostly my boobs. I stared right back, concentrating on his crotch area. Did he suspect that I knew the story of the stolen (though eventually returned) engagement ring? A very faint flush appeared in his cheeks for a moment. He laughed, as though he thought I'd been joking. 'So why are you here?'

'My parents are friends of Sandro's parents,' I said.

'Which ones are they?' As if he gave a toss.

I indicated them. And then Herry. 'So is my brother.'

An expression approaching respect briefly illuminated his handsome face. 'Hereward Quick is your brother?'

'As it happens . . .'

'Good Lord.'

'You sound astonished.'

'I am.'

'Why's that?'

'Oh, we've had . . . uh . . . dealings in the past.'

Something cold finger-tipped the back of my neck. While I wouldn't stake my life on it, I was pretty certain that any dealings this guy had with anyone at all would be on the shady side of legal. If Herry was mixed up with him, it could only be bad news. Hereward, my straight-arrow, white-bread brother . . . had he fallen in with a nest of vipers? Or a single adder, to be precise? I'd have to find out.

The door opened. In blew a gale force ten, straight from the Arctic, via the frozen Russian steppes. The temperature in the room dropped several degrees. The newcomer was thin and sallow, very erect, with an eagle's beak of a nose and greying black hair brushed back from his forehead to reveal eyes which – though I hate a cliché – could only be described as hooded. Like a bird of prey. Like a crocodile trying to decide which bit of its victim to crunch down on

next. From Maddalena's glad cries of greeting, I gathered
that this was the Marchese Cesare Antonio de Farnese de
Peron, her brother, Sandro's uncle and indirectly the genesis
of this gathering.

I remembered Sandro's shiver of apprehension and could
sympathize. *Fierce*, he'd said. Cesare could be *fierce* . . .
Looking at the man now as he haughtily surveyed the company,
I believed him. Sandro seemed mesmerized by the sight of
his uncle, like a stoat caught in the crossbeams of an owl's
attention. He glanced apprehensively round at his friends,
checking that none of them had a sign hung round their neck
announcing I STOLE THE DOGE'S RING. I'd heard somewhere that the Marchese had a long-term mistress in Venice
and a second one in Rome. But looking at the woman standing
beside him – presumably his wife, the Marchese Allegra – it
was hard to blame him. It can't have been a bundle of laughs
to share a bed with such a package of skin-draped bones.

He was a businessman, but also a diplomat. I supposed that
such people are trained in the art of the poker face, the ability
to give nothing away, the deadpan expression. This man was
deadpan from top to bottom, inside and out.

Maddalena saw me staring at him and tugged him over
to introduce us. He bowed stiffly over my hand, murmured
courtesies. Turned out he was a collector, in a small way, of
contemporary North American artists. The arctic permafrost
melted a little when I mentioned Walid Raad and Chuck Close.
I also spoke of Rauschenberg, Lee Miller, Andy Warhol. He
winced again. 'What is your opinion of *him*?'

'The man who flung a can of soup in the public's face,' I
said. I swear he came close to smiling.

I told him about my commission from Darren Carter and
he even went so far as to suggest that if I ever found myself
in Venice, I should rock up to his *palazzo* and enjoy a glass
of prosecco with him and his wife, who nodded unenthusiastic
agreement. And, incidentally, he added, cast a glance over
some of his paintings. It went without saying that the eye
would be expected to be an appreciative one. 'I think you'll
like them.' Despite the unspoken '*or else*' behind his words,
I expressed myself as delighted and grateful for such a unique

opportunity. I wondered if I could get an article out of it. *Venice's Secret Treasures* . . .

Sandro appeared, holding a couple of plates of delicious bits and pieces. 'Here, take this,' he said, handing me one. Then he ushered me to one of two chairs set on either side of a small, marble-topped table which held a bronze statue of some bearded person with a trident in one hand and something fishy in the other. 'Neptune taming a seahorse,' I said. 'Thought a rarity.'

'It's that, all right. At least, according to my English grandfather. It was a twenty-first birthday present from him.'

'Not cast for him by Claus of Innsbruck, by any chance?'

'No idea.' Not picking up my Browning-esque literary reference, his face expressed concern. Was Alex losing it? Had she suddenly developed dementia? 'Have some of these battered prawns,' he said kindly. 'Absolutely delicious. They make the batter with brandy.' He crunched one down. 'Have you met everyone? Of relevance, I mean.'

'Apart from Fabio.'

'Oh, sorry. I forgot to tell you that Fabio phoned from Milan yesterday afternoon to say something had come up and he wouldn't be able to make it today.'

Was that significant or suspicious in any way? Well, of course it might be. But equally it might not.

'Now tell me, Alex,' Sandro went on. 'In your considered opinion, of the guys you've met, which one do you—'

'Hang about,' I said. 'I haven't even had time to *form* an opinion, let alone consider one.'

'No intuitions? No hunches?'

'Not even in crime novels do investigators rely on sixth senses. Not any more. The readers wouldn't stand for it.' I laughed aloud, until I saw he was wrinkle-browed serious. 'No, Sandro. No gut feelings. Nothing came up and hit me between the eyes, I'm afraid. Except that I wouldn't trust your girlfriend's brother with my brush-combings. Want my advice, steer clear of any business deals with that one, for a start.'

'Hmm . . .' He nodded. 'But other than that?'

'Nothing.' The truth was that apart from Tony Hartley Heywood, they had all seemed as clear and transparent as glass. Even Miss Sullen, the brooding model. 'Mind you, I haven't met Fabio yet.'

'It can't have been him . . . he spends nearly all his time in Milano.'

'But you told me your friends are constantly popping back and forth between England and Italy.'

'I know. But somehow I don't feel . . .' He turned his head away and surveyed the room. 'I mean, if Fabio had stolen the painting, why come over to England to dispose of it?'

'That's easy. To divert suspicion, I'd imagine. Cover his tracks.' I ate some of the stuff on my plate. All of it was absolutely delicious. I wanted more. Much more. 'One thing I don't understand . . . why not *sell* the doge's ring? It must surely be a museum piece. Whoever took it in to the pawnshop can't have got anything even close to what it's worth.'

'This had puzzled me also. But perhaps the depositor intended to come back as soon as possible to redeem it. Or perhaps just because it *is* a museum piece. There'd almost certainly be some adverse publicity.'

'Someone temporarily embarrassed, as they say?'

'I guess.'

'It was taking a bit of a risk that the piece would have been sold before whoever deposited it came back to redeem it. As indeed it was.'

'Luckily it was by me!'

'And still no idea who might be responsible?'

'I told you. As far as I know, none of them have any need to steal. Or pawn.'

We both scrutinized the room. Standing by a porphyry column – God, how horrible, why would a young man like Sandro own such a thing? – was Katy Whatever and Uncle Cesare, discussing something in an energetic, not to say forceful manner. Probably art of some kind, I imagined, since he was a collector and she worked in a gallery. Near them, Jack and Harry Jago, the organic kings, were considering an asparagus spear in a thoughtful way. They were cheerful young men, as I had discovered when I chatted to them earlier. Hugely enthusiastic about their enterprise, too. 'If we can get the necessary documentation, we want to add homemade jams and jellies to our catalogue,' one of them had said. Jack, I think it was. The two of them were almost indistinguishable, with auburn-tinted hair and ruddy countryman's cheeks.

At the word 'catalogue', the other had produced as though from nowhere a booklet. 'Never without one,' he said.

'Take a gander at that sometime,' said his brother. 'I think you'll find it interesting.'

Eating Naturally, it said on the front. There was a picture of a rustic basket full of vegetables on a red-checked tablecloth, with a sunny yellow bowl of wholesome brown eggs arranged artfully in front of it and a view of fields full of daisies in the distance. I stuck it into my shoulder bag. 'I'm sure I shall. Tell me, does it cost a lot of money to set up something like this?'

'Pretty much. Start-up money, that is.'

'We were lucky,' said his brother. 'We were gifted the land by our grandfather. The thing was what to do with it?'

'Then we came up with the organic idea.'

'And away we went.'

'Drew up a business plan—'

'With Sandro's help.'

'Cost sheets, feasibility studies, funding, publicity, all that.'

'It's worked out well.'

'Millionaires in the making?' I said.

One of them raised reproving eyebrows at me. 'Maybe it sounds naive—'

'Or even untrue.'

'But we didn't go into it for the money.'

'We're happy enough just to make a decent living.'

'With sufficient for a few extras, of course.'

'Such as affording to get married.'

They had explained that Jack (or possibly Harry) was tying the knot next month.

I'd looked round. 'Is the bride-to-be here?'

The soon-to-be groom shook his head. 'She's gone to Barcelona with some mates.'

'Sort of an early hen party,' explained his brother.

'So she's not part of this crowd?'

'God, no.' The two brothers looked at each other and laughed. '*Christ*, no.'

'But you were all in Venice for Sandro's party.'

'That was different.'

I couldn't pursue our conversation further because I had just noticed my mother looking at me, and went over to join her.

Now, chomping on my last prawn, I said to Sandro, 'I hadn't realized that you were involved in *Eating Naturally*. The Jago brothers' enterprise, I mean.'

'It was only to a limited degree. And only until they got going.'

'Nonetheless . . .' Leave a sentence unfinished and I've often found that people rise like a fish snapping at a fly to complete it, often in ways I couldn't have imagined. Sandro didn't.

'Yeah,' he said vaguely. He stood. 'I'd better go and circulate a bit more.' He hesitated, looking down at me. 'I saw you talking to my uncle earlier.'

'That's right. He invited me to visit him and his collection if I'm ever in Venice.'

'*Cesare* did?' He seemed astonished. 'Why?'

I simpered modestly. 'Because I'm worth it.'

'I'm sure you are, but . . .'

'I also know quite a bit about some of the painters in his collection.'

'I see.'

As he moved away, I caught at his sleeve. 'Sandro, has this happened before? Has stuff gone missing from other houses where your friends have been?'

He frowned. 'Why do you ask?'

'Know what a kleptomaniac is?'

'Of course.' His eyes were suddenly wary, his body poised as though for a blow.

'Is it possible that one of your friends, rich and well-brought-up as they are, might be one?' I tried to keep my voice neutral.

To my surprise, his face reddened. '*No!*' he said explosively, the word sounding like a fired bullet. 'Certainly not.' Which I took to mean, '*Actually, yes.*' It was something I'd have to look into later. But kleptomaniacs don't usually go on to sell the stuff they've lifted. They're more in the nature of magpies, hoarding the stolen treasure, rather than taking it for monetary gain. There was a royal personage, wasn't there, the present monarch's grandmother, or great-grandmother, who was given to helping herself to expensive little *objets* from the houses of her friends, which her ladies-in-waiting would discreetly return the following day?

'I'll go along to the pawnshop tomorrow and see if I can dig up any more details,' I said. 'Though such places are notoriously close-mouthed about the people who take advantage of their services.'

'They'd have to be, in an upmarket area like the West End.' Sandro was looking curiously relieved, as though I'd been Hot, or at least Warm, a moment ago, but had now moved towards Cold. Which made me wonder if I should be looking in a different, though related, direction. And also, if I was correct in my assumption, find out which one of his friends was the possible klepto.

As with an ebbing tide, little pools of conversation were forming and melting into similar but different ones. I saw Katy Pasqualin standing temporarily alone, staring out of one of the tall windows at the cityscape below, and went over to join her.

'Oh, hi, Alex,' she said, turning to me. Clever to remember my name after one brief introduction, I thought. Then I saw there were tears in her eyes. And one moving slowly down her cheek.

I frowned. I had been wrong to designate designer scarves and lava or whale-tooth necklaces. Her pretty dress made no statements at all, and her meticulously manicured feet were in ordinary Prada sandals. Ordinary, that is, except for the price. Which I happened to know was well over six hundred quid. Six *hundred* . . . say *what*? 'What's wrong?' I asked.

'Oh, nothing,' she said. As I could have placed bets she would. She brushed at the lone teardrop.

'Something obviously is,' I said. 'Do you want to talk about it? Do you need to?'

'It's not really the right time or place, is it?'

'Is there ever a right time?'

'True.'

Despite the hair, I'd already marked her down as more mature than her two friends. 'Boyfriend? Parents? Money?'

'Something like that.' She placed the back of her index finger under her nose. Sniffed a little. Gave me a damp smile. 'It's kind of you to be concerned, but really, it's nothing.'

'If you say so . . .' I moved away, leaving an encouraging smile behind me and wondering what on earth could be responsible for the momentary look of sheer terror I had glimpsed lying behind her tears.

Was this the first rift in the lute? There were obviously darker forces at play beneath the privileged upbringing. It had been short-sighted of me to think otherwise. Ahead of me was another floral frock, inside which I recognized Bianca. I had been wrong to peg these pretty feminine girls as . . . well . . . pretty mindless. They were all far from that. 'Hey, Bianca,' I said.

'Oh, hi.' She frowned, obviously trying to remember who the heck I was.

'Alex Quick,' I said. 'We only had the briefest introduction earlier.'

'Of course.'

'You live in London, don't you?' Coming in sideways, so she wouldn't suspect I was trying to pump her.

'I should hope so. I would hate to have to commute every day.'

She had a charming accent, not quite foreign, but equally not quite English. 'So where do you live?' I asked.

'I share a flat in the City. Before you ask, there are two other people, one of each sex.' She gave me a shrewd smile, indicating that she knew exactly what I was doing. Did she know why?

'What about Katy? Does she share too?'

'Not on a permanent basis. She has a boyfriend. James something or other, if you're interested.'

'Is he here?'

Bianca gave an indifferent shrug. Nuff said. Either she didn't like the boyfriend, or didn't approve of him. Or both.

'But not Fabio,' I said. Even to my own ears, I didn't sound as frank and open as I would have liked.

'Fabio prefers the men,' Bianca said. She shrugged haughtily. 'And why not.' This was a new piece of information, though I couldn't see that it was necessarily relevant. Nonetheless, I wondered why Sandro had omitted to tell me.

'Did Sandro tell you he and Katy are cousins?' I asked.

'Probably, since they are.'

She was a daunting young woman. Although there isn't much which daunts me, I found myself not daring to ask if she herself had a significant other.

Edred and Mary joined us. Bianca quickly made an excuse and left.

'So,' I said. 'How's it going?'

'Lots of very pretty girls,' Edred said happily.

'Are you going home tonight?' asked Mary.

'I have to see someone in the morning so I'll stay here. Shan't get back to Longbury until lunchtime.'

'Isn't it time Lena produced that baby?' my mother said. 'I saw her last week and she looked as if she was carrying quintuplets.'

'Octuplets,' said my father.

'Any day now, I should think,' I said. 'By the way, just so you know, I'm planning to go to Venice next week for a few days.'

'Lucky you.'

'I know.'

'Business or pleasure?'

'Mostly business. But just being in Venice is a pleasure.'

'"Once did she hold the gorgeous East in fee,"' said my father vaguely. '"Venice, the eldest child of Liberty."'

'I wonder what Wordsworth meant by that,' said Mary.

'Surely it's obvious.'

'I don't agree. Why the eldest child? Why Liberty?'

Uncle Cesare was approaching and I left my parents to their literary wrangling.

'Signorina, please take this.' He handed me his business card. 'I am leaving now but I look forward to hearing from you when you arrive in Venice. Until then, *ciao*.'

'Thank you,' I said. 'I'll definitely be in touch.'

*   *   *

The next morning, I made my way to the upmarket pawnshop where Sandro had seen his aunt's ring displayed in the window. I pushed open the door and faced a barrier of shiny stainless-steel rods which extended right across the shop, with a small grille which could be opened set into it. As I approached, a person of some kind appeared behind it. Male? Female? Impossible to say.

A man in a flat tweed cap was standing to the right of the shop, examining a wall-hung display case containing necklaces hung on pegboard hooks. His back was very pointedly towards me and I wondered if he was someone recognizable, trying to look both inconspicuous and like the sort of punter who was in and out all day, pawning stuff. He didn't pull it off, really. His behaviour made me determine to linger, once I got outside, to see if his face was familiar.

'Yes?' said the grille person. I still couldn't tell what sex he/she/it was from the voice.

'I wanted to enquire about a piece of jewellery which was recently handed over as collateral for a loan.'

'And you are?'

'I'm with the police.' Put like that, I wasn't quite impersonating a police officer, was I?

As far as I could make out, the expression on the other side of the grille was sceptical in the extreme. *Pull the other one* trembled on its androgynous lips.

'I'm afraid we can't divulge any details at all about our depositors.' The being leaned forward slightly and glanced at the back of the man examining necklaces. He was standing ramrod straight, tension tightening his shoulder blades. 'As you can imagine, once we start giving away information of that sort, our reputation for discretion would be destroyed.'

'Could you give me a rough general description? That's all I need. I'm not trying to track the person down. I just need to know which of three possibilities it might have been.'

Very quietly, the person wrote on a slip of paper and turned it so I could read it. *Come back at 17:30.* Speaking clearly, they said, 'Where theft is concerned, obviously we are more than willing to cooperate with the police as far as we possibly can.'

'But theft is exactly what I'm talking about.'

'We would require much more information about the stolen item or items, and identification of the true owner of the piece. Until then, we have to rigidly respect the privacy of our customers. We can't start changing the rules every time some inquisitive person wanders in.'

'I can quite see that. But I have photos of the missing object and I'm working on behalf of the owner.'

'How do I know you're telling the truth?' The piece of paper had disappeared.

'You don't.'

'Precisely.' The face receded. 'So I'm afraid I can't be of further assistance.'

'Well, thank you anyway. And may I say how much I admire your ethical stance. It must be a great relief for your clients.'

Outside, I crossed the road and stood looking into the window of a place selling butcher shop equipment. Everything from table-top mincers to wood-block tables, every kind of knife you could think of from cleavers and slicers to boning knives and carvers. There were hooks and steels and bandsaws and weird latex gloves. Fascinating. Across the road, Flat Cap Man came out of the pawnshop and swiftly moved away. At the corner of the street, he removed his cap and sunglasses and headed off round into the next street. All I had time to note was the slim build, the fancy designer shoes and the expensively beautiful overcoat.

SIX

The art gallery where Katy Pasqualin was the manager was just off Kensington High Street. I hung around a bit, clocked the shop windows, went into the bookstore directly opposite and glanced through a few of the volumes piled on the front table, at the same time keeping an eye out for Katy emerging for lunch. Of course, for all I knew, she might just bring a sandwich and eat at her desk. Or, given her slim figure, she might skip lunch altogether. But I was betting she'd come out, if only for a change of scene. Otherwise, I'd have to go into the gallery and look at the stuff on display, which would make it a lot more difficult to go into the artless mode I planned, hailing her across the street with phoney spontaneity.

At five minutes past one, she emerged. She was all business today, in a short brown skirt with a long jacket over it. I wasn't crazy about the brass buttons. A bag was slung over her shoulder and she was talking on the phone as she passed the bookshop. I dashed after her.

'Katy!' I carolled, spontaneous as hell. She stopped and looked back.

'Oh . . . uh . . . Alex,' she said. 'Just a moment.' Into her phone, she said, 'Gotta go, hon. Talk later.'

From which I deduced she was talking to the boyfriend. James Something. 'Sorry to barge in on you like this,' I lied, 'but I was in the bookshop, and saw you go by. Can I buy you a coffee? Or even lunch?'

'That's very nice of you. Thanks,' she said.

We walked to a restaurant nearby. Crowded with braying customers. Smelling of coffee and grated cheese. Several of the brayers lifted their hands and waved at Katy. She smiled back at them. We found a table and set ourselves up with coffee. I had a grilled cheese sandwich. She chose a salade niçoise.

'So,' she said. 'What brings you here?'

'I had to see someone whose office is . . .' I gestured vaguely in the direction of the park. 'And then I saw you.' I'm a great believer in the lie direct.

'Right.' She obviously didn't believe me.

In which case, I might as well go for the truth direct. 'It's absolutely none of my business,' I said. 'But you seemed a little upset the other night at Sandro's. More than that. You seemed scared of something.'

'Scared?' For a moment, she held my gaze. Then she looked away. 'You're absolutely right,' she said. 'It *is* none of your business.'

I'd have said the same in her place, if some more-or-less stranger had shown up and started probing into my private affairs. 'Nonetheless,' I continued. 'I don't like to see someone in distress. And as I said last time, if there's anything I can do . . .'

'There isn't.' She folded a leaf of young spinach against her fork and lifted it to her mouth.

I took it as an encouraging sign that she hadn't asked me to fuck off. 'Is it anything to do with the thefts from Sandro's uncle's apartment in Venice?' I said.

That got her. She sat abruptly upright, as though a bolt of lightning had struck her. 'What are you . . .? What do you mean?'

'I think you know. At least . . . I think you know something about it.'

'I'm not a thief,' she said.

'I didn't say you were. I'm only suggesting that you might know someone who is. Perhaps one of your friends.'

She tightened her lips so hard I could practically see the outline of her teeth under them.

'I can tell that you know what I'm talking about.' I kept my voice gentle. Conversational. Quite hard for me. 'The antique ring. The little Botticelli lookalike.'

'Who are you working for?' She stared wildly around. 'How do you know about them?'

'Let's just say I was informed.'

'Who by?'

'I'd rather not say.'

'Was it Suzy? Or Harry?'

'Heavens above! Were you all in it together?' I smiled. 'Sounds like something out of an Agatha Christie novel.'

Which one of the people at Sandro's party could have scared Katy so much? Or was it all down to someone else entirely, someone who hadn't officially been present? Someone she might have caught in the act of stealing something from the Marchese's collection, and been sworn to secrecy by?

I thought she was going to stand up, point at me dramatically and order me to leave. Instead, she crumpled. Her spine slid against the back of her chair. 'Oh *God*.' She buried her face in her hands.

I was about to push a bit harder when a couple of guys in blue-and-white striped shirts and beige linen jackets appeared beside us. One of them glared at me. The other put his hand on Katy's shoulder and bent down towards her. 'Everything all right, Kates?' he said.

'Fine. Just fine, thanks, Edward.' Katy spoke in a strangled voice and sat up as straight as she could manage.

'We'll walk you back to the gallery,' said the glarer.

'I'll pick up the tab,' said Edward. 'As for you, whoever you are . . .' He jerked his head at the door of the place. 'On your bike.'

Let no one say I can't take a hint. 'You know how to get in touch, Katy,' I said softly. I touched her arm and left. At least she seemed to have friends. I would dearly have liked to know what she was so scared of.

Katy was the easiest of Sandro's friends to 'run into' without arousing suspicion. I decided to go for Bianca the Banker next, though she'd be much harder to 'accidentally' encounter. Since I had the address of the financial institution she was employed by, I went down to the City, and found the place. Diving straight in was the best way, I decided. Meet her head on.

The global headquarters of the company she worked for was housed in an imposing building, its massive front door placed at the top of a shallow flight of stone steps. An equally imposing guy in a top hat and a long green coat strewn with medals was standing in front of the door. I walked up the steps, wondering whether he was going to let me in.

After a nail-biting couple of seconds, he did. Phew! I walked into an interior of marbled walls, sweeps of stairways and galleries, acres of black and white tiling, an impression of daily polished brass. There were shiny boards on the walls, proclaiming in gilt letters the different departments and corporations housed beneath this august roof. I spotted Bianca's company, up on the third floor. I could have walked up, but chose to take the lift. Another imposing bloke stood inside, dressed identically to the first one and wearing exactly the same medals. What a coincidence. They must have fought together in the same fields of conflict. Brothers in arms, or what?

When the lift stopped, I stepped out and walked along the corridor until I came to the office where Bianca, according to Sandro, spent her working days. I looked through the glass panel set into the door. And there she was, one of about twenty people, all beavering away at papers on their desks, or staring at computer screens in front of them.

I pushed open the door. As one man/woman, they all looked up at me. Bianca recognized me and frowned. What was this woman doing here, someone she'd only met briefly two evenings ago? And why was she – Alex, was it? – beckoning her over? With an apologetic look at the beavers on either side of her, she got up and walked between desks towards me, still frowning. Unless she was ready for a break, I could see this was going to be an abortive meeting.

No floaty dresses and strappy sandals today. She was wearing a dark-green trouser suit with a girly-pink T-shirt under it. Very plain. Very one of the boys. With just the right touch of femininity. 'What are you doing here?' she said.

I wanted to say I'd just been appointed the Ann Summers rep for the area, but didn't think she'd laugh. 'I'm so sorry to disturb you,' I said humbly. 'It's just that Sandro Grainger suggested I get in touch. It's regarding the dinner party he had in Venice, whenever it was.'

'What about it?'

'He was worried that someone might have walked off by mistake with something belonging to his uncle and asked me to look into it.'

'Why couldn't he ask me direct?'

Good question, Bianca. 'I'm not quite sure.'

'Well, for your – and his – information, I know nothing about anything being removed, whether by mistake or not.'

'You didn't see anyone who might have picked something up to admire it, and then slipped it into a pocket? It's easily done.'

She drew in an indignant breath. 'You – or Sandro – sound perilously close to accusing me of theft. Or if not me, then one of his other guests.'

'I'm certain that wasn't his intention. It's just that a couple of small items did go missing on that occasion, and he didn't want his uncle offended. It might easily have been one of the catering staff, or the cleaners. Who knows.'

She adopted a supercilious expression. 'That's who I'd look at first, if it was me.'

I'll bet you would, I thought. I could easily see just how she'd treat any domestic staff if the opportunity occurred. Accusing hotel chambermaids of stealing her jewellery. Sacking underlings if something important went missing then not bothering to apologize when she later found whatever the item was in one of her drawers or bags.

'Sandro said they were all trusted people who'd catered for his uncle and aunt many times in the past.'

'Oh, well.' She turned to go. 'Good luck, anyway.'

My ex-police officer's antennae had detected no hint from Bianca that she was having me on. But Katy? Leaving Bianca's building, I decided I wasn't so sure about her, despite the fact that like her friend she'd sounded perfectly genuine in her denial of any involvement in the theft. There was that tear in her eye at Sandro's gathering. There was her obvious terror, and her cool reaction to me over lunch. I reminded myself that as Sandro's cousin, she might quite legitimately have gone back to the Marchese's apartment and seen someone nicking the missing objects, or even nicked them herself. I further reflected that neither lightning rods nor antennae are perfect instruments, and it's entirely possible that they're sometimes faulty.

I walked away. And that's when I realized that for once the gods were smiling on me, making my life easier. For, parked in a loading bay in one of the streets leading down to the river, was a white van. Its back doors were open, and guess what: on the side of the van was a picture of a rustic basket full of vegetables, set on a red-checked tablecloth, alongside a bowl full of wholesome brown eggs, with a view of fields in the distance. *Eating Naturally*. The Jago boys. Right where I wanted them. I moved faster.

One of them emerged from a door further down the street and came walking back towards me, swinging an empty box in one hand, not registering my presence. He shoved the box into the back of the van and then stood leaning against the side of the rear door, pulling out a waterproof bag of tobacco and a packet of Rizlas. He rolled himself a fag, and put his paraphernalia away.

'Tut, tut,' I said, as I came abreast of him. 'I thought you were into healthy living.'

'And so I am. This tobacco is more vegetable than tobacco. You could practically fry it with butter and have it for supper.' He smiled at me. 'And how are you, Alex?'

'This is quite a coincidence, isn't it?' I said. 'Seeing you here and all.'

'I guess it is. Or is this your usual stamping ground?'

'I don't even live in London. But I wanted to speak to Bianca—'

'She works somewhere round here, doesn't she?'

'That's right.'

'What did you want to see her about, if you don't mind my asking?'

'It's to do with that dinner party Sandro had in Venice, in his uncle's *appartamento*.'

'Great fun,' he said. 'A great evening.' Did I imagine it or had his eyes suddenly become wary?

'It sounds it.'

'And what did you want to know about it?' He dragged on his roll-up. Trying for nonchalant and not quite making it.

'Well, Sandro was very embarrassed to discover that some small valuables had gone missing after the party, and asked if I could look into it for him.'

'And he thinks one of us might have taken them?' His voice was a mixture of incredulity and contempt. 'One of his *friends*?'

'He didn't go that far. But me being an ex-copper and all, he thought it might be a good idea if I put on my detective's hat and had a word with all of you. Find out if any of you noticed anything amiss, that sort of thing.'

He snorted derisively. 'Like seeing one of us pocketing a diamond ring or some other precious bauble when they thought the others weren't looking?'

'Exactly like that, yes.'

'In other words, if we had, you – or Sandro – want us to sneak on them? That's quite an ask, isn't it?' He was beginning to lose his temper. His freckles seemed to pulse indignantly.

'Not really.' I hardened my voice. 'After all, theft is theft.' *Sneak* . . . I loved it. So prep-school, little boys in cherry-red blazers or bigger boys in tweed jackets with leather patches on the elbows.

I wasn't sure whether it was Harry or Jack, but whichever, he ostentatiously raised scornful eyebrows. 'Can't think where my brother's got to,' he said. 'But I mustn't keep you.'

'You aren't,' I assured him. 'Not in the least.'

'Well, I've got some paperwork to do in the van,' he said. He tossed the end of his roll-up into the gutter, pulled open the van door and climbed into the driver's seat. 'I'll say goodbye, then.' His eyes weren't friendly. 'Really good to see you again.'

Sure it was. 'And you.'

He did a little finger-wave at me from the front seat and bent his head over a file of papers in such an ostentatious way that I had no choice but to leave. And to wonder what to make of the conversation. It seemed reasonable to suspect that he knew something about the objects stolen from Venice. Whether he or his brother was guilty of taking them was something else. I was inclined to think that though they might be aware of the theft, they weren't actually responsible . . . I presumed he spoke for his brother. Or at the very least, would back up or be backed up by him. So here I was. Four or five down and four to go. Suzy. Her brother Tony. Sulky Laura, the model. And Fabio, even though he apparently spent most of his time in Milan. Not that that made much difference. Sandro had made it clear that he and his friends divided their time between Italy and England. If Fabio was the thief, he could just as easily dispose of any stolen booty in London as in Milan.

So who next?

SEVEN

It was three days later that I returned from running some of the boring errands that plague our lives when we have to travel to find six messages on the answering machine. All were from Sandro, each one increasing in urgency and desperation. I pressed in the buttons for his mobile. He picked up after the first beep.

'Alessandra!' He was breathing heavily, as though he was climbing a mountain.

'What's up?' I asked.

'It's Katy.' He groaned. 'Oh, this is terrible.'

'What's happened?' I spoke harshly. In a crisis, people often react better to an abrasive voice than to a sympathetic one.

It certainly seemed to work with Sandro. He coughed, cleared his throat. 'Her boyfriend telephoned me this morning. James Renfrew. They don't live together, but they spend most evenings at one or the other's place. And apparently last night Katy went back to her own place alone, since James had to stay late at work. He phoned her, just to say good night . . . you know how it is, and when she didn't answer he assumed that she'd already fallen asleep, so he didn't keep on trying. And today he went round, and she didn't answer the door. He managed to get someone to open up, someone from the management team, a–and th–they found her.'

'Oh, my God,' I said. It sounded terminally serious. 'What? Tell me.'

Sandro began sobbing. Harsh sounds came at me down the line. 'She was . . . she was . . . in the bath. Dead. Oh, Alex, I can't believe it. I just can't take it in. Not Katy. She was so nice. So sweet. So—'

'When you say she was in the bath . . .'

'She had been . . . she was *drowned.*'

'Oh, God. I'm really sorry. She was a nice kid. Do they know when this happened?'

'Sometime last night, the police are saying.'

It was hard to take in. I'd only seen and talked to her the previous lunchtime. 'Do they think it was an accident, that she had a heart attack or something?'

'No. That's what's so horrible. They're saying someone came into her bathroom and pushed her under. There's water splashed all over the floor and distinct marks on her face where she was held down until she . . .' He gulped and coughed. 'Until she died. And she'd obviously . . . obviously struggled. Oh, my poor cousin. Oh, God. *E terribile . . .* It's terrible.'

'Sandro, I know how upset you must be feeling, but try to think. Could this have any connection to the thefts from your uncle's place in Venice?'

'I don't know. I just don't know. Why should it?'

'Wouldn't it almost have to?'

'It–it does seem like it. And it's my fault.'

'How do you work that out?'

'Isn't it obvious? Whoever is responsible for taking the doge's ring must have been afraid that Katy could identify him or her. If I'd never had that party, she might still be alive.'

'Huh?' If the two events were connected . . . the girl's death and the thefts . . . he might be right, though I couldn't as yet follow the trail. Not until I'd done some research. Meanwhile, poor Sandro would probably live with the unfounded guilt for the rest of his life.

On the other end of the phone, he sobbed bitterly.

'Were Katy and James a together couple?' I asked. 'Got on well?'

'Absolutely. They've been a couple for ages. I've never seen either of them be anything but happy to be in each other's company.' He sniffed. 'They were planning to get married in October.'

'Oh, dear. That must make it that much worse.'

'I know.'

'Look, keep in touch. And I'm so sorry you've lost your cousin, Sandro. I know the two of you were close.'

Snuffles. Gulps. His first brush with the seamy side, I guessed. 'Thank you,' he said in a tiny voice. 'By the way,

I'm going back to Venice this evening with my uncle. So I shan't be around.'

'We can still keep in touch.'

Call ended, I couldn't help wondering. Had someone been waiting for poor Katy when she returned to her flat? Had she invited someone back? Someone who'd been at Sandro's party? She hadn't seemed the type, especially given Sandro's assessment of the relationship between her and James Renfrew. In any case, she would never have undressed or got into the bath unless the person in the flat was someone she knew pretty well. Unless the assailant was already there, waiting for her to return home. But if the boyfriend was responsible, would he have been the one to call in the police? I gave an inward shrug. After all, why not? There'd be no better way to try to divert suspicion from himself. I tried to remember him from Sandro's party, but I couldn't put a face to the name.

With so little information to go on, I tried to push it out of my head. Instead, I got out my reference books to start the preliminary work on Venice and Venetian paintings, but found my mind kept returning to the thought of pretty Katy in her floaty summer dress. Dead. Drowned in her own bath. Why? Did she have information which someone didn't want revealed? Did she know who'd stolen the doge's ring? Or the small school-of-Botticelli? Had she stolen them herself?

I thought back to my conversation with the pawnbroker. I'd returned to the place after five thirty, as I'd been instructed, and been ushered in by a tiny person who suffered from such acute osteoporosis that their body was almost the shape of an inverted U. I still couldn't have said either way whether it was male or female but I opted for female, given the rather beautiful gold and amethyst chain she was wearing. She shut the shop door behind me and swung a sign around which informed the pawning public that the place was closed.

'Now,' she said, 'why do the police want to know about the ring which was pawned a week or so ago?'

I recognized someone hungry for drama. I looked from side to side and bent towards her. 'It could be a matter of life or death,' I said. 'That ring was stolen property and the man who owned it is a pretty fierce Italian nobleman who doesn't like having his stuff nicked.'

'The ring is no longer in my possession,' she said.

'That's because a relative of the guy who owns it luckily happened to see it in your window. He was able to buy it back, and return it before its rightful owner found out. But we need to find out who took it in the first place so they can't do it again. Or,' I said significantly, 'murder might be committed.'

'Heavens above!'

'So can you help me?'

'Like I said earlier, no, I can't.'

'So why the fu— Why did you tell me to come back?'

'I wanted to know what was going on.'

'And you still can't give me a clue as to who brought it in? Male? Female? Young? Old? Anything?'

She shook her head. The amethyst sparkled in its gold setting. 'Sorry.'

'You can't give me even a hint?'

'Sorry,' she said again.

I stood up. Feigned anger. Asked again why the hell she'd told me to come back later. 'Sorry,' she said once more.

'You've seriously wasted my time,' I said, implying a number of postponed meetings. 'And don't tell me you're sorry, because it's obvious you're not.'

'Not English,' she said. She held open the door for me. 'That's all I'm saying.'

I wagged a finger at her as I stepped out on to the pavement. 'If someone dies, you'll be responsible.'

All the way home I had pondered her last words. *Not English* . . . so Italian? It almost went without saying. But since all the people I knew to be involved undoubtedly spoke perfect Italian, certainly fluently enough to convince the pawnshop woman, that wasn't much help.

Now, I reached for my phone and called my friend and former colleague, DCI Felicity Fairlight. I ran over the details of what Sandro had originally told me about his dinner party in Venice, about his discovery in London first of the ring, and then of the little pseudo-Botticelli sketch, and asked what she knew about Katy's death.

'I can make a call,' she said. 'London's not my bailiwick.'

'But it is Joy's.' Joy was Fliss's partner, a long-serving officer with the Met.

'What do you want her to do?'

'She's obviously not running the case. So nothing much. Except find Katy's killer. And whoever it was who had pawned the two items belonging to Cesare, because logically, that person must be the thief. And therefore possibly linked to Katy's murder, since she was the only one of his friends that Sandro told about the thefts.'

'I think I got that,' Fliss said. 'So not a big ask.'

'I'm banging on about it because this inside sort of information is sometimes hard for the investigating officers to obtain, so they might find it helpful when they're questioning the victim's known associates.'

'Thanks, Quick, I'm sure Joy will be happy to pass it on.'

Moving on to more general things, I told her I'd be in Venice for a few days for work purposes, just as soon as I could get my act together. Which was taking rather longer than I wanted it to. 'At least I've got two good contacts right there in Venice, panting to have me round to theirs,' I added.

'Oooh. What for?'

'Not what your nasty little mind is thinking. It's art for art's sake, nothing more.'

'I've heard that one before. When's the lovely Sam coming back?'

'I can't see the connection, but in the next couple of weeks. Or so I believe.' I strove to keep my tone neutral.

'A distinct sound of pique in there, Quick. Hasn't he been keeping in regular touch, the bad boy? Joy and I had *such* a nice card from him last week. Seemed to be having a *whale* of a time. Dating all these *gorgeous* Antipodean blondes. I'm *so* glad he's enjoying himself so much. I expect he'll be quite sorry to get home.'

'Scumbag. Stirrer,' I said, hoping she couldn't tell how put out I felt.

What I was thinking, when I eventually ended the call, was that next time either Felicity Fairlight or Samuel Willoughby came round to my place for a drink – if ever – I would be going pretty heavy on the arsenic. Sam had been away now for seven weeks and three days and hadn't contacted me in all that time. Not once. Pique was the right word. Still, when I thought about it, why should he? I've never given him the slightest encouragement. But I was also damn sure neither Fliss nor Joy had, either, yet he'd sent them postcards. And emailed Edward Vine, as I'd discovered last time I'd dropped in to pick up a bottle or two of Shiraz.

The hell with him.

The phone danced on my desk. It was Fliss again. 'I just had a word with Joy. She says they seem fairly confident it was the boyfriend,' she said. 'And for your information, some female DCI by the name of Carole Leavis is on the case. Ring any bells?'

'Ever so slightly.' Had my love-rat husband had an affair with her? She'd be one of the few if he hadn't. 'Can't remember how or why.'

'She sounds pretty much on the ball. So let's await developments.'

I ended the call. The phone immediately rang again. The Major, a hint of distress in his voice, asked me to come and see him when I had a moment.

'Good news?' I asked.

'Depends what you consider good,' he said gloomily. 'They say those drawings – the old boy and that clown – are probably worth a lot of money. Said they'd be glad to handle the sale of them, if I was so minded. There'd be a lot of publicity, once they had the definitive authentication. Doesn't bear thinking about. I ask you, what am I going to do with all that cash? And I feel a bit of a fraud, d'you see? I mean, they're not really mine, when it comes right down to it. They rightfully belonged to Nell.' Behind him I heard Marlowe start to bark.

'But she gifted the house and contents to you,' I said. 'She must have known about them when she did that.'

'Tell the truth, at the moment I'm living in fear of finding something else equally valuable she hid somewhere in the house.'

'Well, they haven't been completely authenticated yet, have they?' I soothed. 'Maybe someone sold them to her as the real thing, which is why she hid them behind her friend's painting, but they're not actually genuine. Where are they, by the way?'

'Up in London still, thank the Lord. I hardly dared to light a match while I still had custody, in case the house went up in flames and they were destroyed.'

'Major, you've been lighting matches for years without any ill-effects. Why would you suddenly start setting fire to things?'

'Silly, I know. Anyway, I'm delighted that they're not currently in my possession.'

'I'll come down to see you as soon as I can,' I promised.

A couple of days later, when the afternoon had begun to cool off, I went out. I walked along the seafront, up towards the university perched on the hill above the town, then striking right out into the countryside. It took me just under an hour to reach the top of Honeypot Lane. I walked down and into the Major's garden.

I could hear him crooning something. Difficult to say what, exactly. Sounded like his singing voice was on a par with his topiary skills. Poor to hopeless, in other words. But he sounded really happy. As I reached the open kitchen door, I heard another voice joining in. Female, this time.

'Tea for two,' rumbled the Major.

'And two for tea,' sang a higher, clearer voice.

Goodness me. What was this all about?

'. . . how happy we should beee . . .!'

'Tea for two,' started the Major again.

At which point I rapped on the door and said, 'Make that three, if you don't mind.'

Both of the people in the kitchen turned towards me. The Major looked beatific. The other one, a woman, looked startled. She must have been at least in her early sixties, with a huge mop of curly, grey-brown hair gushing from her head and big brown eyes. Her clothes were what you might expect from someone who'd had all of theirs stolen and been forced to resort to a rag-bag of old curtains, torn skirts, discarded blouses. She reminded me vividly of my murdered friend and business partner, Helena Drummond.

'Alex! How lovely to see you, m'dear,' said the Major.

'And you too, Major. Gosh, for a minute there I thought I'd blundered into a private concert.'

He drew the woman forward. 'Do you know Ms Forbes?' he asked.

'No, I don't think so.' I stuck out my hand. 'How do you do? I'm Alexandra Quick.'

She smiled, shook my hand and stepped back. 'I have actually heard of you,' she said. 'Norman never stops talking about you.'

'Nonsense, m'dear.'

Forbes. I realized that actually I did know the name. Philippa Forbes had been the art mistress at the girls' high school. Maybe still was. The one who'd painted the farmhouse behind which the Major had discovered the two Tiepolo sketches. 'Aha,' I said. 'Are you still teaching art?'

'Just about.' She grinned at me, displaying a set of flawless plastic teeth. 'But very much looking forward to retirement.'

The Major was nodding and winking behind her. 'I've made some peanut butter cookies which are to die for,' he said. Unusual phraseology for the Major, I must say.

'And I brought a chocolate cream sponge with me,' said Ms Forbes. 'Homemade, of course.'

'Three for tea, and tea for ten,' I said. 'And what a tea it sounds!'

Later, having consumed two largish slices of cake and three cookies, I said, 'I take it you two have things to . . . er . . . discuss.' Was I supposed to know about the Italian drawings or not? I gave the Major a thumbs up.

'Yes,' he said. He cleared his throat. 'The Tiepolos.'

'Yes, indeed,' agreed Ms Forbes.

'Thing is, m'dear, Flo here dropped by a couple of days ago to find out if I knew about them. We've been discussing our best course of action more or less ever since.' He looked at Ms Forbes. 'Tell her, Flo.'

Flo? I had thought the art teacher's name was Philippa.

Or Fiona. The Major's memory was clearly not in peak condition. I said nothing.

'Yes,' she said. 'Well. Nell and I went on holiday together back in the spring. To Venice. Before she got sick, this is.' She ran her hands through the curls on top of her head. 'It was a great trip. We were in this little hotel, in a back street somewhere, with carved angels above the front door, and a rather grand salon on the first floor. *Piano nobile*, they call it. It must have been an impressive place once. Very simple, lovely.' Her expression was wistful.

'Anyway . . .' I said.

'Yes. Sorry. Anyway, we were rootling round the antique stalls in one of the squares, looking at prints and so on, and those two small sketches rather leaped out at me.'

'But . . .' Hadn't they been found in a bookshop?

'You see, in my younger days at art college, I did a dissertation on Tiepolo for my degree, so I recognized them at once. The style, at least. The execution. I said to Nell that I had to buy them, just as a nostalgic souvenir of Venice and my long-lost youth. Naturally it didn't occur to me that they might be the real thing.'

'Which square was this?'

She looked up at the ceiling. 'Um . . . Piazza di Sant something.'

'Not hugely helpful.'

'Sorry. I'm pretty sure there was a P in there somewhere. Pietro? Paulo? Can't remember exactly. Anyway, I bought the drawings and the man put them between pieces of cardboard, and they fitted very comfortably into my shoulder bag.' She looked at me. 'You've seen them . . . they're quite small.'

I nodded.

'Anyway, we found a nice restaurant for lunch, on a little canal. Sat outside. I had pasta with octopus . . . delicious! People were passing back and forth, smiling and so on. I noticed this one man, because I'd seen him back in the square where we bought the sketches. He was wearing—'

I interrupted. 'You bought these drawings from a stall, or from a shop?'

She seemed irritated. 'I just said . . . from a stall in the piazza di something. This man was wearing one of those flat white caps made of cotton or linen that men on the Continent like to wear. And then he passed our table, which was fine, why shouldn't he? But then he came back again, past us. And then went past again and came back. I'd got my shoulder bag very securely over my ankle, foot in the strap sort of thing, in case he was a pickpocket trying to snatch it.'

'You thought he was a would-be thief?'

'I was quite convinced of it.'

'What did he look like?'

'Well, funnily enough, apart from the cap thing on his head, he looked quite respectable. Suit and tie, polished shoes and so on. Anyway, after lunch, Nell and I walked back towards our hotel, thought we'd have a little nap, since we're both getting on a bit, and again I noticed him behind us. So I said to Nell that we'd walk round the corner and then dodge in at the back gate of the hotel, so he wouldn't know where we'd gone.'

'Though he'd probably have guessed,' the Major said. 'Where else could you have gone?'

'As it happened, there were a couple of other hotels right there. And a patisserie. Even a small grocers-cum-supermarket. Coop, it was called. The Italian version of the Co-op, I imagine.'

'So what did you do then?' I asked.

'It was difficult to know what was best, really. Did he take us for rich tourists with bulging wallets? Was he planning to grab our jewellery? We were far too old . . .'

'Nonsense, m'dear,' came from the Major.

'. . . to be abducted by a white slave trafficker unless it was for a kinky sheikh or something, into old women.' She threw back her head and laughed, displaying a lot of gold fillings at the back of her mouth.

'So then what?'

'It didn't really occur to me that he could be after my souvenir Tiepolos until later, even though we first saw him near that stall. We took as many precautions as we could, and he seemed to move off.' She moved her mouth around, making it clear that her dentures needed adjusting.

'Other fish to fry, I expect,' said the Major.

'Except . . .' She stared at us with eyes opened dramatically wide.

'Except?'

'Except that two days later, when we arrived at the airport to catch the plane back to London, there he was again!'

'Goodness me,' I said, since she obviously expected something in the way of a reaction. 'What did you do?'

'What *could* the poor girl do?' said the Major, sounding all protective and, not to put too fine a point on it, soppy. How did this happen? It was only a few days since I last saw him, and there wasn't any Flo Forbes in the offing then.

'What I did when we got back home was give the sketches to Nell, hidden behind a small painting of mine. If the man had been watching as closely as that, he would have known that I was the one who'd bought them, not her. So it probably wouldn't have occurred to him that they might be in *her* possession. By then, I'd had a really good look at them, and was pretty sure they were originals.' She gave the Major a white-dentured smile and he looked back, I'm sorry to say, like a lovesick adolescent.

'So you see, they aren't mine at all,' he said to me.

'I would have come round sooner, but I didn't want to march in claiming ownership of objects in the house before poor Nell was cold in her grave,' Ms Forbes continued. Her teeth clacked a bit. 'And since she died, I've been away on a number of trips and courses, plus visiting friends and relations all over the place. So it's only now I've been able to come round to see dear Norman.' She put her hand on his knee. I thought he was going to have an orgasm right there on the spot.

How very convenient, I thought. Just after dear Norman had had the Tiepolos evaluated by experts in London and pronounced as worth quite a large sum. Maybe I simply have a suspicious nature, but we had absolutely no way of telling whether her story was true. And given the Major's faulty memory, it was possible he'd remembered all wrong what Nell had told him. But it could just as easily have been Nell who bought them, as she'd told the Major, Nell who was the target of the stalking man in the white cap, Nell who had then hidden the sketches behind the painting her friend had given her. In which case, the Major was in danger of being cheated out of a substantial sum of money. I don't know whether it was the hair or the dentures, but frankly, I didn't believe a word the woman said. Especially after the Major had earlier reported Nell's own words regarding the discovery of the drawings in the Venetian bookshop the size of a coffin. Had he forgotten?

Maybe while I was in Venice, I could try to track down the bookshop and the guy who'd sold them.

When I got home, I rang the girls' high school. The woman who answered seemed very efficient. 'I'm trying to find my mother's friend, Ms Forbes,' I said. 'Florence Forbes.'

'That would be *Philippa* Forbes,' said my informant.

So where did she get off insisting that her name was Flo? 'The one I'm after was Florence,' I said positively. 'Or was it Fiona? She taught, or teaches, art. She was a good friend of Nell Roscoe. Headmistress.'

'I know who you mean. And now, alas, like Mrs Roscoe, poor Pippa is no longer with us.'

Aha! And aha! again. 'My mother will be so sad to hear that. She told me her friend had a big mop of curly hair.'

'The only person I can think of with hair like that is Angela Morton, our old Head of Maths.'

'I see,' I said, although I didn't. 'Perhaps my mother got it wrong. These days she does tend to get confused.'

'Tell me about it! My husband's mother has just come to live with us and . . .' She rambled on for several minutes about her mother-in-law, not in very flattering terms, before I could escape.

If the experts did indeed confirm their authentications, it sounded to me like the Major was about to be fitted up good and proper by the so-called Flo Forbes. I'd have to warn him. *And shatter his new-found happiness, you bitch,* said a nasty little voice inside me.

EIGHT

I went out to do some last-minute shopping before I flew to Venice. I got back to find there were several messages waiting. All of them were from Maddalena Grainger. All said more or less the same thing: 'I need to talk to you urgently. Call me soonest.'

What could have happened? And why did she want to talk to me? She was more my parents' generation than mine. I rang her back but the line was busy. I called her again. Still engaged. I went over to my desk and rootled through it. Somewhere I had a note of her cell phone number, but goodness only knew where. Eventually, after some fruitless searching it occurred to me that in a burst of efficiency, I just might have copied it into my address book – if I could only locate that. Which I eventually did, lost in a pile of old newspapers. I called the landline again, which was still engaged. Then dialled her number on the cell phone, to which there was no reply. I left a message, telling her to get back to me.

Hours later, the phone woke me from sleep. Sleepily checking my clock as I reached for it, I saw that it was one-forty in the morning. Late, by anybody's reckoning.

'What?' I said.

'Alexandra! It's Maddalena Grainger. Thank God I got you at last!' She sounded close to hysterical.

'You'd have got me much sooner if you hadn't constantly been on the phone.'

'That's just it! I haven't been. Oh *Dio, Dio*! Wouldn't you know the thing would choose today of all days to go out of order?'

'What's so special about today? And why're you ringing me at this hour of the night, anyway?' I recollected that she had said that whatever it was that was bugging her was urgent.

There was a gulping silence.

'Mrs Grainger . . .?' I said.

'It's . . . it's Sandro.'

'What about him?'

'That's just it . . . I don't really know. He flew to Italy two days ago, with my brother, to spend a week in Venice. He met a friend for dinner the day before yesterday, and never returned. None of us has heard anything from him since. It's so unlike him that I'm really beginning to worry.'

'And Cesare doesn't know where he is either?'

'No. None of us have the slightest idea where he is or what he could be doing.'

'Haven't you?' I could. Sandro had been a babe magnet since birth. 'How about he met a girl and they've been shacked up together ever since?' I suggested.

'A girl?' Maddalena hesitated, as if for a moment she wasn't quite sure what a girl was. 'I know I'm only his *mamma* but he's always been so reliable. All his life. He wouldn't have gone for as long as this without talking to Dominic and me unless something bad had happened to him.'

'It's only been, what, two and a half days? Forgive me for pointing it out, but aren't you overreacting?'

'No, no. He has always kept in touch.'

'Have you contacted the police over there?'

'Of course. But they refused to take me seriously. They assumed the same as you did, that he must be with some girl. That it's not a very long time since we last spoke to him . . . Perhaps their sons are more careless than mine. Look, Alexandra . . . I know you're terribly busy and so on, but if there was any chance that you could go out there for a couple of days, look around for me . . .' As always when she was agitated, Maddalena's accent was growing more pronounced. 'Dominic and I would pay all your expenses, of course. You can stay at Cesare's place.'

'Well . . .' I began.

There was some more gulping. A sob. 'Oh, God, what on earth is he doing, why hasn't he been in touch with us? I just know there's something terribly wrong.'

'He's twenty-five, so he's fully independent.' I couldn't share my friend's anxiety. 'Able to make his own decisions without reference to Momma and Poppa.' I clamped my teeth around the yawn which erupted from my inner depths, nearly fracturing my jaw as I did so. The first yawn was swiftly followed by a second one. *One-forty a.m.* . . . Give me a break. 'I'll be happy to poke around a bit while I'm there. But I absolutely can't promise anything. For all you know, he might not even be in Venice any more. Or he'll turn up in the morning, apologizing for not getting in touch.'

'That's just what my brother said. It's so unfortunate that he and his wife had to travel to meetings in Rome the day after Sandro got there so they didn't realize he was no longer around until they got back this evening, when the servants told them.' There was the sound of another muffled sob, then she added, 'How soon can you go?'

'I'm hoping to fly out there tomorrow. Should be there by the evening.'

'I'm so grateful, Alex.'

I didn't point out that I was going anyway. 'Bear in mind that he might not still be in Venice,' I cautioned.

'*Oddio!* Suppose he . . . suppose he has been taken to the *ospedale civile* without identification and nobody knows who he is. Or he has drunk too much and fallen into the lagoon and drowned!'

'The hospital is the first place I'll check. As for accommodation, since you've offered and if you're sure Cesare won't mind, I think it would be better to stay with him than in a hotel. He'll know more about the local scene and the best people for me to contact.'

'I will call him immediately. Give me your flight details as soon as you have them and he'll send someone to Marco Polo to meet you. Oh, Alexandra, I'm so grateful to you,' she repeated.

'Please, Maddalena, don't be. I've done nothing yet.'

'But you will. I know you will.'

I hoped that if he found out I had rejected his offer, my new best friend, Renzo Vitali, wouldn't take offence and turn nasty, something I sensed he was more than capable of doing. While talking to Maddalena, I'd had an uncomfortably vivid mental image of him and me holed up in some huge, echoing apartment overlooking the Grand Canal where gondoliers warbled and bells rang, while I fled through room after room of faded grandeur, my Titian-coloured hair streaming behind me with the speed of my passage as he relentlessly pursued me. Oh, those Italians!

Cesare, on the other hand, was not only married but possessed the manner and bearing of an icicle, so I would be safe. Or should be.

'I'll do my very best.'

I was about to replace the receiver when I heard a phone ringing in the background. Behind Maddalena, as it were. A male voice speaking. An exclamation. 'My God, no! Are you serious?'

'What?' Maddalena was shouting. '*What?* Dom, what is it?' She turned back to the phone. 'Wait, Alexandra, wait.' I heard echoing thumps as she laid the hand-piece on the table.

I listened while the two of them talked rapidly. There was a high-pitched, agonized shriek from Maddalena. A soothing reply from Dominic. More shrieks and sobbing. Finally the phone was picked up again.

'Alex? It's Dominic.'

'What's happened?'

I could hear the carefully controlled panic in his voice. 'My wife's brother, the Marchese, has just received a ransom note. The safe return of my son Sandro, in exchange for twenty million euros.'

'Bastards!' I drew in a sharp breath. 'Scumbags!'

'I couldn't have put it better myself,' said Dominic. His tone was dry.

'So the Marchese is back in Venice?'

'That's right. They arrived back this evening and found the note waiting. Got in touch with us immediately.'

'Twenty million euros,' I repeated. I knew Dominic could easily come up with it. Given his wealth and assets, twenty million seemed a fairly trivial sum. Much more importantly, how safe was Sandro? I'd known of too many kidnap cases where the victim had been killed long before the ransom was paid.

'Not that I give a toss about the money. I just want my . . .'

his voice shook slightly, '. . . my son safely home. The thing is, the note tells Cesare that on no account must the police or the *carabinieri* be informed or they won't hesitate to murder . . . to murder Sandro.'

Behind him, his wife screamed and screamed again.

'Why would they contact your brother-in-law instead of you?'

'Basically, I imagine they knew he was there, and thought it would be easier to snatch him in Venice.'

'Which would argue that they're Venice-based. Wouldn't it?'

'Not necessarily.' Dom drew a gusty breath. 'There's also the whole of the Veneto. You've got Padua, Verona, Treviso, all within striking distance . . .'

'Cesare's pretty well heeled.'

'Very.' Dominic suddenly sounded doubtful. 'As far as I'm aware, that is. A couple of financial reverses recently, but nothing serious.'

'And it's him they're asking to pay the ransom, not you, even though he's not Sandro's father.'

'I imagine that's because he's on the spot and I'm not – though obviously whatever payment is made, it will eventually be my responsibility, as is only fair.'

'How are they getting in contact?'

'Apart from the initial note, they're not. They've set out their terms and conditions so now we can only wait until we hear from them again.'

I thought about it. 'What can I do?'

'Maddalena tells me you were going out to Venice anyway, to look for Sandro.'

'That's one way of putting it. I also have some work to do.'

'I'm sorry, I didn't know about that. But Alex, it would be of enormous help to us if you can find anything at all about Sandro's disappearance. This . . . development makes it even more important, urgent, desperate, what you will.'

'Given the wide field of possible operations, I'm not sure how helpful I can—'

'You've solved a couple of murders, haven't you? You could take a kidnapping in your stride. The point is, Alex,' he continued over my attempted disclaimers, 'that whichever bastards took our son, they're not going to suspect some unknown Englishwoman who shows up at Cesare's place, are they?'

'I should think they'd be immediately suspicious. Boy is snatched, ransom note's delivered, police aren't informed but a female stranger suddenly arrives out of the blue. I'd certainly be on my guard, if I was watching out to see what happened. Which is presumably what whoever's grabbed him is doing.'

'I take your point.'

'And I'd also need to know if there are any of the usual suspects in cases like this: disgruntled ex-employees, business deals where your brother-in-law – or you – have done someone down, a slightly dodgy arrangement where some person or other has lost out unfairly, someone who feels resentful, for whatever reason – you know the sort of thing.'

'Off the top of my head, I can't think of anything like that at all.' His voice changed. 'I'll have a think about it. Meanwhile, you're right about not staying with Cesare. Why don't you put up at the Gritti or the Danieli if you think it would be less obvious than staying at Cesare's place? We'll pick up the tab, of course.' His voice began to waver slightly.

'No,' I said briskly. Regretfully. Because I would love to have stayed at either of them. 'They're luxury hotels, very expensive. If I'm going to use my magazine commission for some articles about Venice as my cover, it's highly unlikely that I'd be able to afford either of those.'

Or I could take up Renzo Vitali's invitation after all. I thought about his *palazzo* apartment on the Grand Canal. I thought of the *stanza segreta* and the shifting watery light of Venice. So tempting, but no . . .

'I see what you mean,' Dominic was saying. 'OK, I'll find something more suitable, further down the scale. I believe there are some good small hotels and B and Bs in the Rialto. And you're leaving tomorrow?'

'I'd already planned to go anyway. Obviously you'll need to let me know the name of wherever I'm going to be staying. And cancel Cesare meeting me with his private launch. I'll take the *vaporetto* to the nearest setting-down point.'

'Thank you, thank you.'

'How long are they giving you to come up with the cash?'

'Until the end of the week. Then they'll send directions as to where the drop will take place. They want Cesare to handle that.'

'I'm appalled by all this,' I said.

'As are we.'

'How can I contact you from Venice? I imagine they've got Cesare's phones tapped.'

'I'll buy two or three mobiles tomorrow. Our messenger service will pick one of them up and bring it over to you before you leave. That way, we can hopefully keep in touch without these people being aware.'

'Maybe Cesare can do the same.'

'Maybe. But I don't know how secure that would be. Alex, I'm . . . we're . . .' His voice seized up for a moment. 'We'd do anything, pay anything, to get our boy back.'

'Of course. Understood. Talk soon,' I said, and terminated the call before he broke down completely. Or I did.

Those poor people. What a nightmare, to have a child imperilled, themselves terrorized. It wasn't the money: twenty million euros was probably chump change for Dominic. It was the horror of wondering what was happening, whether Sandro was alive or dead, where he was, what they might be doing to him, in what disgusting, degrading conditions he might be being held.

If I were to come anywhere near the scum who'd taken him, I knew I wouldn't hesitate to kill, if I had to. Sometimes justice needs to be served in the most primitive possible way.

First thing the next morning, I fished out Renzo's business card. Luckily it had a couple of email addresses on it, so I sent a message to both, thanking him for the beautiful roses, and saying, in vague and muted fashion, that I too looked forward to seeing him again sometime. I didn't mention the possibility of meeting up with him in Venice, nor of availing myself of his various offers, both spoken and implicit. After that, I left my phone in answering mode so I could monitor any calls. I didn't fancy getting too hot and sweaty with my

new admirer. Especially when it might not be me at all that
he fancied, nor the colour of my hair, but the putative Tiepolos
that I'd so foolishly mentioned and which he might hope to
have a shot at through me.

I spent the rest of the day packing, and making arrangements
for wheels to keep turning while I was away. The whole time
I worked, the thought of Sandro Grainger in the ruthless hands
of kidnappers lurked like an evil toad at the bottom of a pond.

I rang the Major. 'I'm off to Venice shortly,' I said.

'Lovely. Enjoy yourself, my dear.'

'I'm sure I will.' Oh, Lord . . . my conscience was doing
a lot of smiting. 'Look, Major, there's something I have to
confess.' I swallowed.

'What's that?'

'I hope I haven't done any damage, but I stupidly told
somebody about your possible Tiepolos.'

There was a short pause while he digested this. 'Broke the
official secrets act sort of thing?' he said finally.

'Precisely.'

'Oh, well, can't be helped.'

'Thing is, the man I spoke to is an Italian art dealer. And
he seemed extremely interested.' Although I didn't say so,
there was also the possibility of him being some kind of
high-class crook . . . but surely not.

'Oh dear. But no harm's done, I don't suppose. I presume
he doesn't know anything about me, or where I live.'

'I don't think so.'

'And for the moment the pictures are safely locked away
in London. If anyone should come down here looking for
them, they'll be out of luck.'

Unless they're styling themselves as Ms Flo Forbes. 'Yes,
but . . .' I felt increasingly uncomfortable. What had I done,
blurting out the information about the Tiepolos to a complete
and possibly dodgy stranger? I really didn't want to imagine
the Major naked, tied to a chair with someone applying a
blowtorch to his genitals in the hope of extracting information
concerning the whereabouts of the two pictures, and not
believing him when he said they were in London. To be absolutely candid, I really didn't want to think of the Major's

genitals at all. Those Italian crims would stop at nothing, I knew that. At least, they didn't in thrillers and films. I sat at my computer, typed in Renzo's name and waited for information to come up. And waited. And waited.

Nothing. How could that be? My brother and his wife seemed to know quite a bit about him.

I typed in Vitali, and this time got a host of sites coming up, but none with the combination of the two names. Herry might know, but there was no way I was going to contact him about it. I checked out the Vitali name again and this time came up with some pictures of a recent family wedding, some rather gorgeous youths dancing with pretty girls, a wedding dress like the dome of St Paul's and wedding guests looking distinctly the worse for wear on smooth green lawns in front of a rather splendid castle. Was that the ancient family stronghold, I wondered, or merely a hired rendezvous?

And in some of the pics lurked Renzo himself, burly in black tie, champagne glass in hand or dancing with the bride, ugly as a toad, or smiling like an archangel.

Idly, since I was online, I went to Facebook, to Sam Willoughby's page. There he was, posting short messages about how great New Zealand was and how he wished he'd visited much sooner. *Days of wine and roses*, said one post, and there he was, sitting under a rose arbour, blue hills on the skyline with his arm round a glamorous blonde, both of them holding slender glasses of white wine and looking pretty pleased with themselves. There were several other photos. One of Sam with a sheep. One of him standing with a guy who could only be his brother, Harry. One of him with the same blonde and three sheep. One of him sprawled across a mass of wool with a shivering, naked sheep and a lot of weathered guys laughing. Another of him seated at a table overlooking a shimmering bay with the sun going down, while opposite him sat the blonde wearing one of those jillaroo Akubra hats, holding another glass of wine, the two of them smiling at each other in loving fashion.

Good on yer, Sam, I thought. I was delighted to see him having such a good time. Focusing for a change on someone who wasn't me.

Really, really delighted.

NINE

t was late by the time I stepped off the *vaporetto* from Marco Polo airport. Dominic had chosen a small and inconspicuous hotel for me somewhere in the warren of little streets in Rialto. There was a tiny railed garden in front with two broad-leaved banana trees and an indeterminate palm. The wonderful rippling light of Venice sent splinters of green radiance up and down the walls which lined the small canal on which it sat. I could see at once that it was perfect for my purposes. Shabby and old, even the jumpiest kidnapper wouldn't have suspected the place of harbouring an investigative force hoping to foil their plans for extortion. Inside, it belied its scruffy, peeling exterior. It was clearly an historic sixteenth-century building, and had been extensively and very tastefully renovated. Some of the rooms faced the canal, and I was lucky enough (or Dom had enough clout) to have been given one of those. I unpacked my books and papers on to the small table in front of the window and hung up my clothes. Looking out, I could just see the lighted outline of a *campanile* against the brilliant but darkening sky.

Dominic had given me a whole file of information which he thought might be useful. I'd had a chance to go through it on the plane. There was apparently a witness to Sandro's abduction. Tomorrow I would call Dom, see if there was any further update on Sandro. And meanwhile, I would try to contact the witness, Signora Carlotta Moretti. According to the papers Dominic had passed on, she knew Sandro by sight and had recognized him as she sat on her balcony in the evening, sipping a nightcap *grappa*. Her address was included.

I was hungry. I felt optimistic as I set off down the *calle* to find the restaurant recommended by the *direttore d'albergo* on the other side of the Grand Canal. Venice is a small town, a closed society in which tourists are something of an irrelevancy, apart from the money they bring with them. And the way they turn the tranquil city into a crowded nightmare. It was quite likely that Signora Moretti's evidence could prove helpful in finding out what had happened. Or the opposite, of course. Witness statements are notoriously unreliable.

I ate *linguine pescatore* with a couple of glasses of crisp pinot grigio. Someone was singing somewhere. Not tourist-trap singing but genuine music. It floated down from an upper window and wrapped itself round the tables set out on the pavement, a shifting shawl of glittering notes. The moon was already high in the sky. It would have been perfect had it not been for my desperate anxiety about Sandro.

I was up early the next day. Lots to do. Places to go and people to see. I would leave Signora Moretti until later in the day. Meanwhile, before I left England I had booked interviews with the curators of two galleries and a professor at the Ca' Foscari university whom I'd met at a symposium on contemporary art a couple of years earlier. He'd looked pretty unusual back then; on my way to meet him, I wondered if he had quietened down. Sartorially, that is. When I got there, I saw that he hadn't. He sported skin-tight jeans in a leopard-skin print and a yellow singlet which showed his ribs to advantage. A Mohican coloured red and peacock-blue and a feather dangling from one ear completed the ensemble. And why not? He was not only a real enthusiast for his subject, but was still excited by the whole contemporary scene. Always a plus in a teacher.

A phone call to Cesare's new and unused mobile, the number contained in Dominic's file, ascertained that there had been no further word about Sandro. 'Do we need to talk about anything?' I asked.

'It's all in hand, I think.'

'Seen anything suspicious?'

'Nothing. I'm organizing the ransom money. I'm hoping the kidnappers will make themselves conspicuous one way or another before the day they've set for payment.'

'You're by no means the only rich man in the city,' I said. 'So why you? Or, rather, why your brother-in-law? Which one of you is being targeted?'

'Signora, I just wish I knew.' He sounded very worried.

My meetings went very satisfactorily and I left each one with plenty of material for my commissioned articles. After the third, I headed for a restaurant where I could sit outside and enjoy the *va-et-vient* while I had some lunch. I was drinking coffee when I noticed someone staring at me from two tables away. Young, tanned, well-dressed in a linen jacket, starched shirt and red silk tie. The very picture of a successful businessman. He was reading the *La Gazzetta dello Sport* and pretending not to look at me. Doing a damn poor job of it, too. He couldn't possibly be one of the kidnappers and already on to me. I'd only arrived the evening before, and apart from our brief phone conversation, had made no contact with Cesare.

My spirits drooped a bit when I remembered Tiepolo and the Major's (or – highly unlikely – Ms Forbes') sketches. Was this guy something to do with Renzo Vitali? Renzo hadn't known I would be arriving in Venice, or that I would bring the sketches with me. Why would I? He knew they weren't mine. As the guy folded his newspaper, dropped some coins on the table and got up, reaching for a briefcase beside his chair, I realized I was being irrational. Or was I? As he left the place and set off along the pavement, he pulled from his pocket a white-coloured cotton cap and pulled it over his hair.

What? A white cap? This was too much of a coincidence. Or was it? I glanced around and saw three other guys wearing the same kind of headgear. But they were old, protecting their bald heads from the sun. To see a youngish, smartly clad man wearing an item so unbecoming and old fashioned, almost like a badge, or uniform, was unnerving, especially in light of the Forbes woman's story. If she was to be believed, that is, which I was pretty convinced she wasn't. I wondered if the real coincidence wasn't that I'd chosen this particular café for my lunch.

I finished eating, paid and left, looking for the address I'd been given by Dominic. Signora Moretti lived in one of those typical tall Venetian houses along a canal, crammed together with its neighbours, all peeling plaster and rose-painted walls. The house's faded shutters were closed against the afternoon heat, giving it the blank air of a cemetery. I pressed the bell beside the name Moretti and waited. And waited some more. Pressed again. Some clanking noises took place above my head, so I stepped back and looked up. A face appeared, half obscured by a fascinating display of underwear of a kind I hadn't seen in England for years. Fearsome salmon-pink corsets, vast knickers, suspender belts of pinky-grey, boned bras, vests of the sort people's grandfathers used to wear on the beach at Blackpool and Scunthorpe under handkerchiefs knotted at the four corners. Time warp, I told myself.

The head screeched a question of some kind down at me, and I screeched back my name. A string appeared with a key on the end of it, making its way down through the laundry, getting caught up on some tea towels on the washing line below and being jerked free, bypassing the three blouses below that and eventually landing in my hand. I released the key and watched the string snake its way up again. I assumed I was to use it to open the heavy door, which I did to the accompaniment of approving stridency from above.

Inside the small square hallway were smells of damp and fungi. There were green stains round the lower part of the walls, and the clammy tiles were uneven, forced from their setting by creeping moisture. A narrow stone staircase led to the upper part of the building and, looking up through the coil of the banisters, I could see the screeching woman herself way up at the top, guiding me aloft with encouraging cries. When I reached her landing, she was standing beside her open door, smart in black top and trousers, with a scarf of brilliant emerald green around her neck. Now we were more or less face to face, the shriek was softened into a relatively civilized voice.

'I am Carlotta. Come in, come in,' she said, speaking pretty good English. I'd been afraid she would not only use Italian, but the Venetian version, which is practically a separate language. 'We shall drink coffee together, and I shall tell you what I know.'

It turned out that she had spent time in England in her younger days, first as an au pair girl with a family in Cheltenham and then working as a waitress in a café near Wallingford for six months, in order to perfect her grasp of English before becoming a language teacher.

'Now,' she said finally. She put down her coffee cup and leaned forward. 'What do you want to know?'

'I read a transcript of your statement to the Marchese Cesare, with regard to the abduction of his nephew, Sandro,' I said. 'I'd be grateful if you could go over it again for me.'

'Ah, yes. You see, young Sandro is friendly with Alberto, my sister's son, so I know him well,' she explained. 'There is no question of me mistaking him for someone else. I saw it all. Everything. I was sitting out there, on my *balcone*, enjoying the last of the sunset when I looked down and saw Sandro. He was walking in the direction of his uncle's home, and I was just about to call down and invite him to join me in a glass of *grappa* when suddenly these men appeared from some doorway. Three of them. I thought it was a prank, a joke, when they grabbed him. One put a hand over the boy's mouth. The other two lifted him and hurried along the *calle*. He was struggling. Striking at the men with his hands, but he couldn't get free.'

'Some prank.'

'I know. I still didn't realize it was a real abduction, though, or I would of course have called the police. I don't know where they took him. Once they had turned the corner, obviously I couldn't tell. But I am friends with Signora Elsa, who works as a secretary at the Marchese's office, and when I bumped into her the next day – or was it two days later? – she had heard from one of the staff at his place that the boy had disappeared. At first I was laughing; I still thought it was a joke, you see. Or that he was with a girl. A boy who looks like that . . . *dio mio!*' She waved a hand in front of her face like a fan, as though to cool down the flames of desire. 'So it was a while before I realized that it was serious. That the poor boy really had been kidnapped. And that I had watched it all and done nothing to help him.'

'Can you remember anything about the men who took him?'

'Not really. One was tall, with a shaven head and an earring – I could see that because of the moonlight. The other two were smaller and more – what is the word? – stocky. Jeans . . . I know they were all three wearing jeans, but these days, what does that signify?'

'Did they look like Italians?'

'One of the two shorter ones had light-coloured hair. Not blond, but certainly much lighter than black, which is the colour of most Italian men's hair.'

'Though not all,' I said. 'Which, when you think of Venice's history, is not so surprising. Could you tell what sort of age they were?'

'Hard to say. Somewhere between twenty-five and late thirties, I would say. The tall one was definitely the leader.'

'Did *he* look Italian?'

She moved her mouth about a bit. 'Now you mention it, I'm not sure. Come to think of it, and despite his lack of hair, no, he definitely didn't.'

'But the other two?'

'Local, I would say.'

'Do you think you would recognize them again? If you saw them on the street, for instance?'

She shrugged. 'If I saw all three of them together, I might. But otherwise . . .? I doubt it.'

'Has your friend Elsa had anything more to tell you?'

'Only that the Marchese's household is very upset. Which is understandable. His poor uncle and aunt are distraught indeed.'

I made about-to-leave motions. 'Signora, I must ask you to tell no one that I have spoken to you,' I said in a low voice. 'Not even Signora Elsa. No one at all. It could seriously get in the way of finding Sandro if his kidnappers knew I was here.'

She brought up her hands and pressed them against her mouth. She said, half-gasping, 'Then you are . . .'

I nodded significantly while she lay back in her chair, looking at me as though I was some creature who had emerged from the lagoon. A creature with power. I repeated, 'If you mention my presence here in Venice to anyone, you could gravely endanger Sandro's life.'

She shrank slightly away from me. 'I won't say a word to anyone, I swear.'

'That's good, signora. And if anything else occurs to you, please let me know.' I told her where I was staying.

'Meanwhile . . .' I made a zipping-up gesture across my mouth. She did the same.

As I left the building, pulling the front door shut behind me, I didn't look up. But I was prepared to swear that Signora Carlotta Moretti was watching me from above. What she had told me sounded perfectly sincere.

I walked towards Campo San Polo along streets crowded with every sort of shop, selling all kinds of merchandise from tacky tourist souvenirs to top name brands like Gucci, Prada, Versace, Dior. Coming out of one of these was a Bichon Frise with a two-inch wide jewelled collar round its neck. It was straining at a lead held by one of those relentlessly pared-down women you come across in big cities. Long blonde hair streamed down her back, topped by a black fedora which hid most of her face. Tight black leather trousers descended into high-heeled black ankle boots decorated with buckles and bits of diamante. A vivid black-and-white checked coat swung above her narrow hips. Over her shoulder was a must-have leather bag which probably cost as much as my flat in Longbury. If not more. A gym-honed body couldn't hide the loose skin of her throat.

Like everyone else in the vicinity, I stared at her. Which I imagine was the intention. Call me shallow, but I hated her on sight. Forcing myself to look away, I went on to visit a couple of galleries specializing in modern art. It wasn't stuff I particularly liked, but I picked up brochures and, where I could, explained that I had been commissioned to write some articles on the contemporary art scene in Venice. I added that I would be delighted to mention their names in exchange for information and illumination. In return, I received a mass of usable stuff.

I had set aside the following day for a visit to the white Palladian building which housed the Peggy Guggenheim Collection. I was also hoping to contrive a meeting with Cesare, which we would have to make look accidental in case there were any watchers around. Perfectly possible. After all, I *was* in the city, and we *did* know each other . . . what could be more natural than to shake hands, express exaggerated surprise at bumping into each other like this and at the same time exchange as swiftly as we could anything we felt the other should know.

It was a beautiful evening. I strolled along beside small canals, crossed tiny bridges, squeezed down little alleyways. Birds swung in their cages from vine-covered *altanes* and geranium-stuffed balconies or loggias. Venetians love pets of every kind and their artists have always included them in their paintings of saints and Madonnas, bringing the divine down to the level of the ordinary lives of the city's inhabitants. Dogs, doves, rabbits, lambs, pheasants . . . they're all there, engaged in their domestic routines, while angels descend and holy babes are held in loving maternal arms. And of course there was the Lion of Saint Mark, representing the evangelist St Mark.

I passed various shops selling beautiful leatherwork and paper goods. Sam Willoughby would have loved this, I thought. Maybe he should try to import some of the classy writing paper, notelets and matching envelopes lined with traditional Florentine designs. He could stock them in his bookshop. They'd go like a bomb in Longbury. But, I thought sourly, these days he probably preferred woollen goods produced from New Zealand sheep.

I found a restaurant I'd been to before and sat down. A nice meal, in spite of the various sex pests who stopped at the sight of me. In Italy, it is a truth universally acknowledged (at least among the male population) that a reasonably presentable female on her own must be in want of a male. Difficult as it was, I managed to keep my knickers on as one after another they paused at my table to try their luck. Fortunately I have a fairly impressive Italian vocabulary of put-downs to use if I have to. I've often wondered what on earth they would do if I stood up and said, 'Come on, big boy, let's go, your place or mine?' Run like the wind, probably.

I kept an eye out for White Hat Man, but didn't see him. Had I just been paranoid, imagining that he was following me? The truth was that if the faux-Forbes hadn't mentioned a similar man, I wouldn't have given him a second thought. I also watched for any tall, bald men with earrings to appear, but none did. Where would they have taken Sandro? And why would they have emerged just below Carlotta Moretti's balcony, or close by? I walked back towards her house, scanning to left and right as I went. They must have been taking a hell of a risk, kidnapping poor Sandro in such a crowded quarter. Which would argue, would it not, that they weren't taking him very far? So had they used a boat of some kind and motored across the lagoon to one of the outlying islands? Or up the Grand Canal to the mainland and bundled him into a car before driving him off to God knew where? Or had they simply stashed him in one of the houses close to Signora Moretti's? It was easy to be secretive in a city like Venice, even though, as I had been repeatedly told, it was a place small enough for all the genuine Venetians to know, or at least recognize, each other.

There were stars in the sky as I walked back to my little hotel. Accordion music drifted from somewhere. Evocative. Melancholy. From windows high above my head came the sound of conversations, laughter, arguments, singing, even weeping. I wondered whether Sandro was somewhere nearby, confined to a room, gagged and bound, and if so, what he could see and hear, if anything.

Back in my room, I dialled Cesare on my anonymous cell phone for an update on developments, but he said there had been none. I told him that my movements during the day had corresponded exactly with what I purported to be. With what I *was*. That's to say someone writing about art in Venice. Establishing my credentials. With any luck, I wouldn't be an object of suspicion even if I did 'happen' to see Cesare in the city. Though in any case, I could see absolutely no reason why I should be.

'So let us meet tomorrow,' he said. 'Some time before lunch. I have an appointment with my bankers and financial people, making arrangements for releasing the ransom money. We can meet as though by accident.' We established an approximate time and place.

I showered away the heat and exertion of the day and slept deeply.

TEN

'*Madonna santa!*' A handsome man of some fifty summers or more halted in front of my table as I sat nursing a coffee. 'It *is* Signorina Alessandra Quick, is it not?'

'*Marchese!*' Like him, I feigned astonishment, then stood up to greet him. 'It is indeed! But fancy seeing you – though of course, I'd forgotten that you live here, so it's not all that surprising, is it?' I gave a peal of girlish laughter which, while it didn't fool me, might possibly fool any suspicious kidnappers who were lurking nearby.

'Such a pleasure to see you here in my beautiful city.' Despite his words, Cesare's face was drawn, as you would expect, given the circumstances. His eagle's beak of a nose jutted out sharply between eyes that had sunk deep into their sockets, and his former haughtiness had dimmed.

I gestured at the spare seat at my table. 'Would you like a coffee? Or a glass of wine?'

'No, thank you. I have to get home for lunch,' he said. He shifted position so that he was now facing the canal, his back to any observers. 'Anything new to report?'

I laughed again, throwing back my head. 'Signora Moretti described the kidnappers to me, but wasn't sure she'd recognize them if she saw them on the street.'

He raised his hand, as though pointing out the church across from us.

I nodded vigorously. 'Yes, I certainly won't miss that.'

At the same time, he said, 'We've had a new communication from them. Soon we get instructions about where, when and how to hand over the ransom.'

'Do you think this is only about the money?'

He shook his head. 'I have no idea.'

'I imagine it's fairly straightforward to organize.'

He hesitated. Then said, 'Of *course.*' Over-hearty and under-convincing.

'I'll call you tonight,' I said. And, more loudly, 'It's been great to see you again.'

'And you too, Alessandra.' He shook my hand and bowed slightly. 'On another occasion, I should have been delighted to show you my collection, but now is not the time.' He raised his voice. 'It's a pleasure to see you here in Venice. Enjoy it, signorina,' he said, and continued on his way.

The whole conversation had lasted maybe three minutes and would have appeared as innocent as baby talk if anyone had been watching us. Seeing him go, shoulders slumped, posture defeated, I felt extremely depressed. Not only was it painful to see how far he was removed from the fearsome bird of prey he had resembled at his nephew's gathering such a short time ago in London, but I was also all too aware that payment of a ransom was no guarantee that a kidnap victim would be safely released. I also knew it had been estimated that, worldwide, criminal gangs made up to five hundred million dollars a year simply by kidnap and subsequent extortion. The statistics were not good. On the other hand, ransom victims *had* been returned safely. Hold that thought, I told myself.

I fiddled with my shoulder bag, watching Cesare cross the canal. The people at a nearby table were also watching, making comments of some kind then looking across at me. No doubt they had recognized him and were wondering who I was. I didn't have them down as part of the kidnapping gang: they wouldn't have been scrutinizing us quite so obviously if they were. Much more possible was the all-male foursome at another table, crouched uncouthly over bowls of pasta, shovelling the stuff into their mouths. Two of them were stocky young men with short hair cut close to their heads – so close, in fact, that the pink of their scalps shone through. All of them were *not* looking at me. Was that a studied avoidance, or because they couldn't have been less interested?

Back in the safety of my room, I unfolded the half-sheet of paper Cesare had managed to thrust into my hand when we first met at the restaurant.

I am in despair. This came today, he'd written at the top of the sheet. My eyes scrolled further down.

One word to the police or any other investigator and your nephew is dead. We will send proof of this. There will be no negotiating. You now have three days in which to get the ransom together.

A couple of things struck me immediately about the kidnappers' message. First of all, it was written in English. Secondly, the language was sophisticated: the use of a construction like 'in which to' spoke of someone reasonably well-educated. I began to wonder if the tall, bald man spotted by Signora Moretti could be English. Someone who knew of Sandro's privileged background and decided to cash in on it? In that case, it wouldn't be too fanciful to conjecture that by now Sandro might have been transported back to England. Perhaps by car. Perhaps driven by a third party. It had also earlier struck me as odd that Cesare seemed uneasy, as though he was having a little difficulty in laying his hands on twenty million euros. Given his status and resources, I couldn't believe he'd have had any problems at all, especially given Dominic Grainger's assets to throw into the mix. Not that twenty million wasn't a mind-blowing amount.

Was it possible that the wealthy front he projected was just that: a front? That the loaded Marchese was not rolling in it after all? And with that thought, another followed on its heels. Supposing he were not as affluent as was believed – could he himself have organized the kidnap? It wasn't as crazy an idea as it sounded. Sandro's incredibly well-off parents would be flinging money left, right and centre to get their boy back home. And the boy was unlikely to come to much harm if he was unknowingly in his uncle's custody. It was certainly something to consider. On the other hand, who would the tall baldy and the two henchmen be? Co-conspirators? It didn't seem likely he would be consorting with such lowlifes given the cold, stiff, arrogant persona the Marchese presented to the world. And in any case, wouldn't he be laying himself wide open to blackmail? No, there had to be another explanation.

I sat on the miniature balcony attached to my room, just wide enough for a folding chair and a tiny round table. Bells were ringing at intervals, each peal sending flocks of birds high into the air as though flung by giant catapults. The sky was golden. I felt too restless, too full of good food and wine to go to bed just yet. Downstairs, the woman on duty at the desk watched with disapproval as I approached the front doors.

'It's late,' she said. 'And with all the tourists in the city, there are many pickpockets around. And other criminals.'

'Thank you for the warning,' I said. 'I shan't be out for long. Just going to take a little walk.'

She produced one of those don't-blame-me shrugs and thrust out her lower lip.

Outside, it was a little cooler. From different streets, I heard shouts and laughter. The canals, clogged with gondolas and waterbuses, were as busy as Regent Street at midday. Mind you, it had been pretty much the same in Canaletto's day, judging by his paintings. I was looking for Mr Bald Man with his glinting earring. Venice is pretty compact: the chances were high that I'd catch sight of him. One of these days. Except I didn't have that many days. I hung about in the area but there was no sign of him. Despite the late hour, the streets were still crammed with tourists having a good time. It must be a little disconcerting for the residents, despite the revenue they brought in, to have their city taken over every year, especially with the tourist season getting longer and longer. Oxford is much the same. And Canterbury.

It was as I was heading towards my hotel that I finally saw him. Naturally he was on the other side of a canal so narrow that he would have seen me if I hadn't ducked into a doorway. Peeking out, I saw that he had crossed the bridge and was now walking back towards me. When he had passed my hiding place and sundry others had inserted themselves between him and me, I popped out like a maggot from an apple, mingled a bit with them and followed him. Was I on the trail at last?

Baldy turned round corners, walked down little alleys and crossed another couple of bridges. He ducked through a *soto-portego* into a narrow street, turned into an even narrower one. Finally he stopped. He fiddled in a pocket, looking up and down the confined space of the street, and inserted a key. I walked on past him. I appeared to be part of a group who were talking animatedly, while I nodded and smiled as though taking part in the conversation. At the same time, I clocked the number painted in a black-rimmed white oval above the red door of the building he was standing in front of. 192. Great! Could I possibly have tracked down the place where Sandro was being kept? I'd have to confirm it in some way, or else eliminate it from my enquiries.

I mooched slowly back the way I'd come. I turned and waved at the backs of the group with whom I'd pretended to be walking. I glanced very obviously at my watch. A woman with a purpose. A woman on her way to meet her lover. A woman taking time to stand at the edge of the canal and look down to where lights from the houses on either side were reflected in the murky water. The house with the red door showed a light high up in a small window. A window which I noticed had bars on it. Plants drooped from an *altano*. An empty birdcage hung from a hook attached to a beam. Otherwise, there were no signs of life. I was reluctant to move from my observation point but figured I had no choice. There was no café or restaurant here in this cramped *calle* where I could wait without arousing suspicion. And then the light at the top of the house snapped off. I figured that, as far as action went, that was it for the day.

Having reluctantly walked back to my hotel and plodded up the stairs to my room, I sat out again on the tiny *balcone* and pondered. Should I tell Cesare about this development? If my earlier misgivings turned out to be true, and this *was* the place where Sandro was being held, I might be endangering his life. On the other hand, it could be that I'd been keeping tabs on a perfectly innocent Venetian citizen who happened to have lost the hair battle and liked a spot of gold around the earlobes. Or possibly the Marchese already knew all about the place. Perhaps Dominic, Sandro's father, was the best person to discuss it with. But suppose he told Cesare . . .

If only, I thought crossly, Sam Willoughby hadn't buggered off to New Zealand and, instead of hanging out with blonde girls in Akubras, was around to advise me what to do.

I wondered if the police had nailed anyone for Katy Pasqualin's death by drowning yet. It was far too late to call anyone in England, but I would telephone Fliss Fairlight first thing in the morning.

'Nothing definite yet,' said Fliss the next day. 'They're pursuing several lines of enquiry, Joy tells me.'

'Like they always do,' I said.

'Indeed. Lots of lines to pursue, if truth be told. She seems to have been quite a gal. And somewhat different from what you'd expect. They're uncovering quite a lot of unsavoury information, which doesn't exactly go with the standard English rose image she projected.'

'Like what?'

'Drugs, for a start. Sugar daddies, if you can believe it.'

'Daddies? You're kidding! How many?'

'At least three, so far. All very well-heeled. All desperately denying any connection with her. It's a variation on crowd-funding! The girl gets given all sorts of expensive gifts, including cash, in return for looking good on his arm and yielding up her tender young body when required to do so.'

My mind shifted inevitably to the woman I'd seen shopping in Rialto. A born mistress. And here was another. 'Think one of them might be responsible?'

'Perfectly possible. Or else paid someone to do the dirty deed, which is much more likely. The investigating team hopes to know more when they've had a chance to investigate further.'

'Hmmm,' I said. 'Was she trying to blackmail one of them, I wonder?'

'Officers at the Met are wondering too.'

'What about the boyfriend?'

'He's not around. Gone to the States on business. Or so I understand.'

I couldn't think of much more to say. 'I did tell you that in my opinion she was dead scared of something or someone, didn't I?'

'It's been duly noted.'

'Get back to me if there's any further news.'

'Will do. When are you back from Italy?'

'It slightly depends.' I wasn't going to go into detail right at that moment. 'Probably in three or four days.'

'We'll talk.'

Katy had indeed been dead scared. Scared enough to cry even at a party. But of whom? Someone who had been present that evening? I tried to recall who had been there who might be termed a sugar daddy. There were the husbands of the ultra-chic women with lacquered hair. There was also the Marchese, Cesare. I ruled out Dominic Grainger, knowing that it was highly likely Sandro would invite his own parents to the gathering. Katy was surely smart enough to make an excuse not to attend if they had.

I spent a sleepless night, worrying about what course of action to take. In the end, I'd come to the conclusion that I had two options. Either I did nothing, or I stormed the citadel on my own, did a bit of role-playing, see if I could come up with any details at all that might decide whether Sandro was or ever had been held hostage in the house with the red door.

I'd drunk a contemplative coffee, paid my bill and was preparing to leave when I saw a tall man emerge from a restaurant-bar on the opposite side of the canal and start strolling along the *riva*. A tall, bald man. With a gold ring in one ear. And seen in daylight, somewhere in his middle thirties, if not younger. He was carrying a plastic bag which even from across the water I could see held a stick of bread, some pastries, some tomatoes, a slab of asiago cheese, some salami and a litre bottle of water. Supplies for a prisoner? It certainly didn't look like dinner for a person able to get out and about. I more or less ran – as best I could for the crowds – to the nearest bridge, which unfortunately was in the opposite direction to the one he was going. As for keeping him in sight, it was pretty hopeless. By the time I got across, he'd vanished. Darn, darn, darn!

I scouted about as unobtrusively as I could, stopping to admire doorways and window-boxes, to lift my camera in a pretence at taking photos. Just in case anyone was keeping an eye on me. But no bald men appeared. The one I was after had to be somewhere in the vicinity, but it was anyone's guess as to where. If he were indeed one of the abductors spotted by Signora Moretti, at least I now felt a little more certain that Sandro hadn't been shipped off to distant parts but was being kept somewhere fairly close at hand. Or was I assuming too much? Baldy could simply be going about his perfectly innocent business, bringing in some supplies for his wife and family, the earring one of those midlife crisis acquisitions since in Venice the bright red sports car wasn't an option. How many men just like him were in the city at the moment? Which raised the question again of whether Sandro's abductors were from Venice in the first place.

If I hung about here, on the off-chance of seeing the tall guy again, it would be hard, if not impossible, to maintain a low profile. Trouble was, some of the backwater little canals were often deserted, even in the tourist season. I would stick out like a severed finger in a rice pudding if I hung around too long, or even showed up too often. But if the guy had materialized once and then disappeared in this area, he was likely to do so again. It occurred to me that I might have to extend my stay . . . which would be OK since Cesare would cover my costs, I knew. And I could get more research done for future articles. Pity I couldn't paint or draw. What could otherwise have been more natural than to set up easel and artist's gear, in order to produce a charming portrait of this picturesque corner of La Serenissima?

I was very glad that I had opted not to take up Uncle Cesare's offer of accommodation. Perhaps I would be forced to resort to my secret weapon and contact Renzo Vitali. I hoped not. Though if I thought about it, Renzo would provide excellent cover, and I was quite certain that I had more than enough strength of will – and of purpose – to resist any overtures he might make along the lines of me coming to stay at his place. And I had to admit that I would dearly love to see the *stanza segreta* he had mentioned at my brother's dinner party. A room of glass sounded spectacular. Especially a hidden one.

Back in my hotel room, I wrote him an email, saying I was now in Venice for a few days and would love to meet up for lunch or something. Before sending it, I deleted 'or something'. Didn't want to give the guy any ideas.

Then I went out again, to stroll along the streets, cross the little bridges, drop into churches from which music was issuing. Monteverdi. Mozart. Vivaldi. It was all captivating: the combination of baroque music, stunning architecture, birdsong and flower baskets, houses of old rose, faded red, yellow ochre and pinky orange, the soft movement of water against stone. Above all, the light. A green glimmer in the shadows, a bolder brightness over sunlit canals. And at night, as the soft dusk fell, it would become a glittering radiance of gold and coral and fuchsia flushed with mauve as the sun went down behind the buildings.

I had three more interviews to conduct the next day. Two that afternoon and one the following morning. And a kidnapped boy to find. I'd thought long and hard about the circumstances of his abduction – assuming Signora Moretti's information was accurate – and concluded that it seemed very unlikely the items stolen from Cesare's *appartamento* were not somehow involved. Would I be sabotaging Sandro's relationship with his uncle if I asked about them when I phoned him tonight? Given the situation, I thought not.

When I next opened my email, a response had already arrived back from Renzo, commanding me to meet him the following day, suggesting that we have lunch at a restaurant which I knew to be one of the finest Venice had to offer. Impatiently awaiting my reply. All of it liberally besprinkled with exclamation marks. I sat on the tiny balcony of my room watching the flights of birds wheeling and winging above the bell towers and church spires. I wondered whether Sandro, somewhere not too far away, was sawing off chunks of salami and slices of cheese to eat with bread and tomatoes.

My new cell phone rang. Cesare, of course.

'Signorina Quick . . .' He sounded like someone who has just mounted the scaffold. 'My sister Maddalena called me thirty minutes ago,' he said.

'Yes?'

'She is nearly beside herself with worry about Sandro,' Cesare said. 'I told her that we have matters in hand.'

'I don't suppose that was much comfort to her.'

'Not really.'

There was a pause. Then I said, 'Do you think the death of Sandro's friend Katy has anything at all to do with his abduction?'

'Who can say?' He sighed heavily. 'But it is not a possibility we can dismiss.'

'Look, Marchese . . .' I swallowed. I bit the bullet. 'I hope Sandro won't mind me telling you this . . .'

'What do you mean?' Some of the former frigidity had returned to his voice.

'But I do wonder if it has any bearing on what's going on among that group of friends.'

I explained. Quickly assured him that Sandro had restored the status quo. That he had found it unthinkable that one of his close friends could have committed these thefts. That the use of a pawnshop indicated that the valuable ring would be redeemed as soon as could be. As indeed it had been.

He wasn't best pleased. 'I cannot believe I am hearing this,' he said, his tone arctic.

'I'm aware that it's rather poor conduct from a group of people who should know better but—'

'There are no buts. It is a simple abuse of hospitality.'

'That's exactly what Sand—'

'I'm amazed that these young people could behave in such a way. Stealing from the person who was, in a sense, their host. It's appalling.'

'I know.'

'However, we have more important things to discuss.' He projected such frostiness that even down the phone I felt cold.

We talked some more about tactics. I explained about the follicly challenged guy with the earring. He listened in silence. While we both knew that the situation with Sandro was far more important than the loss – and quick return – of a few costly possessions, it was obvious that he was still seriously pissed off.

After I'd hung up, I noticed a woman sitting on a balcony of the house opposite my room. She was staring across at me, not even attempting to hide her curiosity. I figured that even if she could lip-read, which seemed highly unlikely, I had said nothing which would indicate who I was talking to, nor what I was talking about. I waved. She waved back.

Below me, the crowds of tourists were thinning out, either returning to their hotels before going out to dinner, or finding a café in which to sit and enjoy a glass or two with their friends and families. I would shortly do the same.

Had Sam Willoughby ever been to Venice? I wasn't sure. But I couldn't help thinking what a pleasant travelling companion he would be. Knowledgeable, restful, always ready to share a new experience. Such as shearing bloody sheep.

Mid-morning, I stood right in front of the house with the red front door. There was no knocker so I rapped with my bare knuckles, which was more painful than I expected. While I waited, I glanced to the side of the door where several bells were set one above the other, noting the names beside them. It looked like there were two flats to a floor until the top one. The names seemed to be Italian – Cafarella, di Giovanni – except for the one at the top. Or was it the bottom? Whichever. The odd name out was listed as Jerome Gregory. My nose twitched. There'd been a girl at school called Hanna Gregori who claimed to be of Italian descent. Could this be an Anglicization of the same name?

I waited for someone to answer my knock. Nobody came. I knocked harder and felt the door shift slightly under my hand. I pushed it a bit and, with a hideous creaking sound, like something out of a gothic-inspired horror movie, it slowly opened. I looked up and down the street but for once there was nobody about. Too close to the lunch hour, I guessed. I slipped inside and closed the door as quietly as possible – which wasn't very. Nobody came. The house seemed full of silence.

I was in a narrow hall with shallow stone steps leading upwards. As in so many houses in Venice, there was a faint whiff of sewers and decay. I'd memorized some of the names on the list beside the front door, in case someone suddenly appeared. Then I started up. And continued up. And up some more, until finally I was on the top floor and could go no higher. In front of me was a small window which offered a panoramic view over the roofs and terraces of the city. There were two doors, one to the left and one to the right. The left-hand one was ajar and I went towards it.

'*Buongiorno,*' I said tentatively. 'Hello?' Was Sandro inside? There was no answer. I was beginning to feel kind of creeped out. Why was the door open? Did I dare go inside? I decided I did. I stepped into a room with polished parquet flooring, a table and four chairs and a large TV set. Not much else. Doors led off towards bedrooms and a bathroom. I knew this because all the doors were wide open. I could see someone lying sprawled across a bed. For one heart-stopping moment, I thought it might be Sandro, but no. This guy was short and stocky, with thinning dark hair cut *en brosse.* He was also very dead.

One of those cheese-cutters – a length of wire with wooden handles at either end that old-fashioned grocers use to slice off a hunk of Cheddar or Wensleydale – had been thrown round his throat and drawn as tightly as the strong hands of, say, a tall, fit man without any hair might have wrenched it. The man's dead eyes bulged. His face was blue in colour, cyanosed from lack of oxygen. A small trickle of bloodied drool ran from one corner of his mouth to the edge of his chin. There was no other sign of violence, as far as I could see. Just the bedsheets tangled into a rat's nest by his last desperate struggles.

I laid a finger lightly against his face but his flesh was cold. Of course, I had seen him before. He'd been one of the party of four men at the restaurant the other evening who were pretending not to be looking in my direction. And lying on the floor, under the bed, almost invisible, was one of those charity wristbands which Sandro had been wearing last time I saw him, though I could only read part of the slogan: *elp for He* . . . It was too much of a coincidence to suppose that someone else had accidentally dropped it there. It was quite obvious that Sandro must have been held in this room at some point and had somehow managed to cut the thing off his wrist in order to leave it as a clue. Smart move. It was fairly likely that his captors wouldn't notice it, whereas someone like me happening to blunder into the apartment would be actively looking for evidence that he'd been there.

Back in the living room, I saw the remains of primitive meals: hunks of stale bread, salami sausage skins, apple cores. Cartons which once held prepared pastas. And empty Chianti bottles lying in a heap by the window. Meanwhile, what to do about the dead bloke on the bed? Checking that there was nothing to indicate that I'd ever been there, I hurried down a flight of stairs and banged on the doors of the two flats there. No answer. The same on the floors below. I was just about to descend to the *piano terra* when a woman pushed her way through the front door and started up towards me. She nodded politely and made to pass me.

'Signora,' I said urgently. 'The police, there is a man upstairs at the top, a dead man—'

She gave a little scream. 'A dead man?' she said, in English.

'*Si, si.* Call the police at once.'

'But who are you? Why don't you call them yourself?'

'Because I don't know the number or where the *questura* is. I was just paying a visit when I saw the . . . the – oh, it's too horrible!' I buried my head in my hands, hoping she'd take things on from there.

'You poor thing.' She touched my shoulder. 'I always knew those men were trouble.'

'Do you mean Signor Gregori and his friends?'

'No, no. He is American, only comes two or three times a year. The rest of the time the apartment is rented out. This time to those . . . men.'

'Which men? What trouble?'

'The ones in the top *appartamento*. Four of them. Arguing. Drinking. Swearing. All night long. Look, signorina, I'll go and call the police.'

'Thank you.'

'And you can wait here and tell them what you saw.'

Not bloody likely. I could be tangled up in bureaucracy and suspicion for the next six months. I nodded at her then watched

her hurry up the stairs to the third floor. So she was either
Ms Cafarella or Ms di Giovanni.

As soon as I heard her key in the lock of her flat, I went
out of the front door and hurried away as far and as fast as
I could.

ELEVEN

Venice was very bad for my figure. Despite my worry about Sandro, I never seemed to stop eating. I'd worked in my hotel room for most of the morning, all the time expecting to hear from Cesare, but no call came. That was OK. It gave me a chance to outline a couple of articles for *Nirvana*, Darren Carver's arty mag. Later, I pushed aside my work and walked through the streets to the pretty square, not far from my hotel, which Renzo had chosen as a rendezvous. And there he was. I could see him through the window, perusing a menu, still as ugly as sin.

He saw me. 'Alessandra!' He jumped up and came running out to me, a white napkin tucked into the neck of his shirt, then embraced me in a hug that would have made a bear humble. 'Come. Come.' He took my hand and walked me inside. 'Sit. I have ordered food for you which will make you glad to be alive.'

That was only going to happen when Sandro was safely home. 'Thank you,' I said. Prettily, but not too prettily. We sat down. There were two glasses and a bottle on the table. And a plate of seafood pasta already in front of him. Renzo half-filled our glasses, tipped his towards me in a silent toast and then settled down to the serious business of eating the food which a string of waiters began bringing to the table.

'And after we have eaten,' he said, 'we shall go for a gondola ride.'

Uh-oh. 'Shall we?'

'Sure. I shall call my private gondolier to come and he will take us on a magical mystery tour of Venice.'

'Sounds great.'

The food was wonderful. And way more than I could eat. I wanted to ask for a doggie bag, but felt it would not be in keeping with the upmarket nature of the place. It was as we were drinking our coffees, along with a glass of semi-dry marsala for me and a *mirto* for Renzo, that he put his elbows on the table and inclined his barrel chest towards me. 'So,' he said. And paused significantly.

'So?' I countered. Was he going to ask me to become his mistress?

'Last time we met, you spoke to me of some drawings,' he said. 'Special drawings. By Tiepolo, no less.'

'What about them?'

'I would so much love to have the opportunity to see them.'

If I told him that I didn't have them, that they weren't mine, would he lose interest in me, either as a person or as a woman? I didn't want that to happen. Call me cold and calculating, but I sensed that he could be very useful to me in some form or another while I was here.

'*Ciao*, Renzo,' someone called. A woman. Passing our table. Another of those ultra-smart, tooth-achingly expensive women. He flashed her his terrific smile and jumped up to exchange kisses and hugs. Which gave me time to think. As he sat down again, I made up my mind. 'And so you shall,' I said.

'When?' he demanded eagerly. He put a hand over mine. 'How soon?' And here, all along it was the Tiepolos he was interested in. Not me at all.

I don't generally do coy, but I did try. 'I shall have to retrieve them first.' A meaningless sentence which gave nothing away.

'I understand.'

I laid a finger over my lips and nodded. From the way he took to this cloak-and-dagger stuff, I couldn't help wondering how many of his deals were in some way or another rather shady.

'Are you interested in buying them, then?'

He sipped his *mirto*. Put his head on one side. Nodded. 'Extremely. Especially since I've heard that they have gone missing from . . . from the collection of the person who currently owns them.'

How the hell had he heard that? 'Great art is universal,' I said trenchantly. God, I could be a ponce sometimes.

'True enough. But someone has to be its guardian.'

Yeah, after large sums of money have changed hands, I thought. I nodded again.

'So, if you can't show them to me at the moment, could you tell me more about these Tiepolos?'

'You do understand that this is top secret, don't you?'

'Absolutely.'

'And that they aren't really mine to handle?'

Renzo put one hairy hand over his heart. 'I swear to you, signorina, that I have said nothing to anyone about them.'

'Right.' I set about the business of describing the two I had seen at the Major's house. The old man in red chalk, face half-turned away. The Pulcinella with his clown ruff, the hideous *maschera di carnevale baùta* mask with its grotesque nose and chin, the loose white pyjama suit. With each added detail, Renzo grew more excited.

'Oh, how I wish to see them.' He sighed.

'Well . . .' I smiled at him. 'One of these days . . .'

Finally he called for the bill and signed a piece of paper which I presumed was part of a running tab. At the same time, he made a quick phone call.

'Come,' he said as we stood. He took my hand and led me to some steps at the canal's edge. In about forty seconds a black-painted gondola appeared, guided by a smiling guy in the traditional gondolier costume of red-striped shirt, crimson sash round the waist and straw hat banded with a red scarf. Gold trimmings covered the backs of the seats where scarlet cushions waited to be sat on and a small basket held a bottle of prosecco and two glasses.

'Golly, Renzo,' I said, as the gondolier handed me down with much flourishing and gallantry and showed me on to a fat-pillowed sofa. 'You really know how to show a girl a good time. This is certainly the way to live.'

'I am happy you like it.'

As the gondolier moved out into the canal, Renzo plumped down beside me, filled two glasses and handed me one. 'To us,' he said.

'To Tiepolo,' I added. Meanly. He nearly choked on that one.

The ride around the canals was lovely, though I could have done without the hairy hand on my knee and the hairy arm round my shoulders, let alone the garlic-infused breath against my neck. I figured that if things got too hot, I would ask how his children were. That should put a bit of a dampener on things.

'Earlier you said there were rumours that the Tiepolos might have gone missing from a private collection,' I said.

'Yes.'

'Do you know whose?'

'I know what the rumours say, but whether it's true or not, I don't know. Venice is a city of rumours, after all.'

'Any chance of telling me?'

'If I am to tell you, I would have to invite you dine with me again,' he said lustfully.

Oh, gawd . . . 'I think I could handle that,' I told him, at the same time flashing him a coquettish glance.

'In two days' time? I regret I am in Rome tomorrow.'

'Sounds great.' The Rialto Bridge hove into view and I scrambled forward on my seat. 'Oh, look, there's my nearest *imbarcadero*. Will you drop me off here? It's been wonderful to catch up with you and thank you so much for an amazing lunch. I really look forward to seeing you again very soon.'

I even planted a kiss on his cheek before hopping nimbly on to dry land before he could reach for me, though I felt a brush of hairy fingers on my thigh. What I do for art's sake.

TWELVE

I sat in my hotel room, typing into my laptop some more of the notes I'd taken earlier. It was hard to concentrate on work when my brain was whirring with worries about Sandro and his current whereabouts, the Major's Tiepolos and Katy Pasqualin drowned in her bath. Right from the start I'd felt there was little I could do to solve Sandro's need for information concerning which of his friends might have stolen his uncle's possessions. Factoring in the kidnap, particularly given the restrictions imposed by the abductors, I was being about as useful as a fly swat against a charging elephant. And time was running out. From my days on the force, I felt quite certain that the people responsible for the snatch wouldn't hesitate to carry out their threat if the ransom money wasn't forthcoming. At the same time, I was feeling a little out of my comfort zone. My command of Italian wasn't that good and, in addition, I knew that I had been clocked by the bad guys so, in spite of my years on the force, I might as well abandon any kind of covert surveillance. I needed help.

I used my phone to call Sandro's parents in London. Dominic Grainger answered almost before the first ringtone had ended. 'Yes?' he barked.

'It's Alexandra Quick,' I said.

'What's happening?'

'Basically nothing.'

'Why not?' he yelled.

'Because it's damn difficult to get a handle on anything, given that your brother-in-law has been given strict instructions not to involve the police. But I have a suggestion . . .'

'Which is?'

'That you immediately hire a professional private detective who speaks Italian – preferably one who knows Venice – and get him out here pronto. He could stay in this same hotel you booked me into, which would make it easier for the two of us to collaborate. He'd have much more idea of where to start looking, which is important. And there's absolutely no reason why anyone should connect him to Sandro or the Marchese.'

'Sounds like a good idea.'

'Believe me, it is. And there *has* been a development which might be a step forward.' I explained about Baldy and the house with the red door. Plus my discovery of the garrotted corpse and the half-hidden wristband.

'A corpse? Someone's been murdered? And my Sandro's involved?'

'I'm quite sure he had nothing whatsoever to do with it.'

'This is a fucking nightmare,' Dominic said roughly.

'I know.'

'My son . . .' He made a choking sound, then recovered himself. 'I agree with your suggestion about the detective,' he said slowly. 'I have some connections which could be useful. I'll get on to it right away and call you back with further details as soon as I have them.'

'Fine. The sooner the better. Time is of the essence here. And if I sound strange when you talk to me, it could be that I'm not in a position to be normal. Whatever that is.'

'Understood.'

I felt easier about the prospect of a working professional on the case. It's what should have happened right away, as soon as the news of Sandro's abduction came through.

Joey Preston showed up late that evening, on the last flight from London. When he tapped at the door of my room, I opened it and stepped back in surprise. I have to say my heart sank when I saw him. I'd expected someone more mature, more solid, a man who seemed more of an experienced detective and less like someone who'd just completed a distance-learning diploma in How to be a Detective 101. Preston was young, dark, lanky and looked like a bit of a dweeb. Nobody would give the poor sap a second glance. Which probably made him an excellent PI.

All this passed through my head as I stood aside to let him in to the room.

He grinned at me. 'Fancy a quick one?' he said.

'I *beg* your pardon.' I pretended outrage to break the ice. 'I'm not that kind of a girl.'

He laughed. 'During the flight, I read all the intel Mr Grainger sent over but you can probably fill me in on any missing details.' He grinned again. 'My room or yours? I've got a fifteen-year-old bottle of Bowmore's burning a hole right here in my pocket.'

'Mine, then.'

He produced a bottle from behind his back. 'Here you go. I hope your furnishings include a tooth mug or something. I asked the woman on the desk downstairs for a couple more glasses but she seemed reluctant to provide them. Or we could go out and sit by the water somewhere.'

'I'm easy,' I said. 'We're not far from the Grand Canal. *But . . .*' I raised a hand in a policeman-stopping-traffic gesture.

'What?'

'Should we be seen together? I don't think so.'

He looked crestfallen. 'You're right.'

'Of course I'm right. You need to be doing surveillance and/ or undercover investigation type stuff. And I may already be suspect . . .' I described the four guys who'd been pretending not to watch me at the restaurant. One of whom had just been murdered.

'Got it.' He wrenched open his bottle of whisky and poured us both a tot. He sat down on the chair at the table I was using as a desk, while I scrambled on to the bed and leaned back against the headboard.

'Just as a matter of interest,' I said, 'why were you chosen to come over here on such short notice?'

'Mainly because my grandparents are from Milan,' he explained. 'So my mother is too. My name's Giovanni really, but Joey's easier.'

'So you got the job because of your fluency with the language?'

'That, and a few other skills,' he said modestly. 'So, give me the gen.'

I brought him up to date, including the death of Katy. I described the tall, bald man and the corpse I'd stumbled on, and the Help for Heroes wristband.

'Sounds like your hunch was right and the missing lad *was* being held there.'

'Right. Trouble is the whole thing seems to have escalated from simple theft via kidnap to multiple murder. But the family are still insisting that the police mustn't be brought in, as per instructions, because of the threat to Sandro.'

'As per usual in these cases.'

I frowned. 'Doesn't it seem a bit odd that these people would kill one of their own and leave him in that upstairs apartment, when they've been insistent that the police aren't called in on the case?'

'Thieves falling out?'

'Could be . . . but leaving a corpse behind? It's not exactly street smart.'

'You're an ex-copper, Alex. You must have noticed that most of the toerags aren't very bright.'

'True. Or is someone else involved? Someone we don't yet know about?'

'Seems likely.' He swigged a fair old slug of whisky. 'God, that's good. And it's your considered opinion that the thefts from this Marchese and the kidnapping of his nephew, plus the murder of Katerina Pasqualin in London, are all interconnected?'

'It seems to me that they more or less have to be.'

'At least we can safely leave Pasqualin to the Met. Know what I think? From what I've heard, I'm guessing she knew too much and was applying pressure.'

'Sounds very likely.'

'What's the hold-up in paying the ransom? I was informed that the money was all ready to go.'

'The kidnappers have given the Marchese – the victim's uncle – and Mr Grainger, plenty of time to get the money together.'

'And when's pay day?'

'The day after tomorrow.'

'And when was he snatched?'

'A few days ago. Another piece of stupidity on the part of the abductors. The longer they hang on to him, the more chance there is of him being found before money has changed hands.'

'Talking of which, twenty million euros isn't a huge amount, considering how loaded these two families are supposed to be.'

'*Supposed* may be the operative word. I agree with you about the size of the sum being demanded . . . it's much too small.'

'Perhaps they know more than we do.'

'The uncle is in despair because he can't get in touch with the kidnappers. He just has to wait till they contact him.' I thought of Sandro's bright and beautiful face and felt sick.

'So what now?'

'Going back to the house where I think Sandro was stashed, and also having a more painstaking search for the guy doing the stashing . . .'

'The bald guy?'

He'd obviously been well-briefed. 'That's right . . . Thing is, he didn't look Italian. Not to me, anyway.'

'Do I?'

I considered him. 'Not particularly, I suppose. It's just that the bald one had the colouring of a different culture. Not Mediterranean. Could have been a Scandi, a German, an Englishman. Even a Yank. Whereas you . . .'

'And you think this all goes back to the business with the pawnshop in London?'

'It certainly seems connected. I think the possibility can't be dismissed.'

'And where do you think your young friend has been transferred to?'

I shrugged. 'If they have a car at their disposal, he could have been taken anywhere.'

'Well, we have to assume that, for the moment at least, he's still somewhere nearby.'

'You may have to do the search of the house on your own,' I said. 'I already spoke to one of the residents and don't want to be recognized if she's there.'

'There are ways of getting round that.'

I leaned forward with my elbows on my knees. 'Look, Joey, I was originally drafted in to help out in finding where Sandro was, since he hadn't rung his mother in days.

I was coming to Venice for work purposes anyway, so that
was fine, though since I'm not a local, why they thought I'd
be any good at finding him and what I'd say if I did, I really
don't know. However, before I could get out here, he'd been
snatched and was being held for ransom, and now you're on
the case. So what I'm saying is, after tomorrow, when I finish
gathering the information I came out here to get, there's really
not much reason for me to hang on here.'

He reached out and put a finger on the back of my hand.
'That would be a shame . . .' he said.

Please God, he wasn't coming on to me. I glanced at
him.

'Because two heads are better than one,' he continued.

'That's not always true.'

'Besides, if we're going to apprehend the perps, we might
be able to provide useful cover for each other.'

I shook my head. 'You'll be able to operate much more
effectively if you're independent of me.'

'Probably. Part of the mission is nailing the buggers. The
cash, after all, is easy enough for the family to come up with.
It's the aftermath that's important. Or so I was briefed.'

I suppose I always knew I wasn't seriously going to leave
before Sandro was safely back in the bosom of his family. I
nodded agreement. 'You're right. Though I don't think these
are sophisticated crims doing what they've done several times
before. I just have a suspicion that this is more personal than
that.'

'In what way?'

'I'm not exactly sure. I'm not a believer in gut feelings or
hunches, let alone inspired guesses. I guess it's something to
do with the murder of Katy Pasqualin. It all seems too close
to home, that's all. Wheels within wheels.'

'I can see your point.'

'Anyway, I'm going out to have something to eat. You can
wait a bit and then go to the same place, even sit near me,
but we can't afford to appear in any way to be together.'

Walking to my chosen restaurant, which sat beside the Grand
Canal, I wondered just how good a detective Joey Preston was
if it hadn't occurred to him to take any precautions against

the two of us being seen together. Five minutes later, I was sitting at a table, surrounded by people enjoying themselves. It was a balmy night, light rippling the water, black gondolas prowling like panthers up and down the canal. As always with Venice, there was music coming from somewhere.

A waiter appeared. I ordered a pasta dish in my adequate if simple Italian.

It was then, straight across from my table but on the other side of the canal, that I saw a shining dome. Venice is full of them, but not usually ones with two ears attached, one of which was sporting a gold ring. Baldy, by God. Yet again. I immediately raised my miniature camera to my face and then, for the benefit of any watchers, rubbed at an eye. Got him! Trouble was, I was too far away to get across the canal in time to trail him. I watched the direction he went in, but within half a minute, he had disappeared from sight in the crowds which always swarm around the Rialto Bridge.

At least I could presume that Sandro was still being detained in Venice. Which if I thought about it, he'd more or less have to be, if he was going to be delivered safe and sound after the ransom drop. I hoped that wasn't too big an *if*.

I lifted my shoulders and sighed as I watched Joey Preston emerge from a narrow street and head for the bridge, then make his way to my restaurant.

'We have two more days,' I said to Joey later, as we sat out on my midget balcony, our knees companionably touching. 'And we're still waiting for instructions as to how and where to drop off the ransom money.'

'You just know it's going to involve the canal in some way,' Joey said.

'Exactly what I'm thinking. It seems to me that as soon as we know how it's going down, we should hire a motorboat, ready to take off after them as unobtrusively as possible.'

'The uncle's savvy enough to demand proof of life before he pays up, isn't he?'

'That's what I told him he must do before parting with any money.' I hadn't felt good saying it, but reality had to be faced.

As the once austere, now sadly diminished Cesare fully recognized.

'Can we really chase them across the lagoon? If they take off at full throttle, and we do the same, we're bound to alert them.'

'We don't have to chase. Just follow. Actually,' I said, 'I was wondering whether Murano or Burano or one of the other islands could be where they've taken him.'

'Me too.'

'Then why is Baldy over here?'

'If he's the head honcho, he'll presumably have henchmen to do the babysitting.'

'We've got about twenty-four hours to get our act together, I reckon,' I said. 'Then we'll be sent instructions – or rather, the uncle will – and we may then be able to make a more solid plan.'

'Is it worth scouting round over there across the canal, seeing if by any chance we catch sight of the guy again?'

'I don't think so. Even for Venice it's late. He was probably heading somewhere for the night. Right. I'll meet you tomorrow for coffee and a Danish. But over there.' I gestured to the other side of the canal. 'Then we'll do some checking around. I'll call Sandro's father and uncle first thing.'

THIRTEEN

Before I went downstairs the following morning, I stepped out on to my balcony and looked up and down the narrow pavement which ran along the little canal. A few people were about, mostly locals, scrubbing doorsteps, polishing brass knockers, cleaning ground-floor windows. The woman across the way was hanging out her laundry. An old man in one of those flat white cotton caps was leaning on the bridge, contemplatively smoking a yellow cigarette and gazing into the water. He didn't look like the sort who would have trailed Nell Roscoe and the *soi-disant* Florence Forbes – a woman who was finding it hard to remember what name she was going under – even if her story about it being her who had bought the Tiepolos was true. No reason why it shouldn't have been, of course. But I knew it couldn't be. Not after Nell Roscoe's report to the Major. It would be interesting to know how 'Flo' had learned of the drawings.

Though I couldn't see it from here, I could hear the hum of people's voices coming from the *riva* along the Grand Canal. I picked up my bag and left, not bothering to sample the rather inadequate breakfast on offer in the hotel's little dining room. Outside, the air was warm. I strolled towards the water through streets already heaving with tourists and locals on their way to work, crossed it and found the café where I'd been the night before. I ordered a *caffè latte* and some rolls, which came with butter and a nondescript sort of red jam which could have been made from almost anything, including fruit. I'd bought a newspaper and pretended to be engrossed in it, while I kept an eye out for Baldy. Idly, I wondered whether shaving his head had been a fashion statement or even a misplaced attempt to disguise himself, since any idiot could have told him it hadn't worked. The bald head drew more attention to him rather than less. Especially when coupled with the gold stud.

I saw Joey Preston on the other side of the canal, heading

towards the bridge. And behind him, to my surprise, one
of the guys who'd been sitting at the table in this same restaurant pretending they weren't looking at me. Were they aware
that I was connected to Sandro? This was a worrying
development.

Joey crossed over and came towards me, followed by his
tail, who then suddenly veered away to the right. Was it because
he'd seen me looking at him? Or because he recognized me
from our last semi-encounter? And much more importantly,
was he on to Joey? It seemed unlikely, considering Joey had
only arrived late the night before. Whichever, I wasn't happy
about it.

Joey chose a table well within earshot of mine, gestured at
the waiter, then sat facing the canal. 'I think they're on to us,'
I said softly. I didn't think anyone would notice my lips moving.
At least I hoped not.

'Possibly. But don't let them know that we suspect,' he said.
He ordered the same as I had, plus a plate of sliced sausage.
From his backpack he hoicked out a guide book to the city
and began riffling the pages, acting like an ordinary tourist.
He looked away down the canal towards Giudecca and San
Marco.

'About the drop-off,' I said quietly from my table. 'I'm
getting nervous.'

He turned to another page in the guidebook. 'Don't be
jumpy. We just have to assume that things will go the way we
want them to, and we'll get your friend back safe and sound.
Nailing the perps has to be much less important than locating
the victim.'

'I'm not usually panicky. But it's the thought of what might
happen to Sandro if anything goes wrong.' All too clearly, I
could visualize the effect on the Graingers were they to lose
their son. Pretty much the same as any parent would feel, I
imagined, except that such a loss might actually kill Maddalena.

I spent most of the rest of the morning pottering round
churches and museums, drinking in beauty like champagne.
Neither Baldy nor the henchman – if that is indeed what he
was – showed up again. For a change, I took the Strada Nuovo
in the opposite direction from San Marco. At the rather grand

early Renaissance *palazzo* which housed the Casino di Venezia, I stopped. I'd seen it many times from the canal, but only once from the land side.

I was about to move on when I noticed the woman I'd begun to think of as The Mistress, or possibly her twin sister. She stood just inside the glass entrance, talking animatedly with one of the casino officials. Fancy little pink coat swinging above second-skin trousers with Principal Boy suede boots up to her thighs. So what did that imply? That she was an habitué of the place and therefore familiar to the personnel? Or that the particular man she was conversing with was a friend or relative? Or that she was just a chatty person? The curly-haired white dog moved restlessly in her arms, sunlight glinting on its jewelled collar. Food for thought. Or possibly not.

Later, I walked back to the Piazza San Marco and ate lunch. Veal marsala. I hadn't seen Joey in my wanderings. Nor any of the suspected abductors. Five bites in, my phone rang. My heart began to hammer.

'What?' I said.

'They've been in touch.' It was Cesare, his voice hoarse and rasping.

'And?'

'Tomorrow evening at ten o'clock,' he said. 'Not in Venice itself, but on Burano.'

'Makes sense. There's much less water traffic there.'

'They want me to be standing on a particular bridge and, as they go underneath in a motorboat, to drop the money into it. They've given me instructions on how to package it. I'm to carry two bags with half the money in each. One bag the first time. Then I'm to move to another part of the island, stand on another bridge and follow the same procedure.'

'Much too complicated,' I said. 'Which is good. It means there's more chance that they'll slip up somewhere during the drop and we can nab them.'

'Do you really think so?'

'Definitely,' I said, more strongly than I actually felt. 'Tell you what . . . I'll pack a small bag and go over there early this afternoon. I'll book a hotel or a bed-and-breakfast nearby, if there is one, and see what I can see. And you can probably arrange for the detective whom Dominic Grainger hired to be idling around in his own boat, so that, with any luck, he can follow them. Meanwhile, what's the arrangement for Sandro's release?'

'They said they would give further instructions tomorrow.'

I repeated a question I'd already put to him. 'You've asked for . . .' It was difficult to enunciate the next words. 'For proof of life?'

'Yes. And I've told them that they had better make absolutely sure that Sandro is safe and well, and that I know about it. To which they said they would have to count the money before Sandro would be set free, in case I'd double-crossed them.'

'I don't like the sound of that at all.'

'Nor do I, Signorina Quick. Once they've got it they'd have no reason to bother keeping him alive, let alone releasing him. The longer he's with them, the more chance there is of him identifying them later. I made it absolutely clear if one hair on my nephew's head is harmed, I will personally hound them to the ends of the earth.'

Dramatic stuff, but not inappropriate, given the circumstances. 'Good thinking,' I said. 'By the way, I'm wondering . . . if these are the final stages of negotiations, is it time to disobey their instructions and call in the police?'

'It would make sense.'

'But . . . what about Sandro, if they find out?'

'Precisely. The big obstacle.'

'I don't think you can take the risk,' I said. 'But – with your permission, of course – I'll let the detective know what you've told me. See if he can come up with some kind of plan.'

'Yes, yes, tell him. That is what he's here for.'

'Meanwhile, I'll keep the room in my hotel in Venice and go over to Burano for a couple of nights, if I can find a room somewhere.'

I walked through the city and took a *vaporetto* out to the island of Burano or, rather, the group of four close islands linked by bridges. We passed the melancholy cypresses of the Isola di San Michele, the cemetery of Venice, and other small outcrops of rock and grass, most of them clearly uninhabited. Flocks of black cormorants rose from the water as we approached, or occasionally sank beneath the surface until we had gone. Burano lay on the horizon like a string of coloured beads which, as I grew closer, sorted themselves out into individual houses all painted in the brightest of hues, from rose-pink to crimson to brilliant greens and startling blues to every possible shade under the sun. Burano bills itself as the most colourful place in the world. Not so much a rainbow as an accumulation of every shade of every possible colour. Equally colourful craft of different kinds were moored all along the waterfronts. Their reflections in the water were magical, especially towards the end of the afternoon, when the sun slanted against the house fronts and they were reflected in the ripples of the canals.

I was lucky enough to find a small establishment, somewhere between a bed-and-breakfast and a hotel, which had just received a cancellation and was more than happy to give me the now-unoccupied double room at the front. I figured what the hell if it was twice as expensive as a single room. Cesare – or maybe Dominic – was picking up the tab and the room couldn't have been better placed for covert observation, since the window looked right up the *calle* to the bridge where the first drop was to take place. Although it would be dark by ten o'clock, I might even be able to see and recognize who was piloting the boat, unless Sandro's abductors acquired a touch of the smarts and paid someone else to do it.

And until then, there was plenty for me to do on the island, in keeping with my genuine role. For a start, I wanted to visit the leaning tower of St Martin's Church, and then go inside to look at the famous Tiepolo painting of the Crucifixion. Plus, of course, the lace museum, though lace wasn't really my thing, unless adorning the collar of some dude in a painting. Simple restaurants to eat in, pleasant walks among the colourful streets. I kind of speculated whether Baldy would show up, but he'd have to be incredibly stupid if he did so. I wondered how Joey was getting on – whether he'd found any further information.

And as though I'd conjured him up, my cell phone rang and it was Joey himself. 'Went along to the *questura*,' he said.

'The main cop shop. Explained who I was but obviously not why I was there. Said I'd been sent over privately from England to look into some local thefts. Luckily they didn't ask too many questions. And I just happened to mention one of the suspects, a guy with a shaven head and an earring. Cue sage nods and significant looks.'

'Meaning what exactly?'

'That they knew precisely whom I was talking about. Someone they've come across several times in the course of investigating various burglaries but have never been able to pin anything on to. He and his associates are people they've been keeping an eye on. He's not Italian – they rather thought he was Danish. And not a professional crim, more a petty one. Jens Hansen by name. Or is it Hans Jensen? Works as a baker somewhere in the Giudecca, has a wife and two kids. They even gave me an address.'

'So it's not the house with the red door, near the Rialto?'

'Doesn't look like it.'

'And I should point out that kidnapping's a major crime, not a petty one.'

'I wanted to say something to them, but because of the embargo that's been laid down, I didn't dare.'

'They've been in touch,' I said.

'The kidnappers?'

'Yeah.'

'And?'

I repeated what the Marchese had told me. Outlined my idea that at drop-off time, Joey should be hanging about in a hired vessel of some kind, messing about at the entrance to the particular canal they'd chosen.

'Good idea. Except if you look at a map of Burano that would be just about impossible. They could come in one way and exit into the lagoon somewhere else.'

'Bugger it.'

'Yes, but even if I was at the drop-off point, they'd get a bit leery if my engine suddenly sprang into life when they appeared and I started following them at speed.'

'Understood.' I considered it for a moment. 'Aren't people with boats supposed to spend most of their time messing about? Fiddling with the crank shaft and readjusting the speed dial sort of thing? Couldn't you be doing a spot of messing?'

'That's probably what I'll end up doing . . . unless I position myself at the Venice side of the lagoon and keep an eye out for fast-moving vessels.'

'Joey,' I said, 'would it be a good idea to inform them that the second half of the money would only be handed over as a direct exchange for Sandro?'

He was silent for a moment. 'It could be done,' he said eventually. 'But there'd be a risk. They might decide that ten million is better than nothing, dispose of the victim and exit stage left.'

'We'd have played fair with them up to that point,' I said. 'And all we want is Sandro. We can show them there's no police involved, only the Marchese himself.'

'I'll talk to him. My feeling is there are risks whatever we do. Once they've got the money, they don't really give a toss about their vic, do they?'

'But the big guy is a local, or at least he works locally. And he's got a family here.'

'Maybe he's made plans to decamp immediately once he's been paid off, with or without the rest of the family. With twenty million euros in his pocket – minus the cut he's giving to his accomplices – he can go where he pleases.'

'This is difficult,' I said. 'Look, are you quite sure he's the brains behind this abduction?'

'Not at all.'

'Oh, that's just peachy,' I said.

'Isn't it though?'

When we'd ended our somewhat frustrating conversation, I sat in a café over a cup of coffee and mused. What were the links between Sandro, the thefts from his uncle's *palazzo*, the murder of Katy and the Major's Tiepolo drawings? If any. As I saw it, Sandro was the key. He sat like a spider at the centre of a web of radiating lines. But did any of them connect up? And there was the tantalizing mention from Renzo about the thefts of some Tiepolos. I had found the so-called Florence Forbes' claim to them completely spurious, but even by a gigantic stretch of the imagination, it was hard to see her as a master criminal, involved not just with the drawings but also with the killing of Katy Pasqualin, the abduction of Sandro, the theft of the doge's ring, the bald guy – Jens Hansen, right? Or possibly Hans Jensen – and the corpse in the house with the red door.

But however much I tried to knit the separate threads together, I couldn't. My head began to pound like a bass pan in a steel band. I ordered more coffee. It didn't help. Eventually, deciding that walking might clear my brain, I got up and began to stroll along the canals. There was so much to see and appreciate that it was hard to remember that I was here for a serious and possibly lethal reason. The taste of marsala rose in my throat. Every now and then, crossing a narrow street, I would catch a glimpse of the Chiesa San Martino. Cooking smells floated from windows – cheese, garlic, sausage, tomato – making me feel even more nauseous. Maybe the best thing to do would be to return to my little bed-and-breakfast and try to catch an hour's kip. I could be pretty certain life would still be heaving in the squares and cafés. I strolled past a blue house, a rose house, a glorious ochre one with green shutters and trailing petunias. I turned the corner. And that was it. They jumped me. Three guys, briefly melting out of the shadows, clapping something over my face, grabbing my arms as I tottered, then swiftly lifting me off my feet and in through a doorway. Before I passed out completely, a voice said, 'So, Miss Alexandra Quick, we have you. We shan't—' And that was it. I was gone.

I woke some hours later. I'd been trussed like a piece of rolled English sirloin. Sirloin was one of the few things Mary, my mother, was able to cook. I felt tears in my eyes at the thought of Mary and Edred, their safe familiarity, their increasing eccentricities. For God's sake . . . I blinked them away. More important than tears was to find out where I was and why I'd been brought here.

My arms were tight against my sides. My legs had been tied together. My stomach was roiling. My head felt as though it had been opened and half the contents removed with a rusty spoon. Like anyone else who finds themselves tied up, I tested the knots which bound me, using my fingers, which were mercifully free. Not that I could reach very far. The trussing was pretty good work, but not quite good enough. I found that one knot was less tight than the others, and began to work it as best I could. While I did so, I used my other senses. The room was dark but not completely light-deprived, illumination easing between ill-fitting shutters closed over the window. As so often in this watery location, there was the smell of damp. Outside, sounds of feet, voices, splashing water. I guessed I was in a disused ground-floor room somewhere along one of the canals. I could just make out the rectangle of a door in the wall opposite the window.

Reluctantly, I rolled myself across the filthy floor towards it and awkwardly got my ear jammed up against the lower part of it. Nothing. Not a sound. With great discomfort, I levered myself upright. Was there a handle and, if so, could I reach hold of it? There was, but it was too high up the door and I couldn't reach. Not even with my mouth. The best I could do was rattle it with my chin, which achieved precisely zilch. Suddenly water flooded my mouth and I threw up as neatly as possible. I didn't want to get vomit all over my clothes.

The door was one step above the floor so I sat down on it. There was one small crumb of comfort in that my bindings were coming looser, but at such a tediously slow rate that I reckoned I'd be celebrating my sixtieth birthday before I got free.

Two people stopped outside the window, chatting. A couple of English teenagers, I guessed. Sniggering about some girls they knew, the way male adolescents the world over always do.

I moaned loudly, all I could manage with a disgusting gag in my mouth.

'What was that?' one of them said.

'Dunno,' said his friend. 'Anyway, she's standing there . . .'

A party of Japanese came by, squealing and barking with excitement, drowning out any sound I might be able to make. And by the time they'd gone by, the lads had also moved on. My captors must have known I'd be unlikely to attract attention from my prison. They'd also known my name. Were they aware of my connection to Cesare? For Sandro's sake, I prayed that they weren't. Yet would I have been abducted if they hadn't? '*So. Miss Alexandra Quick, we have you. We shan't—*' Shan't *what*? Gouge my eyes out? Gang rape me? Cut off my boobs? I threw up again.

My stomach began to settle. My head was slowly clearing. They had left my watch on my wrist and I twisted my arm round within its bonds in order to squint at the time. Quarter past nine. How long had I been out? From the light on the other side of the shutters, I assumed this was still the same day I had been taken, since I couldn't possibly have been out for more than twenty-four hours. I wondered whether Joey Preston or the Marchese had tried to phone me. And if so, when I didn't answer, suspect something was wrong. And if so, what they would do about it, if anything? Looked at rationally, what *could* they do?

All this time I had been working on the loose bit of rope which bound me. When I say 'loose', I mean that it was merely a fraction less tight than the rest of the fastenings. But now, abruptly, it pulled away from the piece to which it was supposedly attached. I bent my head and tugged at it with my teeth, pulling as hard as I could, difficult as it was with my mouth full of rag. It wasn't hugely helpful. I tried to tongue the gag out, but again, it was almost impossible. I was still caged in rope, and beginning to feel pretty pissed off about it. The backs of my hands were swollen. The flesh of my arms bulged between the restraints. I was trying not to think of gangrene and blackened tissue. Fingers dropping off. Suppurating sores. Limbs falling. I shivered. Not just because of the gruesome images in my head, but also because I'd come out with nothing more than a light top and the damp of the room was getting to me.

I carried on working on the knots. They were gradually opening up. Eventually I got a hand free, which meant I was able to pull at the ropes round my legs until they were loose enough for me to walk. Which I did. Fast. Over to the door. Tearing out the gag as I moved, trying to get some moisture into my mouth. I listened again at the door, ear flat against the wood. Nothing. I found the handle and carefully turned it. Tugged. Couldn't shift it. I was trapped. And frankly, I could see little prospect of getting out until the bad guys chose to release me. If release was what they had in mind.

Don't think about the alternatives, I told myself. *And keep your wits about you.* Given the opportunity, I reckoned I could take on any of the stocky fellows who'd grabbed me. The bald man was a different prospect. One blow to the head from his massive paws and I'd be out of the equation.

I shuffled over to the shuttered window again. Could I somehow shatter the glass? Apart from my own head, I had no weapon and I knew from sad experience during my days on the force how hard it was to break windows without one. Outside, the daylight was fading and been replaced by gleams from the faux-quaint lamps along the pavement. I drew back my head, already wincing, and banged it hard against one of the glass panes of the window, which achieved nothing except a large lump in the middle of my forehead. And for my next trick, I thought . . .

Voices were fading off into the distance and being replaced by new ones, but fewer now and further away. Were those bastards going to feed me, give me toilet facilities, leave me in this damp cellar all night? And then, back sitting on the damp concrete step over by the door, I finally heard the sounds that I'd been waiting for: movement on the other side. Voices. Steps. A key being jingled. I had a plan. I readied myself.

A weak light flowed into my dank quarters as the door opened. A man stood there, above me, although I could only see his outline. Not the Danish baker, thank God, but one of the stocky guys on his team. As he lifted his arm to chuck a bag containing, by the sound of it, a plastic bottle of water and, with any luck, a loaf of bread or some sausage into the darkness, I grabbed his calf, at the same time jerking him forward and into the room. He fell heavily, hitting his head hard with a satisfactory clunk as skull met floor. It winded him although it didn't knock him out. But I was on him like a hungry tiger, stuffing my already removed T-shirt into his mouth then grabbing his arms and tying them tightly behind his back with some of the rope which had previously bound me. Same thing with his legs. I wasn't skilled at knotting up a rolled sirloin roast but I did a pretty good job. And call me vindictive, but in the weak light coming through the open door, I was delighted to see that the guy's cheek was pillowed in one of my chloroform-induced pools of vomit. I pulled off his shoes, tore off a smelly sock, retrieved my T-shirt and replaced it with the sock, and was gone. I did some rattling of the key as I locked the door, in case anyone was listening. No raucous male voices, no mobiles beeping. I was now in a narrow passage, with the front door of the house no more than a tantalizing dozen steps or so from where I stood. Walls that had once been green but were now leprous. Rubbish blown in from the street: leaves, a paper bag, half a ticket. Trapped behind the front door was some more: a torn tissue, a bit of red plastic. As I headed quietly towards it, a door on the floor above opened and two men came out, talking in rapid Italian and heading for the stairs.

I ran.

I was terrified that the door would be locked, but as I wrenched at the handle it flew open and I half-stepped, half-tumbled out into the street.

There were still lights on in some of the houses and I ran for the nearest one, several down from where I'd been held. I banged on the door, screaming for help at the top of my voice as I did so. Looking back along the street the way I'd come, I saw two men emerge from the house I had just escaped from and then start towards me, but at the same time the door of the house in front of me opened and a burly man looked out.

'What? What?' he said. 'What's the matter?'

'Let me in!' I shrieked. The more noise I made, the better. 'Those men have just kidnapped me. Let me in. *Please!*'

By now, people were leaning out of windows and pulling back hatches on one or two of the houseboats, with heads materializing. That had been my hope all along. Seeing that they had been spotted, my captors retreated rapidly into their own house and slammed the door behind them while my rescuer pulled me into his hallway, a mirror image of the one I'd just raced out of.

He must have realized from my dishevelled appearance that I was telling the truth. 'I don't know exactly who they are,' he said, speaking English. 'But I *do* know that is not their house. The owners – Enrico and Maria – are away in the States, visiting their son in Texas.' He nodded and smiled slightly. 'Bet you anything that their no-good worthless cousin Beppo is behind this.' He then uttered a string of Italian words, of which *figlio di puttana* was the least offensive.

I wanted to tell them to call the police, but once again I didn't dare risk Sandro's life. At least I had a possible name: Beppo. By now I'd been ushered into the kitchen at the back of the house and been joined by the man's wife, plump in a dressing gown and nightdress, and various of the neighbours, who were letting themselves in through the front door. Glasses were being placed on the table, *grappa* was being poured, and I was being urged to tell my story, which I did, with considerable embellishment and a kind of dramatic flair. The members of the drama group in Canterbury to which I used to belong would have been astounded to witness it.

I knew that both Joey Preston and the Marchese would be worried stiff at not being able to contact me, but there was nothing I could do about it, with my phone gone and neither of their numbers in my head. And abruptly came the reaction. I shook as though I was standing naked in a snowstorm. My teeth chattered. My hands were shivering so badly that I had to put my glass down on the table, under which my feet and legs were dancing a fandango to music I couldn't hear. I needed to get back to my hotel, though the thought of leaving the safety provided by these people was terrifying. I smelled of vomit and sweat and damp plaster, And, I'm not ashamed to say, of fear. For myself, as well as for Sandro. I honestly had not thought I would leave that shuttered room alive. The thought of a long, hot shower was far more intoxicating than the alcohol which was being pressed on me by my hosts and their friends.

There were clucks of concern and compassion. Someone brought a blanket and put it round my shoulders. Someone else held my hand and squeezed it sympathetically. I could feel the *grappa* burning down through my oesophageal tube, soothing my stomach and cheering my brain. I simply couldn't help playing to the gallery, which was increasing with every minute. More bottles were being plonked on the table. Plates of sliced sausage and prosciutto had appeared, along with sticks of bread, dishes of olives and *cornichons*. Beer was being served. It had turned into a party, despite it being in the early hours of the morning. I'd have enjoyed it a whole lot more if I hadn't looked or smelled the way I did.

There was talk of a vigilante group going down to Rico and Maria's place and confronting Beppo, if indeed it was he who'd been responsible for my imprisonment in the house, but thank God that petered out into another refill of glasses and a discussion of Venezia's chances in Lega Pro in the coming season and the desperate need for a new stadium. Every now and then someone would turn to me, check that my glass wasn't empty and say 'Arsenal' or 'Chelsea' in encouraging tones, at which I would nod and smile. I even managed to say 'Juventus' which had some of them cheering, and 'Lombardi', really establishing my credentials, though I know nothing at all about football. I desperately wanted to get back to my little hotel and have a shower, but didn't want to break things up when everyone was having so much fun.

FOURTEEN

It was almost four thirty in the morning by the time I was back in my rented bed, showered and clean, my filthy clothes dumped in a corner for washing when daylight came. I'd had to do a bit of elaborately stifled yawning and eyelid-blinking, but eventually a couple of obliging young men at last night's impromptu party had walked me through the streets of Burano to my hotel. They greeted the sleepy night porter with friendly cries of recognition and blow me if another bottle of *grappa* didn't emerge from under his desk. With profuse thanks, I left them to it.

At eight forty-five, there was a tapping at my bedroom door.

'Yeah?' Sleepily, I raised myself up on one elbow. 'Who is it?'

'Joey.'

I stumbled out of bed and walked stiffly across the room. Every muscle in my body seemed to ache and my bones were doing a good job of joining in. I got to the door. Unbolted it. Said, 'Count to ten before you enter,' then staggered back to bed.

Once in my room, with the door closed behind him, Joey stared at me, buried under the bedclothes.

'What's going on?' he demanded.

'What are you doing over here?' I mumbled.

'Nobody could raise you yesterday, so the Marchese decided I'd better hop over here and find out why.'

I started to explain what had happened, but my voice began to shake. To my horror, weak tears sat in my eyes. I definitely don't do tears, let alone weak ones. But I honestly hadn't believed one hundred per cent that I would survive the cold and damp in the room where I'd been imprisoned. I don't suppose I was there for more than an hour or two, but it had seemed an eternity. It was the not knowing that was so deadly, so terrifying. Wondering if they were just going to leave me there to rot, or starve to death.

I wanted to hear the shaven-headed guy speak English. If he had the same voice as the person who'd spoken to me just before I blanked out, I was going to find a means of hurting him in some way. Badly. Not necessarily cutting off his todger, but pretty close. Something really painful, just like Sandro had promised he would do when he discovered who had been responsible for the thefts from Cesare's apartment. At the thought of Sandro, my bruises throbbed. Where was he? More importantly, was he still alive?

'What's the drill tonight?' I asked, my voice returning. I sat up, pulling the bedclothes up under my chin. I'd have killed for a cup of tea.

'Hasn't changed. Burano, launch coming by, half the ransom money dropped in from the bridge, the Marchese hurries to the next designated bridge, other half dropped into the boat and off it goes. Heading, we presume, for the big city.'

'And where's Sandro in all this?'

'That's going to be the problem. The Marchese has arranged to have a boat posted at each departure point across the lagoon, so wherever they go, we can follow them. But they're not going to bring him with them, are they?'

I shook my head. Then wished I hadn't. 'You do realize that they're on to us, don't you? Even if they weren't before.'

'Which you'd assume they must have been or they wouldn't have snatched you last night. Nor addressed you by name.'

'Joey, you said the police had given you the baker's address. Have you—'

'I staked the place out most of yesterday. According to the neighbours, they've seen him around recently but nobody's seen the wife and two children for about five days.'

'Scarpered? Or murdered?'

'The former, I hope. And I'm reckoning he's due to join them as soon as he's collected the cash.'

'Somewhere in Scandiland?'

'So I should imagine.'

Aching, I pushed back my covers. 'Excuse me, Joey, but I need to get dressed.'

'Oh, don't mind me, doll.'

'Out!'

'Spoilsport. I'll be downstairs.'

Fifteen minutes later, feeling a little better, I was washed, dressed and more or less ready to roll. In the mirror of the small bathroom, I could see there were bruises all up and down my body. Those bastards must have just chucked me into the boarded-up ground-floor room like a sack of melons.

Downstairs, Joey was lounging about in the tiny foyer. 'Let's walk along the canal before we go back to the city,' I said. 'I'd like to try and identify the house where they were holding me.' As we went, my eyes hidden behind sunglasses, I scoped the place out, checking to the left and the right for stocky men or shaven-headed bakers. One of the stocky bastards might even have bruises all down the side of his face. But I saw nobody.

Nor could I be absolutely certain exactly which side street I'd been on the corner of when I had been snatched, let alone to which of the narrow, bundled together houses I'd been taken by my kidnappers. At night, and despite the street lamps, they'd all seemed identical. Under cover of my dark lenses, I surveyed the houses from across the canal but could see no identifying characteristics, although I could narrow the choice down to four or five. It was the same with the house to which I'd run. Although I was able to narrow it down to one of four with reasonable certainty, I couldn't possibly say which one it had been. Joey and I crossed over the canal. It was easy enough to knock at the doors of the houses in question, but nobody seemed to be home at any of them.

As we walked away, there was no point pretending Joey and I weren't together. With the theft of my mobile, the bad guys were now several steps ahead of us in the grim game that was being played out. I didn't know how long they'd been aware of why I was in Venice before they took me off the streets, but maybe they'd picked up on me from the moment I arrived – though logic told me that wasn't possible. How could they have been, unless they were art lovers? Which was a stretch too far for me. And even if they were, they can't have known of any connection between me and the Marchese. Mainly because there wasn't one. Not really. Unless . . . I would have to get on to Renzo Vitali again, find out more about the rumour he'd hinted at concerning stolen drawings. I was beginning to think that the Tiepolos, too, had been lifted from Cesare's *appartamento*.

I figured that if we drew a blank at the address we were heading for, we could always go back to the house with the red door, if the cops hadn't sealed it off as a crime scene. Sandro *had* to physically be somewhere, almost certainly right here somewhere in the Veneto, and if we could find him before Cesare paid the ransom, so much the better.

We took a convenient *vaporetto* back across to Venice and started walking. When we reached the bald man's home address, it was obvious we weren't going to find our quarry there. All the shutters on the house were up. Some strands of wilted leafage and dead geraniums hung forlornly down from a balcony. The place looked as though it had been unoccupied for years.

Joey banged on the door of the neighbour's house and asked if there had been any sighting of Baldy since yesterday, and she shook her head. Did some of that Continental shrugging, using a lot of body motion. Retreated back into her house and shut the door. Not rude, simply uncommunicative.

'A woman of few words,' I said.

'But nonetheless informative.'

'So I guess it's back to the red door.'

'Exactly.'

As before, we found the front door slightly ajar. When we pushed at it hard, it grudgingly screeched open again, just as it had the last time I was there. We walked into the tiny front hall. To my surprise, there was absolutely no indication that the police had ever been there. We climbed the stairs to the top and found the same thing. The door to the apartment was firmly closed. Though Joey knocked several times, there was no answer. He turned the handle and pushed, but the door was locked.

We walked down to the next floor and were met by a woman – not the one I'd encountered on my last visit here – who was standing by her open door and wanted to know if she could help. Subtext: *What the hell are you doing here?*

Joey immediately launched into a spate of Italian, telling her that he and his wife – here he indicated me – were in Venice in the hope of catching up with his mother's cousin, who hadn't been in touch for a while and the family was getting worried about him.

'You mean the man from – where is it – Sweden?' she asked, speaking hesitant English.

'Sweden, yes. Stockholm,' said Joey, his accent subtly adopting faintly Scandinavian overtones. 'We need to tell him that Farmor – his grandmother – is dying and desperately wants to see him again before she goes to join the angels.' It was very neatly done.

The woman looked sceptical. She pointed upstairs. 'Believe me, *there's* someone who won't be joining the angels when he goes,' she said.

'Oh dear,' Joey said, looking downcast and slightly shaking his head. 'Has my cousin – how can I put this? – taken up with the . . . uh . . . wrong kind of people?'

'All I can say is the men who come up and down these stairs don't look like nice types, much more what my husband calls "undesirables". Certainly not the sort of people we want living here.'

'Oh dear,' said Joey again. 'My mother will be very upset to hear that. The family really hoped he would make a fresh start here in Venice.'

The woman snorted.

'You don't have any idea where he might be, do you?' Joey asked hopefully.

'I believe he works somewhere on the other side of the Rialto Bridge,' she said. 'But I couldn't tell you where, or what at.'

Joey turned to me and shrugged sadly. 'We'll just have to go on looking for him, then, darling.' To the woman, he added, 'If you see him, please tell him that we'd hoped to catch up with him and why.'

'And you are?'

'Niels. Niels Rasmusssen,' said Joey. 'And this is my wife, Helga.'

She nodded at me in a friendly fashion. As she turned to

go back inside her apartment, she said, 'If you want my advice, I would leave him alone.'

'One moment, signora. My mother's cousin . . . just to make sure . . . we *are* talking about the same man, aren't we? Not very tall, about my wife's height' – he pointed at me – 'with reddish hair and a bit of a limp?' He gave a sad little laugh. 'A relic from the time he jumped over a wall after burglarizing a neighbour's house!'

'Oh, no,' she said. 'No, this man is tall, quite big and burly, with a shaven head and an earring. And a tattoo on his neck. A black spider, quite horrible.'

Joey looked at me in feigned surprise and I looked back ditto. 'Helga,' he said. 'We've been given the wrong address, I think.' He turned back to the woman. 'Definitely no red hair, no limp?'

'Definitely not, signor.'

I desperately wanted to ask if a body had been found upstairs, whether the police had been in the house, but to do so would make it clear that I'd been there before, which would blow our cover story right out of the water. So we thanked her profusely and went on down the stairs. Outside, I said admiringly, 'Mr Preston, I have to admit that you're pretty slick. What I don't quite understand is what happened to the body I found when I came here before. How could they have spirited it down the stairs and away, without leaving the slightest trace, before the police arrived?'

'Perhaps they never did.'

'What?' I stared at him in astonishment. 'But I specifically asked the woman on the landing below to call them.'

'Perhaps she had her own reasons not to do so.'

Frowning, I thought about it. It was a possibility which hadn't occurred to me, though I suppose it should have done. As an ex-cop, I knew how many people hid dark secrets beneath perfectly respectable-seeming exteriors. I remembered the florist in Maidstone who had a thriving business growing – and selling – cannabis in between the Interflora activity, the wedding business and the bouquets for other special occasions. And the popular publican of a pretty village pub near Whitstable who had three Romanian women chained up in the beer cellar

under the saloon bar and let the local riff-raff in after hours
to use them in whatever repulsive way they saw fit.

Meanwhile, here we seemed to have drawn a blank. And
time was running out. If we were to find Sandro before the
ransom was paid, we needed some kind of a lucky break. It
wasn't the payment which bothered me – Dominic could easily
afford it – it was the need to see justice done, unscrupulous
villains brought to book. We live in a society, which necessarily means there are rules which have to be obeyed. No
society can prosper if individuals choose to ignore the rules
and behave as they please.

We walked on. My thoughts turned to the other semi-criminal
events which had recently taken place in my life. The doge's
ring, the small almost-Botticelli. The Tiepolos. And – it came
back to me in a rush – Renzo's hint that not only did he know
about the drawings which had gone missing, but that he also
knew where they'd gone missing from. And as we rounded a
corner into a small cobbled square, there, by golly, was the
man himself, ugly as sin, eating lunch on his own at an outside
table and frowning over some papers.

'You're not with me, Joey,' I said quietly.

Joey was quick. Without a glance at me, he carried smoothly
onwards, frowning at his watch as though late for an engagement, while I surged across to Renzo's table. '*Ciao*, Renzo!'
I cried, all girly and excited.

'*Caro!*' he said. He stood up, holding his napkin to his
crotch. 'What a pleasure.' He indicated the empty seat at
his table. 'You will join me, of course?'

I smiled, shook my head and sat down. 'But a glass of wine
would be *lovely*,' I gushed.

'So how are you?' he enquired tenderly. Over-tenderly, in
my opinion, but I had to go along with it until I could extract
the information I needed.

'A little tired,' I said. 'But otherwise . . .' I flipped my hand
back and forth.

'Too much partying, eh?' If I'd been closer to him, he'd
have nudged me in the ribs in a roguish fashion, which, given
my bruises, would have been painful.

'Actually, I'm here for work,' I said.

'Ah, yes, I believe you said so when we met at your brother's house.' One of his hairy hands clamped itself to my wrist. 'You shouldn't overdo things, though.'

'Oh, I know. Venice is far too beautiful to spend all one's time working. I went to see the ceiling frescos in I Gesuati, this morning. Very beautiful work.'

'Indeed it is.'

A glass of prosecco had appeared in front of me and I lifted it, tilted it towards him and then took a sip. Very nice.

'You like Tiepolo, obviously.'

'Who doesn't?' I leaned my elbows on the table and linked my hands beneath my chin. 'So,' I said confidingly. 'You mentioned last time we were together that you thought the drawings I've seen, which have been attributed to him, might have been stolen from some collection or other right here in Venice.'

'I didn't exactly say—'

'I'd really love to know where you thought they might have originated. This is so I can go back to England and tell the person who currently owns them – or thinks he owns them – that he doesn't. Strange as it may seem to you, a dealer and collector of some renown, he'd be extremely relieved to have them off his hands. He's a simple man, and would be the first to agree that he knows nothing about art or artists.'

'Well . . .' Renzo looked around the little square, checking to see that no one was listening in to our conversation. 'This is only a rumour, mind you, but I'm not breaking any confidences if I tell you that the Marchese de Farnese de Peron may have been the victim of a robbery – including the Tiepolos.'

Given the fact that the ring and the little Botticelli had been stolen, I'd suspected that the Tiepolos were another outrageous theft from the Marchese's art collection, but I opened my eyes as wide as I could. 'How amazing. Are there rumours of thefts from any other private collections?'

'None that have reached my ears.'

'Do you think that the Marchese has been targeted for some reason?'

'It does rather look like it.'

'Any idea what that reason might be?'

Renzo paused to shove some more of his lunch into his

mouth, while I took another dainty sip of my wine. 'I don't know if you've ever met him,' he said after a moment or two, 'but he is known far and wide as a hard man. Hard and controlling. Maybe someone has taken exception and decided to hurt him where it would wound him most – that is to say, by stealing his possessions.'

'It doesn't look as though the thief is after money, does it? The places where these precious artefacts ended up weren't exactly going to make him – or her, of course – rich.'

'I will tell you what it is, Alessandra. It is an insult. A calculated insult.'

'You really see it that way?'

'I do.'

'Not just to the Marchese,' I said. 'To Tiepolo as well.'

Renzo dabbed at his mouth with his napkin. 'You are absolutely right.'

Having got the information I wanted, I tossed back the last of my wine and prepared to leave. Once again, a hairy paw attached itself to my wrist, looking like one of those huntsman spiders you get in Australia. 'How much longer are you staying in Venice?' he asked.

'I'm not sure. I have to get back to England pretty soon . . . articles to finish before their deadline, and I have a talk to give to one of our local schools. I just heard that my poor old mother has come down with pneumonia. But I'll be back very soon. Apart from anything else, I'm anxious to see your *stanza segreta*.'

'Not as anxious as I am to see *you* again, signorina.'

Oh, Gawd . . . I extricated myself as best I could, with many a false promise and flirtatious smile. Then proceeded in the direction I'd seen Joey heading. I was guessing he'd been keeping an eye out for me and, sure enough, there he was, musing over a coffee a square or two away.

'Oh la la!' He batted his eyelashes at me and coyly put his head on one side. 'Oh, Mr Italian Man,' he said in a high falsetto. 'You are *sooo* very wonderful.' He indicated the empty seat beside him, and I sat down.

'You can laugh,' I said. 'But I got the info I was after.' I sighed. 'What one has to do as a seeker of truth.'

'I thought at one point you were going to strip off and beg him to take you right then and there.'

I ignored him.

'Any idea what your friends of yesterday evening were planning to do with you?' he said.

'None at all. I mean, what could they do?'

'They must have thought you could be used as some kind of bargaining chip.'

'I can't see how. What use could I possi—' I broke off. Crossing the corner of the square was the bald Scandinavian. 'Joey,' I said urgently. 'Look . . .' I jerked my head. 'Can you get after him, see where he goes?'

'Do my best.'

'I really need to hear him speak,' I said, although I instinctively felt that his would not turn out to be the voice I'd heard when I'd been snatched off the street.

'Not sure how I'll manage that.'

'Perhaps you could find out which bakery he works at, and then I could go in and order a couple of *cornettos* or a ciabatta or something.'

'If he's the baker, is he likely to be fronting the shop? I don't think so.'

'You're right. But it's worth a try.' I explained about my need to track down the genderless voice which had spoken to me when I was first snatched. 'The more I think about it, the more impossible it seems to pinpoint its sex. One thing I'm fairly sure of: it wasn't one of Sandro's friends. At least, not one of the ones who were in Venice the night those things went missing from the Marchese's *palazzo*.'

With some difficulty, thanks to my bruises, I lifted my arm and glanced at my watch. Five hours before Cesare was due to be standing on a bridge in Burano, carrying twenty million euros about his person.

'We're already in countdown mode for the money drop,' said Joey.

'And, please God, Sandro's safe release.' I frowned. 'I'll tell you something that's been bothering me, and that's why the bad guys have only demanded twenty million. A hundred would be more likely, given how loaded Sandro's uncle and father both are. Or,' I added, 'are supposed to be.'

'Twenty mill's a tidy sum,' said Joey. 'And much easier to get hold of than a hundred.'

'True.'

Joey turned down the corners of his mouth. 'Wish I didn't feel so uneasy.'

'Me too.' We stared at each other, trying not to dwell on the possibility of things going disastrously wrong later that evening.

FIFTEEN

I t was coming up to zero hour. I had travelled back to Burano, determined not to let the events of the previous evening unnerve me. I took it as an encouraging omen that the *vaporetto* which carried me had the name Tiepolo painted on the prow. By the time I had arrived at the grassy area of the *embarcadero* and started to walk to my hotel through the brightly painted streets, they were beginning to empty of overweight or camera-toting tourists, most of whom were heading for the *vaporetti* which would take them back to Venice. Locals, too, seemed in short supply as the dinner hour approached. Windows were beginning to glow in the colourful little houses here and there along the streets and canals.

Across the lagoon, the light was fading behind the towers and domes of the city, sunset turning the sky a flaming red, making it appear as though the whole horizon was on fire. Flocks of pigeons wheeled around and between the spires, their wings suddenly golden each time they turned and caught the last of the sun. Back in my double bedroom, I set up watch at the window, giving myself a clear view up the *calle*, but sitting further back enough that I wasn't visible to anyone walking on either side of the buildings below. I'd borrowed a pair of binoculars but, given the lack of daylight, they weren't much help.

Was Sandro still alive? The question pounded insistently against the shell of my skull. What had begun as a kernel of apprehension and unease was growing like a tumour, more sinister and dangerous as the minutes plodded by.

Darkness had well and truly fallen by the time I saw the Marchese emerge from a side street and walk up the steps to the middle of the bridge and stand looking up and down the canal. He was carrying two bags, one a briefcase, the other – somewhat incongruously for such a distinguished figure – a backpack slung across his shoulders. In a soft leather blouson jacket and a pair of well-pressed tan chinos, he stood out sharply among the people still strolling around. What might happen if they realized he was transporting – as I assumed he was – twenty million euros in cash?

Traffic up and down the narrow stretch of water was slow now, almost non-existent at this late hour. Despite the darkness, I couldn't see how the kidnappers expected to get safely away with the ransom. Or pick up the second half of it. Burano's main streets and *rivas* were too open. They couldn't possibly not have expected the Marchese to have organized some form of surveillance, or set up watchers to keep an eye out for the people collecting the ransom, so that they could easily be identified and followed. After all their earlier precautions, it seemed very unlikely that they'd operate without taking preventative measures to minimize their risk. One obvious assumption might therefore be that they would be perfectly content with only half the ransom that they'd demanded. After all, ten million euros was still a tidy sum. The more I chewed over the possibility, the more feasible it appeared.

And then . . . I leaned forward. Behind Cesare, the bulky figure of the bald man materialized like a ghost from the gloom of a narrow street running towards the canal. Like the Marchese, he started to walk slowly up the bridge and stand looking down at the reflections of the houses in the glimmering water. He was wearing a white polo shirt with an embroidered emblem on the left breast – an antlered deer, a golf club? Hard to tell from my vantage point – and beige cargo pants. I looked at them and thought idly how very handy all those pockets would be, supposing you wished to stash away wads of illegitimate cash. Ditch the briefcase, stuff the pockets and away you went.

At which point it hit me!

After so much obfuscation, I was suddenly prepared to bet every one of those euros that right this minute Sandro Grainger was imprisoned in the very same house where I'd been kept. And at the same time, that hint of something red caught in the swirl of rubbish at the foot of the stairs which I'd noticed

as I fled the place clarified itself in my brain into one of
Sandro's charity bracelets.

That clinched it for me.

Now all I had to do was work out which was the right
house.

Cesare was still displaying a spurious interest in the canal,
which led directly to the night-covered waters of the lagoon.
I tied my hair up and shoved it under a shapeless fold-up sun
hat. Wrapped a scarf round my neck. Tried to make myself
as unrecognizable as possible, then made my way out of the
hotel at a fair old clip, trying to retrace the steps I'd taken
before menace had emerged from the shadows days earlier.
It had all been so quick. I'd barely had time to register where
I was before the chloroform they'd clapped over my nose and
mouth had taken effect and I was out cold. I remembered only
a whirring kaleidoscope of colours – rose, emerald, sapphire,
ochre – and a melange of shutters, doorways, white-framed
windows. It would more or less have to be in one of the side
streets leading up from the canal since they could hardly have
carried a semi-inert body very far without remark. And for
the same reason, it surely would have to be at the end nearest
the canal.

As I crossed the bridge and approached the Marchese, I
said *sotto voce* to his back, 'Don't turn round but keep an eye
on me.' Then carried on, down the steps to the *riva* on the
other side.

He wasn't nearly as good at non-reaction as Joey. He started,
half-turned, opened his mouth, then shut it again and turned
back to lean again on the bridge. Meanwhile, I passed a green
house, a sunshine-yellow wall, a forget-me-not blue frontage.
Rose-coloured doors, emerald shutters, tawny-painted plaster,
petunias trailing from a flat roof, bright green stucco and dark-
blue window fra— I stopped. Dark blue . . . I retraced my
steps.

Green shutters. Ochre walls. Petunias. This had to be the
corner from which I'd been abducted. The more I looked,
the more certain I grew. Gazing up the street, I tried to
calculate how far along it I'd gone or been half-carried before
passing out. Five houses? Six? In case someone was watching

out for me, I strolled nonchalantly along, stopping to admire a display of geraniums, an elaborate brass knocker on a shiny black door. Nope . . . despite the chloroform already curdling my brain at the time, I was pretty sure I hadn't passed either, which narrowed my choice down to just a couple, since it hadn't been the first two or three. Both houses had shuttered windows on the ground floor. Both looked shabbier and more rundown than their neighbours. One had a faded dark blue door; the other had some peeling paintwork round the windows.

As inconspicuously as possible, I took in what details I could as I passed, but absolutely nothing recognizable leaped out at me. And then a light went on across the way, behind white net curtains, and I could see into a small room with a central table covered in a white lace cloth with a vase of plastic flowers placed in the centre. A woman was standing just inside the door, her hand still on the light switch as though she had come into the room after hearing unaccustomed sounds and was checking the place out. I ran across the street and banged her knocker.

The light in the front room went out. Seconds later, she opened the door. 'Beppo?' I said, uncertainly, waving my arm at the row of houses behind me. 'I'm looking for Beppo.'

She nodded, adopting a kind of resigned grimace which made it abundantly clear that people were always looking for Beppo. 'Number six.' She spoke in accented English.

Aha . . . the house with the peeling paintwork. I thanked her and turned to look at the house. A light burned in a top window; otherwise the place was dark. 'Many visitors,' she said, still using English. 'Many men. All days.' She shook her head.

Did she mean the place was a house of ill-repute, with randy men constantly banging at the door? Or did Beppo simply have a lot of friends? I nodded, as though privy to his social calendar.

'You are friend?' the woman asked.

'No.' I shook my head vehemently.

'He is not good man. Much police.'

I shrugged, like one well used to Beppo's negative behaviour.

'I just need to find out if he has seen my brother,' I lied, trying to imply a brother gone or going to the bad under Beppo's malign influence, myself the knight in shining armour come to rescue the misguided youth.

'There was . . .' She broke into a flood of Italian, from which I rescued enough words to grasp that a pretty young man had been glimpsed briefly by the neighbours about a week ago, not the usual sort of caller at Beppo's premises, and that he had not been seen since.

'Did he have black hair?' I asked.

'No, no. This boy was blond.' She waved a flattened palm from side to side. 'Dark blond. Like paintings. Titian, Tiepolo.'

Funny how Tiepolo kept cropping up. I stared at her. Though not a believer in signs and portents, I nonetheless felt that in some complicated way this was yet another encouraging connection. It had to be meant.

'Good,' I said. 'That means it can't have been my poor brother.' I thought of Hereward, safe in his Chelsea house, unaware of how his existence was being bandied about, and hoped all was well with him and Lena. As well as, with any luck, it would – please God – eventually be for Sandro. *Had* to be.

Quickly I made my way back up to the little bridge where Cesare was still standing. The bulky bald guy had disappeared. Cesare was still there, trying hard to look as if he fitted into the scene. Luckily by now there were very few people to notice that he didn't. I slowly walked on up, gazing soulfully into the canal as I went, as if that was what I was really interested in. I even added what I hoped was a touch of authenticity by leaning right over to scrutinize absolutely nothing in the water below us.

When I was standing right beside him, I murmured, 'I think I know where Sandro is being held.'

This time, he managed not to react in any obvious way. 'Where?'

'See that row of houses, with the blue house on the corner? Three houses up, there's one painted yellow, with green shutters and a plant hanging down. I'm fairly sure he's there now.'

I straightened up and strolled onwards, still staring into the water as I went.

And then, ducking out of a side street and walking towards me was Joey. 'Hel-*lo*!' he said brightly. And loudly. Presumably for the benefit of any unseen watchers. 'What are *you* doing here?'

'I think I know where they're holding Sandro,' I said. 'I don't want to turn round, but looking over my shoulder, is anything going on? Can you see the Marchese?'

'Can't see anything . . . Oh, hang on. There he is. He's talking on the phone. Now he's walking over the bridge to the other side of the water and along on the other . . . turning up a side street . . . stopping by a yellow house and pulling out a map, making like he's a tourist.'

'At this time of night?'

'Whatever helps.'

'How much longer to zero hour?'

He looked at his watch. 'Not long. Twenty minutes tops.'

'I wonder what the bad guys suspect. How close they think we are. They were obviously aware that I was here on the island.'

'And probably of your connection to Sandro. In fact, I suspect that they're fully aware of all of us – you, me, the Marchese, I mean. And also where we are at almost any given moment.' He stared over my shoulder. Then suddenly stiffened. 'Christ on crutches!' he exclaimed. 'They're mugging him!'

Oh my God! Had that been the plan all along? To take the money and run, rather than wait for it to be dropped into a passing boat, the boat being simply a subterfuge? Why hadn't we at least considered it as an option? I turned so suddenly I nearly went spinning into the canal. I checked out the scene, then sprinted back across the bridge and raced to where the Marchese had by now been knocked down and was lying on the cobbles, still managing to hold on tightly to his briefcase, the backpack firmly supporting him. Despite his determination not to let go of the handle, two thugs were trying to wrest it from him. A third hovered, looking for an opening into the mêlée. I was delighted to see that he had an ugly-looking wound on his forehead and heavy plastering across his nose. He must be the guy I'd tied up before making my escape.

A few tourists hung about, unsure of whether they should intervene. I karate-chopped the neck of the thug kneeling above Cesare, liking the graceful way he folded up on to the ground. I snatched the briefcase and cradled it against my chest while the second mugger stared uncomprehendingly at his unconscious colleague, until Joey socked the side of his head with a bunched-up fist and he too went down. I started after the third man, who was way out of luck in his attempt to escape, since two American college kids had grabbed his arms and weren't about to let go.

'We saw what happened,' one of them said.

'They knocked the old guy down and tried to snatch his stuff.'

'You're heroes,' I told them. 'Thank you.'

Two policemen appeared and took over while Joey and I helped Cesare to his feet and brushed him down. At the same time, a boat zoomed down the channel and drew up in a spray of foam. Four policemen leaped across the moored vessels on to the *riva* and roughly manhandled the guys who'd attacked the Marchese into their craft and zipped away.

The people still around were loving the action. One elderly woman asked me if this was a scene being shot for a movie. I told her it was. 'Out next year,' I said. 'Starring Tom Hanks and Bruce Willis.'

She looked round. 'Where are they, then?'

I shrugged. 'Gotta go.'

Four more guys appeared. Good ones. Two of them had weapons in their hand. Cesare gave them directions. A minute later, as I ran to join them, they were kicking down the door into Beppo's house.

'Please,' I said aloud. 'Please let Sandro be there – and alive.'

Following Cesare's men, I reached the fallen door and trod across it to the foot of the staircase leading to the upper part of the house. I could smell the dank air of the place as I ran upstairs, Joey close behind. The house was dark and silent, except for the sound of footsteps on the uncarpeted stairs.

There was a cry of triumph from somewhere higher up and I knew immediately what it meant. My spirits lightened for the first time since the news of Sandro's abduction.

'Sandro!' I shouted. 'Oh, Sandro. Thank Go—' But before I could finish my sentence I heard the sound of gunshots somewhere in the darkness above me. 'Sandro!' I screamed.

Two sets of footsteps were suddenly pounding down towards me, someone was swearing, there was a tremendous thump as something fell heavily to the ground. I only had time to wonder whether it was a body before two people pushed clumsily past me. I tried to grab the sleeve of one or other before I was shoved to one side of the rough wall of the staircase, my cheek painfully connecting with the plaster. The two men – I knew they were men from the smell of stale sweat from neglected armpits and the must of unwashed clothes – carried on dashing down to the ground floor. They trampled fast and noisily across the fallen front door and were out into the street.

I sprinted as fast as I could to the upper floor. As soon as I was at the right level, I saw a body lying on the landing. The bright hair told me at once that it was Sandro. Oh, no! God, no! Tears spilled from my eyes as I stood over him. Beautiful Sandro, with his golden eyelashes, his Pre-Raphaelite mouth, his satiny skin. I knelt down beside him. He had been gagged and blindfolded, and his hands were tied together behind his back. I shook my head as my mind grappled with the horror of breaking the news of his death to his uncle and his parents. 'Oh, Sandro . . .' I said despairingly. Something dazzling and beautiful had been destroyed. For what? Greed, avarice, the transient and deceptive lure of money.

Then from below came a full-throated roar as the Marchese yelled his nephew's name. And as though the sound had released him from an evil spell, Sandro's hands began to twitch and his head to turn from side to side.

'Sandro!' I tore off the blindfold, removed the gag as Cesare appeared up the flight of stairs, still shouting at the top of his voice.

'*Zio* . . .' Sandro stared up at his uncle through narrowed eyes. I wondered how long he'd been kept with a blindfold over his face. '*Zio* Cesare.' His voice was hoarse, uncertain.

The Marchese knelt on the other side of his nephew. He stroked his cheek then suddenly began sobbing, while one of the henchmen who'd raced up the stairs behind him produced a knife and began sawing at the ropes round Sandro's wrists.

I could hear sounds of altercation outside in the street. Presumably the men who'd been left to guard Sandro had now been taken into some sort of custody. But they were still only minor players, like the guys who'd been detained by the police just a few minutes earlier. So where was the boss? The big, bald baker? If indeed he was the mastermind behind this whole cruel scheme intended to intimidate, terrify and extort? Only minutes before, he'd been standing almost side by side with Cesare. Had he realized that his plan had failed and legged it?

'Baldy was nearby just minutes ago,' I said urgently to Joey. 'Have you told the cops about him? If they telephone their pals in the city, they could probably catch him before he has a chance to escape to Sweden or wherever.'

'I'm on it.' Joey spoke in rapid Italian to one of Cesare's men, who pulled out a cell phone and spoke even more rapidly into it.

Cesare was helping Sandro to his feet. 'Oh,' he said, his voice breaking with emotion. 'I heard the gun and thought that they had killed you.' He embraced his nephew, who still wasn't quite with it.

I frowned. 'Why was the gun fired in the first place? Is there someone else here?'

'I don't know,' Sandro said. He was pale, his lips bloodless. 'I don't care, either.' He put his arms around Cesare and rested his head against his uncle's broad chest. He began to shake. 'I thought I was going to die,' he whispered.

Joey was peering into the other two rooms. He came out of the second one and jerked his head at me, indicating that he wanted to show me something. The something was another body, lying behind the door and bleeding profusely. 'We should call a doctor,' he said.

'Should we?' I felt little sympathy for any of the gang. However, one of Cesare's men had followed us and was already on his phone, calling up medical reinforcements.

I raised my eyebrows at Joey. 'We should go,' I said. 'We can catch up with Sandro tomorr—'

'Don't go.' It was Sandro, sounding much stronger. He held out a hand. 'Please don't go, Alex. Not yet.'

'Absolutely. I insist that you come back to the *palazzo*,' Cesare said. 'We owe you so much – both you and Joey. My wife will . . .' He broke off. Shook his head as though words were insufficient. Put a hand on Joey's shoulder. 'Come. *Andiamo*.'

SIXTEEN

'd last met the Marchese's wife, Marchesa Allegra de Farnese de Peron, at Sandro's party back in London. Tonight, she looked even more like a corn-fed chicken carcase than she had then: more bony, more yellow, more unwilling to smile. She was also wearing a lot less bling than the last time I saw her. I knew the Marchese wasn't exactly a pillar of fidelity and, given my experience with the unfaithful Jack the Love Rat, I was hardly one to condone his behaviour.

She greeted us with cool gratitude, her husky voice a testament to a million cigarettes smoked over the years. Offered us brandy in huge balloon glasses. Spoke of her happiness at having her beloved Sandro back in the bosom of the family. It wasn't a bosom I'd have wanted to be clasped to, but clasp him she did, while Sandro submitted to her embraces with his usual good grace.

'So,' she said. 'Signorina Alessandra, have you completed your work assignment in Venice or have you more to do?' Her manner wasn't chilly. Glacial would have described it better. Was it the embarrassment and scandal of her noble family being dragged through the criminal mud like this? She must have been relieved that the papers hadn't got hold of it. So far.

'I'll be here for a couple more days.' There was Renzo to catch up with, and his *stanza segreta* to see. Unless I put that on hold until the next time I was here. Meanwhile, there were a couple more galleries I'd made appointments to visit which I'd had to put on hold.

'Then back to London, no?'

'No, I live near . . . Canterbury,' I said, trying to find a reference point for her.

'Ah, yes. Such a magnificent cathedral. And when does your next book appear?' She turned, displaying the tendons of her neck, to indicate a tall mahogany bookcase. 'You will see that we have all your previous ones.'

'I'm flattered.' I gave her my best smile. 'As for the new one, it's in production, as they say.'

'I look forward to seeing it.' Graciously, she started to turn away as, belatedly, I remembered that Katy Pasqualin had been her niece. 'Marchesa, excuse me.' I laid a hand on her black silk arm. She looked down at it with astonished hauteur and I quickly removed it. 'I just wanted to say how sorry I was to hear of your niece's death.'

For a moment, she looked as though she didn't understand. Then she gave a small nod. 'Yes. It was very sad. *Very* sad. Thank you.' She moved off to talk to Joey.

Temporarily alone, I gazed round at my splendid surroundings. This might only be an *appartamento*, but it didn't look like any flat I'd ever lived in. It truly was more like a *palazzo*. The painted ceiling featured the usual rose-edged clouds cluttered with naked *putti*, some winged, some not, pointing with chubby fingers at the rays of brilliant light streaming from a central figure of a bearded elder in scarlet robes, seated in a golden mist, one hand raised in blessing or admonition. From his expression, it was hard to tell which. Was this God the Father? Or the ring-bestowing doge ancestor? Or someone else altogether?

At the far end of the room, a huge and magnificent tapestry covered the wall, portraying a hunting scene. Stags leaped between stylized trees, huntsmen blew horns, a pack of hounds chased after the stags. There was other game, too. Cheetahs and leopards slunk around the edges, a tiger bared its teeth from the mouth of a cave, hares looked interested among harebells and poppies, a lynx stalked behind a bush of something prickly. Three life-size solid silver lions stood on the polished marble in front of the scene.

Giant candelabra stood here and there along the side walls. Old Masters gleamed dully. A cabinet contained what looked like a priceless collection of coloured glass. Three immensely long refectory tables stretched the full length of the room, laden with bowls of fruit, elaborate flower arrangements, many examples of heavily chased ceremonial silver – bowls, caskets, goblets, candlesticks, wonderful pieces of porcelain, including what looked like an entire Flora Danica dinner service. The place seemed more like a museum than a family salon. I wondered how comfortable it was to live in, whether there was a cosier place where you could kick off your shoes, put your feet up on a coffee table and watch a lightweight movie.

And glancing round, indeed there was one – a little anteroom off the main salon with ordinary furniture, a coffee table piled untidily with magazines, and a TV flickering in one corner.

In the main *salone*, there were glasses, red and white wines, fruit, chocolates and sweet pastries. A couple of bottles of '95 Bollinger sweated in a silver bucket. The Marchese seized one and expertly worked off the armour of the cork with his thumbs, removed the cork, filled some glasses and handed them round.

'Please raise your glasses to our beloved Sandro, safely back in our midst,' he said. His eyes glistened. He glanced at him with what seemed to be distaste. At his side, Allegra stood with bowed head, hands nervously twisting the silky material at her waist. In her plain black dress, she looked less like a member of one of the oldest families in Venice and more like someone's victim. Her husband's, I guessed. The man was plainly a domestic tyrant. Fierce, Sandro had called him. Despite the tears he'd shed earlier over his nephew, Cesare seemed to be reverting to type.

'And also to Alessandra Quick and Giuseppe Preston,' the Marchese continued, 'for their invaluable help in recovering him.' Visibly aged by the events of the past few days, he nonetheless managed to lift his champagne flute and look round at us. We all drank to the successful completion of the exercise.

'All we need now is to catch the people behind the kidnap,' I said.

'We're fairly sure who they are, aren't we?' said Joey.

'Why don't you arrest them, then?' It was Allegra, raising her head at last. 'If you know who they are and where they live?'

'Proof,' said Joey. 'We have no proof.'

'We have witnesses,' I added, 'but a clever defence lawyer would have no problem proving them unreliable – even if they haven't already got on their tourist buses and been driven away from here to Florence or Naples or Assisi.'

By now it was late and I was longing to get away, back to my original hotel in the Rialto. I'd managed a few words with Joey on our way here, but he didn't know any more than I did whether the baker had been apprehended. 'At least they didn't get away with the cash,' he'd said.

'So what would they charge him with? I'll bet he stayed well in the background so that Sandro couldn't identify him.'

'One of the sidekicks will break, I'm quite sure. Rubber hoses, water-boarding – whatever it takes.'

'You *are* joking,' I'd said.

He'd shrugged. 'Maybe.'

When we were finally able to leave, after further protestations of gratitude from Sandro and his aunt and uncle, we walked beside the Grand Canal in silence. It had been an exhausting and jittery few days, always edged with the underlying terror that Sandro wouldn't make it. Now that he was safely back, I felt the anticipated sense of anti-climax, so much so that I felt I could hardly put one foot in front of the other. Joey seemed to realize this. He pulled my arm around his waist and put his round mine. At the hotel, he helped me up the stairs, found my key and got me into my room, where he proceeded to remove most of my clothes before pulling back the covers and pushing me gently on to the bed.

It wasn't a surprise to find him lying beside me shortly after that, wearing nothing but a pair of jockey shorts – silk, no less! – which he very quickly removed. What followed was brief, businesslike and extremely pleasurable. Just, in fact, what the doctor ordered, had a doctor been consulted. I don't think either of us saw it as anything other than a one-off exchange of bodily fluids, a way to celebrate a job well done. Afterwards, I felt relaxed for the first time in what seemed like weeks. I'd have enjoyed it just a tad more if Sam Willoughby's image hadn't intruded quite so insistently.

It was late when I awoke the following morning. I was alone. Joey had gone. Suddenly, I began weeping. Not for Joey's absence, but for my own pathetic inadequacies.

Lonely, unloved, divorced, rapidly turning into an ageing spinster, I snivelled away, overcome by the meagreness of my current existence. I should be building a life with someone, having babies, working for pleasure rather than in the hope of earning barely enough to live on through my puny and futile efforts, rather than snatching at sex with relative strangers.

What was wrong with me? I very rarely indulged in self-pity. Reaction to the tension and stress of recent days, perhaps. After a while, I heaved myself out of bed, showered away my angst, dressed then went downstairs. There was no sign of Joey. The concierge handed me an envelope as I passed his desk, which I shoved into my bag. I had two hours to kill before my first appointment, so I went out and found a small cobbled square set among tall buildings, where I was able to order a coffee. I pulled out the envelope the hotel concierge had handed me and started to open it. From Joey, I imagined. *Last-night-was-fun* sort of thing. Or *bye-and-thanks-for-all-the-fish.* Instead, I fished out a thick wad of one-thousand euro notes, dozens of them, and a stiffly embossed card showing the Marchese's coat of arms. *Thank you so much*, he had written. *My wife and I are immensely grateful.*

I was pretty grateful myself. There was enough money in the envelope to keep me in chocolate and red wine for the next three years, let alone pay all my real living expenses, like utility bills, council taxes, food bills and the boring like. More importantly, remembering my woeful morning tears, here was the perfect opportunity to do something different, indulge myself in some of the dreams I'd had over the years. Travel across the Gobi Desert on a camel. Join a circus. Have a year out and live in Prague or Barcelona or Marrakesh, or even Venice. Learn to tap dance. Take up the cello. The world was, or could be, my oyster. Such a pity I don't like oysters.

I whipped through my remaining appointments. Then I rang Renzo and apologized profusely. Said I'd been called back to England on an urgent family matter. ('Ah, your *mamma*,' he said sympathetically, to which I agreed after remembering that Mary was supposed to be seriously ill with pneumonia.)

I promised I would return to Venice very shortly and, when I did, he would be my first port of call. He protested routinely at my departure, but not overmuch.

I was back in my flat the following day.

I set up my computer and checked my emails. A long list of them had arrived while I was absent but none of them was from Sam Willoughby. There was, however, one from a woman I'd never heard of, exclaiming over a picture she'd received from him. Say what? Who the hell was she? How had she gotten hold of my email address? *Looks like Sam's found true love at last!* she wrote. *About time too. A lovely guy like that shouldn't be on his own.*

Nor, I thought crossly, remembering my depression of yesterday and slamming down the lid of my PC, should a lovely woman like me. 'Huh!' I said into the bleak emptiness of my sitting room. 'Some friend *you* are, Mr Willoughby.' Thinking of him, I was surprised at how much I missed him, at the realization of how much I depended on his company, his reliability. I didn't want to think about him staying permanently out there in New Zealand, shearing sheep alongside his brother and the blonde jillaroo.

The following morning, I called Fliss Fairlight regarding Katy Pasqualin.

'Nothing definite yet,' she said, 'but the Met's turning its beady little eye back to the boyfriend.'

'Yes, it almost had to be someone she knew well. Someone she felt comfortable enough with to remove her clothes and take a bath.'

'Or this other person dropped by, was invited in for a cuppa, and then departed – or so Katy thought.'

'Hm, yes, that's a possibility.' I could easily envisage the scenario: a sweaty journey back from work on a crowded tube or bus, then someone she knows well knocks at the door and is invited in, Katy giving a cuppa or whatever and then insisting she herself has to have a relaxing soak before the evening gets underway. Or perhaps using the bath as an excuse not to have to talk.

'I'd like to know a lot more about these so-called sugar daddies,' I said.

'So would we.'

'I mean, is it a straightforward business arrangement? I pay for your serviced London apartment, gym membership, holidays, designer clothes and so on, in return for access to your gorgeous body whenever I want it?'

'More or less exactly that. And don't forget the boob jobs.'

'What? When I met her, she didn't look like someone who'd had a boob job, more like someone who'd never had boobs to have a job done. Nor was she toting a designer handbag. Didn't the word "blackmail" rear its ugly head at some point?'

'It did. Thing is, according to Joy, they're having a hard time identifying them. Nobody seems to have any idea who they might have been.'

'Who mentioned them in the first place?'

'One of her friends . . . Suzy Hartley Heywood, I think.'

Sandro's girlfriend. It all seemed a bit incestuous to me. Luckily, now that Sandro was safely back on home turf, I wasn't involved in any of it.

Later, I walked into town to restock my fridge. About to pass the bookshop, on impulse, I went in. Alison, Sam's assistant and temporary manager, was dealing with a customer, so I waved at her and went to scrutinize the second-hand shelves, looking for something undemanding to read while I spent the next couple of days putting myself together after all the recent stresses.

'Great news, isn't it?' she carolled across the shop when the customer had departed.

'What is?'

'About Sam, I mean.'

To say my heart plummeted in my chest would be to employ a cliché which described exactly how I felt. 'Yes,' I said. Fuck. He was going to emigrate to New Zealand.

'About time he settled down, don't you think? He's such a lovely guy.' Double fuck. He was going to marry the blonde jillaroo.

'He is indeed,' I agreed. A lot lovelier than I'd previously appreciated. I picked out a book at random and took it over to the sales counter.

Alison raised her eyebrows as she rang it up. 'I hope you enjoy this,' she said.

'What do you mean?' I picked it up. *How to Improve Your Sex Life: 20 Easy Tips Towards a Better Work/Life Balance.* 'Sorry . . . must've pulled the wrong book out by mistake,' I mumbled, pushing it aside. I didn't like the way she was smirking.

Out in the High Street, I walked towards the Fox and Hounds, hoping to find the Major ensconced in the bar. And there he was. 'Hello, m'dear,' he said. 'I was hoping to see you. What can I get you?'

'A G and T, please,' I said. 'With a double gin, if you don't mind.' I normally wouldn't dream of drinking alcohol at this time of the day, but I needed it this morning.

'Something wrong, Alex? You look rather down in the mouth.'

Damn Sam. 'I am a bit, I guess. But I'll bounce back. And how about you?'

'Very well, thank you. Apart from some blasted fellow hanging round the gate. Told him to clear off but of course the lane is public property, so if he wants to loiter I can't really stop him. In the old days, I'd have loaded a shotgun shell with rock salt and discharged it at him. That would have sent him packing PDQ, I can tell you. Painful, but non-lethal, d'you see?'

'Do you think he's casing the joint, hoping to break in when you're not there?'

'He's welcome. I've got nothing of any value, really. Except . . .' He began rummaging in a tatty old army-issue canvas haversack at his feet and came up with a square envelope. 'Here. I'd be so grateful if you'd take these under your wing, while I decide on my next course of action.'

'These?'

'Those dratted Italian drawings. I'd like to get them off my hands asap.'

'But . . . didn't Ms Forbes say they really belonged to her, since she was the one who bought them when she and Mrs Roscoe were in Venice together?'

He assumed an expression which combined sorrow,

derision and resentment. He snorted harshly, setting his
moustache all of a quiver. 'She may well have done, m'dear.
But I'm a strong believer in the old army maxim: never take
anyone at their word. Always verify their credentials. And
even then, take nothing for granted. So I checked the woman
out. Went on that spiderweb thingy which my son gave me.
Called the high school. They said she'd died a while ago. I
doubt if the woman even knew poor Nell, let alone ever went
on holiday with her.'

'Wow! Impressive detective work.' I was delighted that he'd
found this out for himself, so that I didn't have to break it to
him.

'Yes.' He looked modest.

'But how do you think she knew of the existence of the
drawings in the first place?'

'Maybe Nell showed them round in the staffroom at
school – look what I bought on my holidays, chaps, that sort
of thing. And one of the staff members knew this other woman,
and talked about it to her. The woman might even be a bona
fide expert of some kind, as well as a con artist.'

'Or a professional art thief. She somehow hears about
the stolen sketches, makes it her business to find out all
about Mrs Roscoe and the contents of her will, comes down
here with a believable cover story and tries to con you into
parting with them.' I cast my mind back. I'd pulled the
notion out of thin air, but it nonetheless had a plausibility
about it. Change the eye colour with contact lenses, pull
on a mop of unruly curls, dress up like one of the raggle-
taggle gypsies and, with any luck, no one would give you
a second glance.

'You could be right.' He smoothed his moustache. 'Not that
it matters. Believe me, whoever she is, the next time she came
nosing round here, enquiring about those sketches, I gave her
the big heave-ho in no uncertain terms.' He seemed briefly
regretful.

'If you don't mind me saying so, that was probably a good
idea. How did she take it?'

'Badly. Started shrieking like a fishwife, if you can believe
it. Accused me of every crime under the sun, from theft to

pederasty. Pederasty . . . I ask you. Had to shut the door in her face in the end.'

'Oh, dear.'

'No way to treat a lady, I know, but if you'd heard the language she was coming out with you'd realize she was no lady.' He sighed reminiscently. 'Makes a rattling good chocolate cream sponge, though, I have to say.'

'It was good, wasn't it?'

'Anyway, got a big favour to ask you.'

'Ask away.'

He bent his head closer to mine and dropped his voice. 'Just wondering if I might be able to persuade you to be so good as to look after the sketches, drawings, whatever, just for a short while. I'd be eternally grateful.'

'Well . . .'

He fossicked in his backpack and brought out an envelope. 'Looks like one envelope, do you see, but in fact it's two. Just in case one of them got lost – not that I'm implying for a moment that you might be careless enough to . . .' He paused, unable to finish the sentence.

I wasn't that thrilled at the idea, especially if there was a new ingredient now added to the mix, namely a person loitering at the Major's gate, with or without intent. Nonetheless, I reluctantly took the envelopes and pushed them both deep into my bag, figuring that should such occur, I'd probably be as good as the Major at repelling attacks of various kinds, if not better. I gave a semi-salute. 'Wilco, Major,' I said. 'Now, let me buy you the other half.'

Turning from the bar with the Major's glass of beer in one hand and a cup of coffee in the other, I was nearly knocked off my feet by some drunken moron with a watch cap pulled low on his head. Trainers which might once have been white and green were now dirt and grime, jeans well past their wear-by date. He lurched past, barging heavily into me as he went. 'Here, watch it,' I said to his retreating back, concentrating on not spilling our drinks. He didn't even bother to apologize, just waved a hand behind him and carried on out of the door of the bar, where I saw him stand and glance up and down the High Street as though wondering where the hell he was.

'What an idiot!' I said when I reached our table.

'There seems to be more and more of them about these days,' said the Major. 'Living off benefits at the taxpayers' expense, gambling on the horses, drinking themselves stupid or getting high on illegal substances. It wasn't like that in my day, I can tell you.' He fingered some froth from his moustache. 'At least, not all of it.'

We chatted of this and that. My earlier gloom had been swept away by the alcohol which was now coursing lightly through my system. If I banished Sam Willoughby from my thoughts, I felt much more cheerful. Eventually I looked at my watch.

'Time to go, I think.'

He half rose from his seat. 'Thank you for your company, Alex.'

I patted the bag slung over my shoulder. 'And I'll take very good care of these for you.'

'Thank you, my dear. Now all I have to do is figure out the best course of action to take with them.'

'Right.'

SEVENTEEN

I arrived home just as the sun began to descend below the horizon, tingeing the evening clouds a rosy pink and staining the sea crimson. Before opening the door to the communal entrance hall, I cast a beady look behind me. I couldn't see anyone lingering, let alone loitering. A few prams heading for home, a dog-walker or two, some giggling teenagers taking selfies in front of the fishing boats, a couple of bicyclists heading for the university up on the hill.

I picked up my mail and took it upstairs. I looked out of the window before I turned the lights on, but there were no suspicious figures to be seen. I therefore drew the curtains across, switched on a couple of lamps and fetched myself a cup of good strong coffee before checking my correspondence. The only item of any interest was a card informing me that although the police had not yet released her body, Dominic and Maddalena Grainger would be holding a small assembly in honour of Katy Pasqualin.

After that, I tugged on a pair of disposable gloves and pulled out of my bag the two envelopes the Major had given me – or at least tried to. Tried but didn't succeed. Like it or not, one of them had gone missing. A flush of heat and apprehension swept up from my knees to my neck. A tingle of embarrassment fluttered along my arms. It was impossible! I'd been entrusted with something really precious and I'd already managed to lose part of it.

I emptied my bag on to the table. No sign of a second envelope. How the *hell* could this have happened?

Over and over again I went into every compartment of my bag but no second envelope magically appeared. I sat down, closed my eyes and went over what I'd done after I left the Major. Came up with nothing. After leaving the Fox and Hounds, I'd bought a loaf of bread from the specialist baker behind the castle. Picked up two beef tomatoes, a bag of new potatoes and an oak-leaf lettuce from the greengrocers. A piece of fillet steak from the butchers, and cheese from the French cheese shop. At no point did I delve into my bag, since I was carrying cash in the zipped pocket of my anorak and therefore didn't need to. So where was that second envelope? And how was I going to tell the Major that I'd lost it?

Once again, I emptied my bag. Once again, I dug into all the compartments, felt for a torn lining (there wasn't one), shook the bag, slapped it. The second envelope still failed to materialize.

Where was it? Could someone have nicked it? It seemed unlikely. I'd taken special care to shove both envelopes deep into the recesses of my bag. I'd separated them as I did so, so that in the extremely improbable event of one of them going missing, at least the other, in a separate compartment, would still be safe. But how could a random pickpocket have known that either of them contained a valuable piece of art? Unless it wasn't a random theft but a highly focused one.

Belatedly, alarm bells began to sound. Suppose someone had been watching me? Suppose someone had seen the Major passing me what appeared to be a single envelope and was pretty sure what it contained? Suppose another someone had been turning away from the bar with her hands full of coffee and beer, and had been fallen against by a half-drunk punter in grubby jeans and a moth-eaten sweater with a watch cap pulled down over his ears? And suppose that second someone was trying to keep her drinks from spilling, how easy it would be for the first someone, who was only pretending to be pissed, to fish an envelope out of the second someone's bag?

I tried to recall him. Tallish, well-built, but not by any means the Bald Baker of Burano. I hadn't noticed his features, only his clothes, plus a definite impression of surliness and belligerence. Was it him who had taken the Tiepolo from my bag? Looking back, it seemed increasingly likely, especially since I couldn't see where else the loss might have occurred. More importantly, since he must have been the errand boy for someone else, who was it that was pulling the strings? And what was likely to be the reaction when it was discovered that only one drawing had been stolen from me, not both of them?

Considering the risks already taken, it seemed there was more at stake than mere money. But I couldn't begin to work out what it might be, or who the ruthless puppet master was. On serious reflection, none of Sandro's friends seemed to fit the bill. On the other hand, back in Venice on the occasion of Sandro's ill-fated dinner, it would have been all too easy for any one of them to have snuck around the Marchese's *salone* and found the drawings. Small and easily portable: which of them would be most likely to recognize their worth? Certainly Katy Pasqualin had the requisite knowledge . . . could that have been the reason she'd been murdered? Or did she know who was after them, and possibly even why? Maybe actually caught the thief in the midst of nicking them? Even though Nell Roscoe had purportedly bought them from a coffin-sized bookshop in Venice.

Could I see Katy herself stealing them on the night of Sandro's dinner party and the next day flogging them somewhere in Venice? She was half-Italian, after all, niece of the Marchesa Allegra – she would know her way around Venice. In retrospect, I could easily see how it all went down. Tears or no tears. She was the kind of girl who had perfected the craft of eye-welling and lip-trembling from an early age. Thinking back, her demeanour when she and I had lunch together had not only been coolly collected – for the most part – she had also exhibited signs of guilty knowledge of the doge's ring and the missing Botticelli. And for all her innocent manner, there were those sugar daddies to take into consideration. Not to mention boob jobs. Neither was something you'd associate with the shrinking violet persona she presented to the world. The long blonde hair, the big blue eyes, the air of fragility were probably no more than a front to help her achieve whatever it was she was after. Money, probably. On the other hand, the terror and the tears she'd displayed, and tried to hide, at Sandro's party in London had not been fake in the least.

I wondered what, if anything, the boyfriend had to say about her. I dialled Fliss Fairlight's number.

'Fairlight,' she said.

'Did Pasqualin's boyfriend come up with anything useful?' I asked.

'Hello to you, too.'

'Hello, Fliss. Did he?'

'As far as we could tell, nothing particularly germane to her death,' she said.

'The girl was very different to the image she projected. Actually, a bit of a tough cookie,' I said.

'So they've discovered.'

'On the other hand, she was genuinely scared of something or someone.'

'We've already taken that on board.'

'Does the boyfriend know about the older man or men in her life?'

'Not sure. He mentioned how lucky she was to have several generous uncles and how close she was to them. We're still not certain whether he was having us on or is just suffering from a serious dose of naivety.'

'Or perhaps he knew and didn't mind.'

'There's that, of course.'

'Well, good luck with the investigation,' I said, and broke the connection.

I rang Sandro, now safely back in London and presumably reunited with his doting mamma. 'Oh, Alessandra,' he said, when he heard my voice. 'Thank you again so much for all you did for us.'

'My pleasure,' I said. I didn't feel it necessary to mention the euro-stuffed envelope which his uncle had forced on me. 'Sandro, there are still so many questions left to answer.'

'Such as?'

For heaven's sake . . . 'Such as whether they've found out who was behind your kidnapping,' I said patiently. 'Or whether they've discovered who killed your cousin.'

'My cousin? But Val is—'

'Who's talking about someone called Val? I meant Katy. Katy Pasqualin,' I added, in case he didn't remember.

'God, yes. I'd almost forgotten, what with recent events and so on. Poor, poor Katy. This has all been so terrible. And the police still have no idea who was responsible. Are we going to see you the day after tomorrow?'

'Most certainly,' I said. 'What time?'

I wondered who else would attend this get-together to mark the untimely death of a young woman. I also wondered how many were aware of her proclivities. And also who stood to benefit monetarily from her death.

I called Fliss again. 'Hel-*lo*,' I said, exaggeratedly. 'I've got another question for you. Any idea how much Katy Pasqualin had in the bank – or anywhere else? Or whether she had made a will?'

'Funny you should ask. With a bit of pressure applied and some finagling – all above board, I may add, we – the police, that is – have just managed to get information from her financial manager, who—'

'Financial manager?'

'One of those guys who manage your financial affairs,' Fliss said kindly.

'I haven't got any financial affairs for anyone to manage.'

'Me neither. But Katy Pasqualin did. I suppose when you're looking at well over quarter of a million quid, someone needs to—'

'Quarter of a million *quid*?' I said. 'But she was only twenty-three years old.'

'And according to her parents, hasn't been left any money, as far as they know.'

'Are we thinking blackmail?'

'I think we are. The bugger of it is that we have no idea who she might have been blackmailing. If indeed she was. At this point, it's not much more than conjecture. Our experts have been through all the papers and documents they could find, and there's no clues, nothing.'

'No encoded entries in diaries? No lists taped to the underside of drawers?'

'Nothing. Or if there is, they haven't stumbled across it yet.'

'Would logic suppose that there might have been more than one bank account?'

'Logic would, and indeed has. But it's hard to know where to start. And she was obviously pretty astute. About her financial affairs, I mean.'

'Has her bank – the one we know about – been helpful?'

'Yes, but not, unfortunately, informative. They say that she used to show up every now and then with wodges of cash and pay them into her account.'

'Wodges?'

'Not so large that she could be considered to be breaking any laws. They started to wonder about money-laundering of some kind, but they couldn't quite see how. The one time the manager did ask about it, she shrugged her pretty shoulders – this is the bank's words, not mine – and murmured something about gifts from relatives, or a lucky streak at cards.'

'Her family's pretty well-off, isn't it?'

'Yes. So, it seems, are most of the people we've questioned. Her friends. The boyfriend-stroke-fiancé. Her wider family . . . There's a whole network of cousins, aunts and uncles.'

'I'd dearly love to know who these sugar daddies are.'

'So would we, if only to eliminate them from our enquiries. You're on intimate terms with at least some of her friends, et cetera, so if you get any leads, let us know.'

'Will do.'

Sugar daddies, I reflected as I ended the call. How many sugar daddies can one girl handle? I was aware that these days students quite often peddled their bodies in order to get their fees and university expenses paid. Nothing wrong with that. I'm not a prude about prostitution, when entered into willingly. If you have a saleable commodity and someone's willing to buy, why not? It's one way to earn a living. But when you get right down to it, this was the higher end of the scale. Much further down the sexual ladder, the consequences could be dire, the victims acquired and manipulated by unscrupulous gangs, the women turned into hopeless junkies and forced to sell themselves, sometimes just for their next drink or fix.

A few days later, at the home of Dominic and Maddalena Grainger, the mood was sombre and heavy with grief. There was some black draping, as though we'd been transported back to Victorian times, and various arrangements of lilies and white carnations standing here and there. Sandro's friends were there, plus the one I'd not met before, Fabio, the Milanese fashion designer. Uncles, aunts, quite a lot of cousins. The Marchesa, black-veiled and be-pearled. No diamonds today. No husband, either. The young folk I'd met before. There was some sniffing, a lot of tears. I felt a little weepy myself. Poor girl, cut off so young.

There were three or four excruciatingly thin females with immaculate make-up and hair becomingly arranged beneath hats of black straw or felt. In their early forties, I'd have said, and doing everything they possibly could to hide it. I wondered, as I always did when I saw women like that, what sacrifices in the way of fun and enjoyment they made in order to remain so fat-free. And whether the time and expense involved was worth it. Were they wives, or mistresses, or just women who felt they needed to look like that? They were drinking sparkling water, making believe it was prosecco or something. Not that it was the kind of occasion where people were knocking back the booze.

I expressed my condolences to Katy's parents, and, belatedly remembering he was her cousin, as well as the only attendee at Sandro's dinner party in Venice to whom I hadn't spoken, introduced myself to Fabio, a nice-looking man in an obviously self-designed suit of black velvet embellished with big silver buttons and hoops of black velvet all over the sleeves, like a melancholy jockey. As a great believer in the striking of hot irons, I managed to bring up Sandro's dinner party in Venice. He seemed to think it had been a sparkly occasion, everybody on their best behaviour, excellent food and drink, as always with one of Sandro's events. Although he was wearing four rings of various kinds on his fingers, I was prepared to bet that he had absolutely nothing to do with the doge's.

'Sandro,' he said. 'He is a . . . um . . . *bon viveur*, that one. Always happy, always kind and . . . um . . . smiling. Even when Valentina came in so unexpectedly.'

'Valentina?'

He jerked his chin at one of the water-sipping pencils. 'Senora Bassano de Guisti. A friend of the Marchese. And his wife, of course. And a second cousin to me and to poor Katy.'

I looked again, more closely. Wasn't she the woman I'd seen crossing a square in Venice with a bejewelled Bichon

Frise on a lead? Even if not, she was certainly a clone of the other three, who had clumped together, eyeing the company through heavy black false eyelashes and making no attempt to express any kind of sentiment whatsoever. In case, I presumed, the *maquillage* splintered. Two of them had high-heeled ankle boots, another wore black suede boots which came up over her knees and a crotch-skimming black dress. Very suitable attire for a solemn occasion like this.

'She and Katy were very friendly,' Fabio continued. 'Being so close in age.'

So close? In Valentina's dreams, I thought. There must have been a good fifteen years' difference between the two.

I could see the Marchesa staring at me and frowning. I wasn't sure why. I hadn't felt that she'd taken to me when I'd met her in Venice, but she looked like the sort of person who didn't take to anybody much, including the Marchese. 'When you say Valentina came in unexpectedly when you were attending Sandro's dinner party, what exactly do you mean?'

'We were having champagne before we sat down at the table to eat, and she appeared at the door of the *salone*. She seemed astonished to see us there. As we were to see her. Naturally Sandro offered her a glass but she refused it, said she was so sorry, she had not realized anyone was there and had only come to pick up a pair of gloves she had left behind the last time she had visited Allegra.'

'Who is her aunt, right?'

'Or her cousin. I'm never quite sure of the relationships among those noble families.'

'But you yourself were Katy's cousin, weren't you?'

'Yes, but on my mother's side.' To my dismay, his eyes filled. 'I was so very upset to hear of her death. It seemed so unnecessary. So cruel. But then, signorina, the world is a cruel place, *non è vero*?'

'It is indeed.'

Jack or Harry Jago appeared beside us. He took my hand, from which I deduced he was the other twin since the last time I'd met his brother, delivering vegetable boxes from Eating Naturally, he'd been pretty unfriendly. 'Nice to see you again, despite everything,' he said.

'You too,' I said.

Someone discreetly tapped a glass and we fell silent. Short tributes were paid from various members of the company. Katy's father spoke briefly, thanking us all for coming. He held a white handkerchief in a hand that trembled. Poor man.

'We are, and shall always be, devastated at the loss of our beautiful daughter,' he said. 'I should like to be able to say that we have nothing but pity in our hearts for the person responsible, but it wouldn't be true. Nobody has the right to deprive another of his or her life. Especially a life as promising, as vibrant, as Katerina's was. I cannot believe that that person will find it easy to live with the burden of what they have done, not only to our daughter, but also to her family.' He glanced around at us all. 'Thank you again for coming to say goodbye to her.'

His eyes filled and without embarrassment he lifted the white handkerchief to blot them dry. Most people were in tears. I saw the one called Valentina detach herself from her coven and run over to hug him, and then his wife. All three of them stood in a small circle, heads bowed. It was very moving.

I stood alone beside a rather beautiful fruitwood credenza – if that was the right word for it – and surveyed the room. I was pretty certain that among the assembled people there was at least one thief and one murderer. They might even be one and the same person and I really wished I could pinpoint whoever it was, but none of the sorrowful faces indicated criminality. It's perfectly possible to compartmentalize one's feelings, of course. The murderer might be genuinely anguished at the death of Katy Pasqualin, which wouldn't make him or her any less or more guilty. The thief might feel no shame at standing in the same room as the person from whom she or he had lifted the Marchese's possessions.

Would we ever find the answer? It seemed to me that the person or people responsible had been remarkably lucky not to have been identified by now. I hated to think of Katy's final moments as someone she trusted – and maybe loved – had come into the bathroom and, as she turned to smile or make some innocuous remark, had simply pushed her under.

Moments of startled disbelief would have been followed by a frantic struggle, followed by desperately diminishing awareness and, finally, by blank darkness. What would you think of in those last minutes? Almost certainly not of anything but the impossibility of what was happening to you.

I shuddered.

When the gathering began to disperse, I said goodbye to those I had been talking to. Outside, the expensive Chelsea air was brisk but still warm as I turned towards the nearest Tube station. Something caught my eye as I walked: a flash, a shine. Someone was coming towards me, and it was only after I'd gone by that I realized I'd just passed – was it possible? – the bald man of Venice.

'Please,' I said aloud. 'Don't tell me that it's someone else, or that this is a tremendous coincidence or anything ridiculous of that sort.' Nobody did.

I turned. He continued to walk unhurriedly away from me, before he turned the corner into a side street. I started to run, then stopped, removed my shoes and took to my stockinged feet. But by the time I'd reached the corner, he was gone. What was he doing there? The logical answer was that he was waiting for someone who had attended the Graingers' little assembly. But who? Any one of the Italians who were there, obviously. But why not use the phone or text or email? Why would he have flown to England? Could he possibly be the person who'd killed Katy? Even if he was, why would he have been hanging around outside the Graingers' place?

I lurked for a bit, for nearly forty minutes, in the hope that he would return. But he didn't, and in the end I took the Underground to my station and travelled back home to Longbury.

EIGHTEEN

'I simply don't know what to do,' I said. With much squirming embarrassment, I'd confessed to the loss of the Tiepolo drawing. My distress was clear enough for the Major to twist his moustaches about then lay a hand on my arm.

'It's really of no consequence,' he said. 'Glad to get rid of the dratted things, if you want to know the truth.'

'I'm fairly sure I know who they legally belong to. If only I knew who'd pinched them.'

'Any suspects?'

'Several. But that's just speculation on my part. I've got no proof.' I reached for another of his peanut butter cookies and mumbled, half of it in my mouth before it collapsed in crumbs all over the Major's carpet.

'Did you ever find the place that woman said she'd bought the drawings?'

'Not really. Though we don't really believe a word she said, do we?' I frowned. 'I wonder how she knew Nell Roscoe had those drawings.'

'The art mistress, the real Mrs Forbes, who Nell travelled with, perhaps?'

'Very possibly. Except she died. Are you sure Mrs Roscoe didn't give you any other clues as to the place she bought them from?'

'None at all.' The Major frowned. 'Thing is, Alex, Nell would hate all this skulduggery. She'd want everything to be above board. She wasn't into anything dodgy. I really can't see her taking much notice of some tout *psst*ing at her on a street corner.'

'I agree. On the other hand, if she was with the real Philippa Forbes, the art teacher might have thought the drawings were worth at least a second look, dodgy or not. I can quite easily imagine that. And Nell ended up buying them because she liked them, not because she thought they had any particular value.'

'Yes. That's plausible.'

'And then, when they got back to their hotel or home to England, the art teacher takes a closer look at them and says, "Hang about, Nell, I think these are worth a bob or two and you should have them authenticated."'

'And before she could do anything about it, the poor old girl starts getting really unwell, and stashes them behind Mrs Forbes' oil painting until she can decide what to do with them, goes off to the hospital and never comes home again. Doesn't bear thinking about really.' The Major reached for another cookie. 'I wonder why she didn't tell me when I visited her in hospital.'

'She probably forgot. After all, she had a lot more on her mind by then than a couple of nice little drawings which she'd bought as a holiday souvenir.'

'Tell you what . . .' The Major smoothed his moustaches and frowned. 'We still don't know how that woman – you know who I mean – cottoned on to the fact that Nell had them in the first place?'

'We'd have to find out who she really is, and then trace her connection to Nell, if there is one.' I mused a bit. 'Could she have been a nurse at the hospital where poor Mrs Roscoe died? Or a friend of Mrs Forbes, who heard about them from her?'

'She had to be someone who knew either Nell or the art teacher,' agreed the Major. 'Stands to reason.'

'What do we know about the real Mrs Forbes?'

'Very little. She was like Nell Roscoe, not married and no children. There might have been a niece—'

'Which would imply a sibling,' I said. 'Who might have heard about the two sketches and shown up here on the off-chance and decided to try her luck.'

'Doesn't bear thinking about,' the Major said faintly. 'It's sad that both ladies are no longer with us. And frustrating, too.'

'But Nell must have told someone about them.'

'Who passed the information on, unwittingly or otherwise.' His expression brightened. 'When you think about it, it would almost have to be someone connected in some way to the girls' high school. Nell didn't have much of a social life, apart from her school interests. She might have taken them in when term started again after her holiday . . .'

'And when Nell died, your – ahem! – friend might have remembered hearing about them and thought that with Nell no longer on the scene—'

'They would make a nice little supplement to her income—'

'Not so little. Did you contact the school again?'

'I did indeed. And it looks like you might be right about Curlilocks, the maths teacher. When I described the woman, they came up with a name immediately. Thing is, the lady retired a year ago and didn't leave a forwarding address.'

'Suspicious in itself if you ask me.' I thought of Joey Preston, private dick. 'Shouldn't be too difficult to trace her. Meanwhile, I'll just have to try and get the missing sketch back from whoever pinched it out of my bag. I'm not sure how, though.'

'And meanwhile, you could return the one you still have to its rightful owner,' the Major said hopefully. 'Since you think you know who that is?'

What was the best way to do that? I pondered the question all the way back to my flat. Then telephoned Sandro. 'Any idea when your uncle Cesare will next be in London?' I asked.

'He's coming over four days from now.'

'So that would be next Thursday?'

'Yes. He'll be staying at the Connaught, I imagine, since that's what he usually does.'

'Not with your mother?'

'Um . . . no. It's sometimes . . . erm . . . easier for him to conduct his . . . er . . . business meetings in a hotel than in a private house.'

And, I thought, to engage in a little extra-curricular business on the side, should he so wish. 'I can quite understand that,' I said.

'Why do you want to know?' he asked.

'I just wondered.' It sounded a deeply implausible thing for me to be wondering about, but Sandro said nothing more.

I put a call through to the Connaught and checked that yes,

the Marchese Cesare de Peron was indeed expected sometime soon but that they could give me no further particulars, nor would they, if they could, since it wasn't hotel policy to divulge details concerning their guests, past, present or future.

'And quite right too,' I said heartily. 'Carry on the good work.' I switched off.

All I had to do now was to ensure that I was at the Connaught in four days' time, would hand over the Tiepolo and explain the circumstances of how it fell into my hands. I decided not to mention that there had once been two sketches and not just one. I couldn't see how I would ever trace the ostensible drunk who'd clearly pickpocketed me in the Fox and Hounds. I would alert Sandro, once I'd returned the remaining drawing.

Four days later, I was at the Connaught bright and early. I figured Cesare would have got in late the night before, or even scheduled a business arrangement of some kind. But at eight o'clock in the morning, he should still be in his room.

A busload of Asian tourists fortuitously drew up and out they clambered, clad in black raincoats and weird little hats, and poured into the hotel. I poured in behind them then strayed towards the lifts and took one to the fifth floor. I'd taken the precaution the night before of calling Maddalena and extracting some info about her brother's whereabouts. I knew she would humour me – after all, I had more or less rescued her boy for her *and* indirectly saved her and Dominic a shitload of money.

On the fifth floor I stepped out of the lift and turned right, then left, then right again. I knocked on the door of Cesare's room, and after a moment, he shouted, 'Come in!' So I did.

His back to me, he was sitting in his dressing gown at a fancy desk set into the window recess, his computer open in front of him. There were trees outside the window, with sparrows hopping about in their branches.

'Just put it on the table,' he said, without turning round, obviously assuming that I was room service.

A woman lay on her elbow in the big double bed. Wordlessly, I stared at her. Wordlessly, she stared back. A grey satin night-dress strap had edged down one shoulder in an enticing manner. And I'm here to tell you that at that time of the day, she appeared a lot older than she'd looked the other times I'd seen her, tit-tupping across the Venetian cobbles or at the remembrance gathering for Katy Pasqualin.

Valentina Bassano de Giusti. I'm not a fortune-teller but, if I were, I'd predict that her days as Cesare's – *any*body's – mistress were definitely numbered. I just hoped she'd managed to stash away a nice little nest egg for her 'retirement'. And then it struck me. As the Marchesa's cousin or niece, she was the woman who had keys to Cesare's apartment, which meant she could come and go as she pleased. And indeed did so. Had she added to her retirement fund by nicking small, portable items belonging to the Marchese whenever she could, before flogging them off at a fraction of their worth? Had she been observed committing one theft or another by Katy Pasqualin? I remembered, too, that I'd seen this woman emerging from the former Palazzo Vendramin-Calergi, otherwise known as the Casinò de Venezia, and seemingly on friendly terms with the personnel inside. Was she one of those women who slinked up and down the gambling rooms in backless sequins, to attract and entice would-be players of blackjack or roulette? Almost certainly not. Although I'd never been inside, I'd heard that the casino was very small and often under-occupied. So unless she worked there in some other capacity, the probability was high that she went there to gamble.

And she was a woman who was purported to be extremely friendly with Katy Pasqualin – in fact, she was Katy's cousin or aunt, certainly a woman in front of whom Katy would have had no problem in taking time to strip off her work clothes and get into a bath in order to wash away the day's grime before going out on the town. Perhaps a woman who was already being blackmailed by Katy, or frightened that it was only a matter of time before she was.

On the other hand, would you remain close friends with someone who was blackmailing you, bleeding you dry for whatever reason? I don't think I would. Unless I already had murder in mind.

I'd have to give the situation some thought. Meanwhile, I judged it best to retreat from the Marchese's bedroom before he turned round and discovered that I had not come bearing coffee and biscuits but was an intruder. So I left. But not before I'd scoped out the expensive leather bag on the coffee table – the *really* expensive must-have leather bag – and the small travelling bag beside it. Why couldn't I afford such luxuries? Well, partly because however meagre it was, I preferred my way of earning my living to Valentina Bassano de Giusti's. And because, let's face it, nobody in their right mind was going to pay through the nose for the exclusive use of *my* body. As I quietly pulled the bedroom door to behind me, I smiled to think of the Marchese expecting a cup of fresh coffee. And then wondering who it was that had come into the room and then so abruptly left it. Well, I thought, as I walked along the passage to the lift, Valentina could explain it.

Once back downstairs in the lobby, I asked if I could telephone upstairs and tell my good friend the Marchese de Farnese that I was here. They dialled the number for me and when Cesare answered, I explained that I urgently needed to speak to him, that it wouldn't take long and that I was waiting downstairs.

'I am not dressed,' he said crossly.

'I don't mind.'

'I am not in the habit of receiving people in my dressing gown.' His voice was arctic.

There was a pause. Finally, although I don't like reminding people of good turns I've done them, but remembering the huge pile of cash I'd recently saved him from having to fork out for Sandro's release, I said quietly, 'I think you owe me a favour. Besides, the favour is for you, not for me.'

Another pause. Then he said, 'Very well. I will come down. I'll be there in about ten minutes.'

Eleven minutes later, he was crossing the shiny floor to where I sat on an upholstered chair, leafing through a magazine full of stuff I couldn't afford nor had any use for: designer coats, designer watches, jewellery, perfumes, shoes. A different world.

I extended my hand to him. '*Ciao*, Cesare,' I said, as he bowed over my fingers and sat down. 'I wanted to return this to you.' I offered the envelope containing one of the two Tiepolo drawings.

He opened the envelope. Drew out the sketch of an old man in two colours of chalk. Studied it for a moment. Frowned. Looked hard at me. 'How . . .?' he said. 'How . . . Where did you get this?'

'It's a complicated story,' I said. 'But this ended up in the temporary possession of a friend of mine, who felt he had no right to it, and was anxious to return it to its lawful owner – who I believe is you – as soon as it could be arranged.'

'And how did you know that it belonged to me?'

'It was an informed guess, really. There were rumours floating up and down the Grand Canal when I was there, and for a number of reasons, I made an assumption.'

'I very much dislike my private business being turned into the stuff of daily tittle-tattle,' he said. He seemed nonplussed. He stared down at the drawing, turned it over to examine the back, looked at it once more. 'To tell the truth, Alexandra, I did not have the slightest idea that it had even been stolen. And who is your so-honest friend who wishes to return this to me?'

'He's a retired Major, lives near me in south-east Kent.'

'And how did he acquire this?' He gently tapped the Tiepolo.

'He inherited it from his next-door neighbour.'

'How is that possible?' He shook his head. 'I am not following this story at all.'

'I told you it was complicated.' And made even more so by the fact that now one of the two sketches had been stolen from me. Not that I was about to tell Cesare that.

'Please give me your friend's name and address,' he was saying. 'I would like to reward him for his honesty.'

I'd been on tenterhooks in case I let slip that there had once been two drawings, not just the one. 'That would be most kind,' I said. I piled on the pathos a bit. 'And as an elderly man living on his army pension, I know how very much he would appreciate it.'

'I have a better idea. Wait here.' Cesare stood up and made his way to the check-in counter. A little later, he returned with an envelope that looked pretty much like the one I'd been given at my hotel in Venice. 'Please, give this to your friend.'

I hefted it. Not anywhere near as thick as the one I'd received, but pretty good all the same. 'I'd be more than happy to. The poor old boy will be delighted!' I didn't think the Major, far as he was from being a poor old boy, would feel too many scruples about accepting it. Now all I had to do was locate the other sketch, return it to the Marchese, and I would be free and clear.

Meanwhile, I had a book to get on with, some notes to transcribe, and a couple of articles to write.

I got back to Longbury at around three o'clock and stopped at the fancy baker's shop – or *patissier*, as it called itself – to get some sinful pastry to eat with a cuppa. I picked up my mail, groaning slightly to see two auctioneers' catalogues. I find the best ones very useful as research tools, since they provide an opportunity to winkle out the lesser-known paintings which could come in useful for some of my themed collections, but there had already been some waiting when I returned from Venice, so there was a lot of flicking through to do. I changed into exercise pants and a loose top, intending to put my feet up, and totally chillax. So it was bloody irritating to hear someone knocking gently at my door just as the kettle boiled. So irritating, in fact, that I padded down my little hall without even asking myself how anyone could have entered the building and come up the stairs. Ready to expostulate with my caller, or at least make it clear I did not wish to linger in idle chat, I pulled open the door.

Outside stood Mrs Gardiner, the old girl who lived on the ground floor of the building and owned two very small, yappy dogs. 'So sorry to interrupt you,' she fluted. 'But I felt I ought to let you know that three days ago, while you were away, someone tried to break in to the building.'

'Really?'

'The rest of the tenants are aware, but I did undertake to inform you as soon as you returned.'

'That's most kind. Did this would-be thief actually manage to get in?'

'Not as far as we're aware. But it behooves us all to be extra vigilant in these lawless times.'

'You are so right, Mrs Gardiner. And how are the dogs?'

'In the very best of health, I'm glad to say.'

'That's great.'

'Anyway, I urge you to keep eyes and ears open.'

'I shall certainly do so.' Especially, I thought, closing the door on her, as the intruder was almost certainly after the Major's sketches.

> Sandro, I wrote, you need to send me a definitive list of all your friends – at least, the ones who attended your Venetian and London dinner parties. Plus all close relatives and anywhere they overlap with any of the others. Plus anyone with any connection to anyone even marginally involved with you or anyone else. Plus whatever you know about Signora Bassano de Giusti. Soonest.

I tapped the right button and sent the email off to Sandro, hoping that he would respond very soon. We all needed to find a final solution. Discover whether Valentina was the one behind Katy's death – not to mention my being bonked on the head, knifed and kidnapped. Whoever the culprit was, and Harry (or Jack) notwithstanding, they were a pretty violent crowd, and I felt that the sooner whoever it was had been taken off the streets, the better for all concerned.

I called DCI Fliss Fairlight once again. 'Valentina Bassano de Giusti,' I said, after exchanging preliminaries.

'What about her?'

'Ever heard of her? Well, no, I'm sure you haven't. But that pal of yours in Interpol . . . might he have done?'

'Do you mean the French guy who's always pinching my bum?'

'Probably. And much good may it do him.'

Fliss laughed. 'I'll see what I can come up with. Any more intel?'

'She's the mistress of the Marchese de Farnese de Peron who lives in Venice. Got a face I swear she hangs up at night and puts back in the morning. Owns a Bichon Frise—'

'That should come in useful for identification purposes.'

'You never know.'

'Anything else?'

'Not at the moment.'

'I'll see what I can do. By the way, it's great that Sam Willoughby is having such a good time out there in New Zealand. I really thought he'd be bored out of his mind, especially without you around.'

'Don't know what that means . . . we're not an item, you know.'

'No, of course you're not.'

'Good*bye*, Felicity.' Bitch . . .

'Goodbye, Alexandra.'

NINETEEN

It was a relief to have some time to get on with my work, after the recent excitement and tension. There had been no further word regarding the abduction, nor about Katy Pasqualin's death. I was able to produce two articles for Darren Carver and submit a third for a prestigious American quarterly. I'd just about prepared all the artwork for my next anthology, plus the text to go with it, ready for submitting to the publisher. With any luck, it should be ready to hit the Christmas market later in the year.

Not that luck had much to do with it. I worked damned hard to see that I got everything correctly sourced and attributed, and that while there were plenty of familiar paintings, there was also a good sprinkling of less familiar images intended to stimulate and interest those who bought the books.

It was also time to start thinking about my next anthology. To which end, eight days later I found myself leafing through my backlog of auctioneers' catalogues, looking for inspiration. What about a travelling theme? Planes and trains and auto-mobiles . . . with boats, oceans and sailing thrown in? Or extend the idea to embrace all forms of travelling and those who travel? A convincing case for the theme could definitely be made.

Or there was the perennially fascinating subject of cards, dice, games of chance, so often celebrated on canvas. But perhaps not often enough. Hogarth and the Flemish painters notwithstanding, I wasn't sure I could gather enough material to put together a worthwhile production. But it was certainly worth considering.

I almost didn't see it at first. Had to turn back several pages. And yes, there it was . . . a folder of half a dozen small drawings, splayed like a hand of cards. And one of the six items for sale was, as far as I could see, the missing Tiepolo drawing of a beruffed clown in a grotesque carnival mask.

It was half-obscured by a black-and-white etching of bare-branched trees beside a stream, but I recognized it at once. No details about any of the other pictures in the file were provided. They were being offered for sale at a small and obscure auction house somewhere in Norfolk in a week's time, and I instantly knew I would have to attend the sale. It didn't occur to me for a moment that it wouldn't turn out to be the Major's Tiepolo. Or more correctly, Nell Roscoe's. Or even more correctly, the Marchese's. The mere fact that I'd even noticed the lot being offered was an unbelievable coincidence – though I knew from experience that most coincidences are. And I had an accustomed eye.

I tamped down my excitement. This might be the only chance I had of finding out anything more about what had been going on, since the Met had so far drawn a blank on Katy Pasqualin's death, though they were doing an excellent job of hiding the fact.

'They're fairly confident that it was the boyfriend,' Fliss Fairlight had told me recently. 'It's just a question of finding enough evidence to prove it. They've already brought him in once for questioning and had to let him go. Joy says it's eggshell time at the moment, with everyone being very wary of having a wrongful arrest suit slapped on them. Can't afford anything like that nowadays.'

'And it cuts out the old rubber hose option too, I imagine,' I said.

'Quite. Trouble is the buggers are far too well aware of their rights. It was so much easier in the olden days.'

'You'll get him in the end,' I said. 'You always do.'

'We had a look at that cousin or mistress,' said Fliss. 'Valentina di Wotsit and Thingmabob. Jeez, what a piece of work *she* is. The only question I wanted to ask her was how many hours a day she spends getting herself ready to face the world.'

'Most of them, I suspect.'

'And the really sad thing about it is the world doesn't give a toss.'

'As long as the guy who's paying the bills does.'

'Actually, I never thought about it before but it must be damned tiring, being a mistress. Always having to look like a million dollars, whatever you feel like. Never able to spend the holidays with him. Probably not able to get married to anyone else – unless you want to end the relationship, of course. Nor have children. God, no, who'd be a mistress? Always having to skulk around like a second-class citizen, no life of your own.'

'Dunno where you get the skulking bit from . . . as far as I could make out, everybody knows about the liaison. Including the wife?'

'Probably,' agreed Fliss. 'Anyway, the point about the woman is that we couldn't find anything at all to link her to Katy that evening, even though they're second cousins. She was over in London visiting some friends, told us what she'd been doing and where she'd been, said she and Katy had dinner together the night before, but she hadn't seen the girl after that. It all hung together. Witnesses for the relevant times and so on. She lives most of the time in Venice, has a couple of kids who live in Geneva with her former husband, and possesses no visible means of support.'

'Interesting – or is it?'

'Whereas the boyfriend couldn't come up with any kind of convincing alibi. Just mooching about, he said. Had a drink in a pub in the West End but couldn't find anyone to corroborate it. Bought a Chinese and ate it at home, by himself. Went to bed early because he had to be up at sparrow's fart the next morning in order to drive down to Wales to see a client.'

'He could be telling the truth,' I said. 'How many of us could prove our whereabouts on any given day?'

'Granted. Especially if we live alone. But I have to say I still like him for it. We've spoken to their friends and the whole set-up sounds a little too perfect. And he himself is as cool as a cucumber.'

'Perhaps he's innocent enough to believe in the notion of British justice.'

'More fool he.'

'God, you're cynical.'

'Trust me,' said Fliss. 'Once we've found the chink in his armour . . .'

'Poor chap,' I said.

I wasn't surprised to discover, three days later, that James Renfrew had been arrested and charged with Katy Pasqualin's murder.

'It wasn't him!' Sandro Grainger sounded almost as distraught as he might have been if he himself had been charged.

'How do you know?'

'Anyone who'd ever seen them together would testify to his innocence. There's absolutely no way he would have attacked Katy. Honestly, Alessandra, the police are making a big mistake here.'

'Unfortunately there's nothing I can do about it.' I agreed with Sandro. From what I'd seen and heard, the boyfriend couldn't be more innocent of murder.

Meanwhile, I was making plans to attend the auction in Norfolk. It seemed unlikely that the person putting the Tiepolo sketch up for sale would also be present, but it seemed worth taking a punt on it. I told Sandro that he was to come with me, and explained all the ins and outs: that there had been two stolen Tiepolo sketches, that one had been safely returned to his Uncle Cesare, and that as far as I knew, Cesare was not yet aware that there had been a second one.

Sandro insisted that we drive up together the day before, which was fine by me. I figured that someone would foot the bill for my accommodation in a local hotel, considering the amount of ransom money they had not had to cough up for Sandro's safe return. Then I called Joey Preston. Told him what I planned to do. Asked if he had any comment.

'Not really,' he said. 'Especially since the seller is unlikely to be in attendance.'

'True. But if you came along, I thought that with your detective skills, it might be easier for you than for me to winkle out who he – or she – is. You could pretend to belong to some organization involved in tracking down stolen art.'

'No pretence needed. I do.'

'That's great. Do you want to come with us?' I explained that Sandro would have a car.

'Better I go alone. Just in case.'

'Fine. See you there.'

'Any further news of the guys who kidnapped you?' I asked Sandro as we pulled away from London and set off towards the Lincolnshire Wolds.

'Very little. At least, they picked up a couple of the . . . small fry, if that's the right word. The underlings.'

'As always in these matters. But not the kingpin?'

'Not yet.'

'Did the situation impact on you in any way?' I asked.

'Not really. Maybe I'm too naive – or too optimistic.'

Naive was the word. 'So no nightmares or anything?'

'No.'

'And no idea who was behind it?'

'No. But I've promised myself that one way or another, I will find out. And then . . .' His voice tailed away.

I didn't ask, '*And then what . . .?*'

We sat silent for a while as Sandro's Ferrari roared its way towards the flat lands beyond Cambridge. Then I said, 'I'm not sure what we expect to accomplish by attending this auction.'

'I was wondering that myself.'

'But I figured that if we could find out who's selling your uncle's Tiepolo drawing, it might somehow help to identify the person who killed Katy. Or kidnapped you. Or both.' I'd already decided not to mention Joey Preston.

'Was that list I sent you helpful? Showing as many as I could remember of the relationships between my friends and their relatives?'

'I read it carefully, but so far, nothing's leaped out at me.' This was a lie. I wanted to drop my probing questions delicately, like a man dropping flies on the surface of water beneath which salmon loitered. 'But who knows? Still waters run deep, as they say.'

'Talking of waters, I'm flying over to Venice next week to

see an opera at La Fenice. *La Traviata*. My aunt's a patron, on
the board there, and she's sent me some complimentary tickets.
Want to come?'

I was surprised how much I wanted to say yes. My recent
visit could hardly be said to have been completely enjoyable,
so it would be good to have a more peaceable one. And if I
went, I could always chalk it up to research and, if nothing
else, claim it on my tax forms as a legitimate expense. 'You
could stay at my uncle's place, too,' Sandro continued. 'Or
he's offered to put you up at one of the really fancy hotels,
since on your last visit you had to skulk in the backstreets of
the city – his words, not mine,' Sandro added swiftly as I
opened my mouth to protest.

'Actually, I'm extremely tempted,' I said. 'And there could
well be loose ends to tie up, though I can't think what they
might be. How long have I got to give you a definitive
answer?'

'Like . . . ten minutes.' He grinned.

'OK, you're on. I'd very much like to come.'

'Our treat. My aunt insisted.'

'Well, thank you very much.' I smiled with pleasure. 'What
a luxury; I'm extremely happy to accept.'

'That's good.'

'Tell me more about your aunt,' I said. 'Your uncle is such
a . . . *strong* character that it's hard to get to know her.'

'You mean he overwhelms her?'

'A bit, wouldn't you say?'

'Yes. It's a slightly odd relationship, really. They both come
from old wealthy Venetian families. My aunt is very conven-
tional, as you may have noticed. Very proper.'

'Very *beneducato*?'

He missed the irony. 'Exactly. She is, as I said, a patron of
La Fenice, and a very generous one, too. My uncle is always
criticizing her for being extravagant, saying there's plenty of
other money, both public and private, to support the opera
house and no one expects her single-handedly to keep the
place going.'

'If all her friends are doing the same thing,' I suggested,
'maybe she doesn't want to appear ungenerous.'

'Or maybe it's a way of compensating for . . . for the way her life has turned out.'

I said nothing for a moment, then murmured, 'She doesn't strike me as a particularly happy person.'

'No, my uncle . . . uh . . . my uncle . . .' He swallowed audibly. 'He is what my mother would call "difficult". And he has many . . . friends.'

'Of the female persuasion?' I said.

'It's . . . uh . . . acceptable over there.'

'I see. And these are Italian female friends, are they?'

'Mostly. I know that years ago he . . . um . . . got involved with an *au pair* from Norway or somewhere similar, working for the family of one of his colleagues, who kicked up a fuss and had to be paid off. I think that in Italy, as long as the . . . um . . . proprieties are observed, these matters are acceptable.'

'What about your aunt? Is it acceptable for her to have male friends?'

'As long as discretion is maintained . . .' He shrugged. 'Why not?'

'What would the Marchese say if he knew?'

'He'd be furious, I imagine. But what *could* he say?'

'Sauce for the goose?'

'Something like that.'

'It's none of my business, but I wonder why the two of them never had any children.'

'I believe my aunt had a very traumatic miscarriage at some point.'

Backstreet abortion, I thought. Did it have any bearing on anything?

'Apparently, she nearly bled to death. And after that, she couldn't get pregnant again.'

'Sad for them both.'

We didn't say much for the rest of the ride. When we reached it, the auction house was the usual large brick building set along a wharf. There was already a crowd milling round inside and out, as people inspected the objects on sale and made marks against certain lots in their catalogues. I noticed a number of London dealers wearing man-of-the-people flat tweed caps and Barbour jackets, as though they were genuine Norfolk farmers. Or simply hoping not to be noticed. Were they after the Tiepolo? If so, it stood to make a tidy sum.

Inside, I scanned the crowds, searching for Joey's gormless face, but couldn't see him. With the catalogue in my hand, I pushed my way towards the table where Lot 134 waited on a small easel, enclosed in a folder. The top sketch showed a watercolour of some indeterminate herbiage standing by a red-roofed barn while what I took to be a cow bent its head to some grass.

Under the eye of a man in a brown overall, I took a pen out of my pocket and used it to turn over the six drawings on the easel one by one. The Tiepolo clown was the fourth one. I ascertained that it was indeed the one I was after by noting the mark I'd made in the bottom left-hand corner so many days before. I was burning with curiosity about the route the sketch had taken to fetch up here. The remaining drawings were nothing more than three or four undistinguished water-colours and a couple of pencil portraits of an old woman in an upright chair.

Behind me, a man spoke to his friend. 'A piece of tourist tat, if you ask me. Pick 'em up on every street corner in Italy. The wife bought two or three of them clowns, if that's what they are, when she was on a coach tour of Venice back in the spring, and now we've got the bloody things hanging on the wall of the lounge.'

'Sooner you than me, mate.'

'Enough to give you nightmares, innit?'

The two of them moved off.

A man across the room was giving me the eye and I turned away. 'Want a cuppa, Sandro?' I said as I moved to the makeshift tea counter. 'Tea, I mean. The coffee will taste like sewage.'

I paid for two plastic cups which were filled with grey liquid from an urn, and handed one to Sandro. 'Here. For what it's worth.'

His patrician lip curled as he sipped at the edge of the cup.

'Tell me,' I said, 'can you see a man on the other side of the room staring at us? Dark beard and moustache, red scarf round his neck? Act nonchalant.'

He peered over my shoulder. 'I see him. Over by a table with three marble busts on it and what looks like some kind of animal under a glass dome.'

'A red squirrel, is it? Stuffed and mounted on a branch? Or with a nut in its paws?'

'Yes.'

'The Victorians were very keen on home taxidermy as a harmless domestic hobby,' I said. 'They liked to stuff small woodland creatures like weasels or pine martens and display them under those glass domes in their so-called natural habitat. Do you recognize the man with the beard?'

Sandro frowned slightly. 'Kind of. But not really.' He stiffened and scowled. 'He's coming over. Want me to fend him off?'

'Let's find out what he wants first.'

People were beginning to clump round the various surfaces which held the items for sale as the auctioneer, smart in a three-piece suit of fine tweed, appeared and started fussing over papers on his rostrum. Men in brown cotton coats were shifting things about and conversing in low tones. I turned my head slightly as the black-bearded guy passed me and said 'Psst!' as though he wanted to sell me a bunch of dirty postcards.

I drew myself up haughtily to show that I was *beneducato*, and he said, 'For Pete's sake, it's Joey.'

And when I looked closer, of course it was. 'Didn't realize you were such a master of disguise,' I said.

'Seemed a good idea to present a different facade,' he said.

'The plot is thickening.'

Joey raised his black eyebrows. 'This is assuming that the Tiepolo sketch has something to do with the kidnapping.'

'Has to have.'

'I wonder where the principal is.'

'I wonder *who* the principal is.'

The auctioneer was banging his gavel, preparing us all for

Lot One, a fine example of a late-Victorian *epergne*, having a wide, crimped-edge bowl, a tall central trumpet and three side trumpets, nicely etched. Or so it said in the catalogue. If you like that sort of thing, it wasn't half bad.

We waited with some impatience for Lot 134. Joey said, 'I'm going to exercise my masculine charms on the sales office, see if I can find out who the seller is.'

'Take Sandro with you,' I said. 'That bright hair marks him out.'

'I'll lend him my watch cap. Come on, guy, let's go.'

The two of them headed off while I stayed put, pulling a scarf round my face and pushing my hair about, hoping not to be recognized. As we inched towards Lot 134, there was a strange wavelet of movement as the men in flat caps moved closer to the folder which held the miscellaneous drawings. By now, two women had joined them, both wearing shrouding coats, with, in one case, a scarf covering her hair, and in the other a black trilby.

Finally, Lot 133 was gavelled down and one of the cloth-coated men eased the small portfolio on to an easel and swung wide the two sides.

'Miscellaneous drawings,' the auctioneer intoned. 'Attributed to various artists, no records available. To be sold as a single lot. What am I bid? A hundred? Eighty? Sixty?'

When he was down to fifteen pounds, the bidding started. Someone obviously either knew the value of at least one of the drawings or was prepared to take a punt on it. The bidding climbed higher and higher and the atmosphere in the room changed from a generalized sort of lethargy to a sudden sense of anticipatory excitement.

'Dunno what they're on about,' a man standing behind me said to his neighbour. 'I had a look earlier – just a bunch of little drawings. Reckon my five-year-old could do better than some of them.'

'Yer,' said his companion. 'What you after, then?'

'Lot two hundred and twenty-three,' the man said. 'Picture of a shepherdess and some sheep. Could make a nice little profit on that if it goes for the right price.'

'Doesn't go, you mean!' The two of them chortled.

Meanwhile, at £1800, the bidding for the miscellaneous drawings had slowed down. 'Blimey,' said one of the men behind me. 'Musta bin something in there I didn't pick up on.'

'They're still bidding,' said his friend. 'Go on, have a go.'

'At that price? You gotta be kidding.'

'I'm bid one thousand nine hundred pounds,' said the auctioneer. 'Are there any more – two thousand I'm bid at the back. Two thousand . . . any advance on two thousand? Two thousand five hundred. Three. Three thousand five. And four. Four and a half. Five . . .'

He finally banged down his gavel at £6700 and we all craned behind us to see who had offered such an enormous winning bid. Hard to say, really, since everyone behind me was looking poker-faced, pretending to be waiting for the next lot. The auctioneer himself seemed a trifle stunned.

Six thousand pounds plus. It was a tidy sum, especially for a small place like this one, but not a whole heap of money, given that I knew what the sketch purported to be. What would the Marchese say if he knew what his drawing had gone for? I wondered even more who it was that had put the drawing up for auction.

Maybe Joey had found out. 'Want the bad news or the bad news?' he asked, when I left the hall and found him waiting with Sandro by the front door.

'The bad,' I said.

'Whoever's selling it is operating under some kind of anonymous umbrella company.'

'And the bad?'

'It's an Italian name. Italartico. Whether it exists or not is something we can find out later.'

I immediately thought of Renzo Vitale. All of a sudden, it seemed so obvious. Like me, he would have been sent copies of catalogues from all over the world. Like me, he would have leafed through them. Unlike me, he might well have been searching for anything that might resemble a Tiepolo drawing. And having found it, would have either come himself, or sent a representative to bid for it. On the other hand, how was he going to dispose of it? As soon as anyone knowledgeable saw it up for sale, Cesare, I had no doubt, would have been informed. And how did it relate, if at all, to Sandro's abduction?

'Any Italians passed this way?' I asked.

Sandro and Joey shrugged.

'Not so we noticed.'

'I suppose we might as well drive back,' I said. I was anxious to get home in order to do some intensive research on my computer. As I lowered myself into the passenger seat of Sandro's car, I looked back. The woman in the pseudo-flat tweed cap was standing just outside the auction house's doors, staring at me. No mop of greying curls this time, but I recognized her at once. She hadn't managed to get the Tiepolo drawing from the Major but I had no doubt that the man who'd lurched into me in the Fox and Hounds was working with her. I raised my hand ironically. Six thousand pounds, minus fees, wasn't a big return for the amount of work involved in stealing it.

It was around six o'clock when I got home, where I went straight over to my machine without even taking my jacket off. I switched on and keyed in Italartico.

A series of references popped up, and among them I was gratified but unsurprised to see the name of Vitali Fratelli. Underlined and in blue. I clicked on the name and, sure enough, there was Lorenzo Vitali. And, to my surprise, the Marchesa Allegra. Did *she* know about the missing Tiepolos? Had there been dirty work at the crossroads somewhere in there? How much of a connection could there possibly be between her and Renzo? Despite the fact that Renzo had all the hallmarks of a villain, he was unlikely to have been behind the theft of the sketch from my shoulder bag – a theft which had obviously been targeted, which meant I was being or had been watched – because if he had, why bother to put it up for auction when he could just have kept it or sold it for much more later in one of the clandestine operations of which I was sure he was a master? But even if he was behind the theft, I couldn't really see the logic behind the sale at auction. He could just have kept it and then attempted to sell it on the art markets.

But if it wasn't him, who was it? In the end, it didn't matter who had bought it. Much more important was who was selling it. And if Joey Preston couldn't coax anything more than a company name out of the auction house, I very much doubted that I would succeed where he had failed.

At least I was no longer in possession of the drawing. And neither was the Major. So I could sleep easy. I needn't expect any more nasty surprises.

TWENTY

There were twenty-six of us, a mixture of people on the
board or patrons of La Fenice and those who administer
the Venice in Peril funds, both here and in England.
With much ceremony, our gold-bedecked soup plates had been
borne away and small dishes of lemon sorbet placed in front
of us along with small golden spoons. The Marchesa had really
pulled out all the stops to entertain this group. She sat at the
head of a long table, all angular collarbones and heavy black
velvet, despite the fact that early summer was greening the
city and gilding the domes and towers. She wore a diamond
necklace and matching diamond earrings, and on her delicately
bony hands was the doge's ring, its emerald stone glinting in
the light from five elaborate candelabra set along the spread
of white damask which stretched between her and her husband.
I wondered if she'd been aware that it had turned up in a
London pawnshop and been redeemed by her dutiful nephew.

The Marchese was equally magnificent in an immaculate
dinner jacket over a double-breasted waistcoat with a heavy
gold watch-chain looped across his chest, and some kind of
bejewelled decoration hanging round his neck from a maroon
ribbon of silk moiré. The other guests were equally splendid,
including, I liked to think, myself. I'd borrowed a beautiful
evening gown of yellow silk embroidered with green and white
lilies from my Swedish sister-in-law and had my hair styled
by someone at the Hotel Danieli where I was being put up at
the Marchese's expense. Personally, I thought I looked pretty
damn cool. I only wished Sam Willoughby could see me now
– he might have second thoughts about that jillaroo of his. I
was sorry that at the last minute Sandro had not been able to
be here, but that wasn't going to prevent my enjoying myself.

I was seated between a Venice in Peril person on my right
hand and one of the opera house's big wigs on my left. I knew
he was a big wig because he told me so. He also told me that

without the Marchesa Allegra, La Fenice would be in poorer shape than it currently was. 'She is a tireless patron,' he told me ponderously. 'And a most generous and indefatigable fundraiser.'

I nodded sagely. It seemed to have been enough response.

'As I'm sure you are aware, signorina, the opera house was burned down some years ago and it has cost millions to rebuild.'

'It was arson, wasn't it?' I asked.

'Sadly it was. Two electricians, cousins, who were falling behind in their renovation work, couldn't afford the penalties and thought the best solution would be to burn the place down. Disgraceful!'

'They got them both in the end, I believe.'

'They did indeed.'

Dishes were removed. More plates appeared. Waiters moved from person to person, offering veal slices in a green sauce, asparagus, tiny potato puffs, slender green beans. It was all delicious. There was cheese, too, if anyone wanted it, and a radicchio and avocado salad with a minty kind of dressing.

My neighbour on the left-hand side smiled benignly. 'I understand you will be joining us tomorrow evening, after the performance.'

'I'm really looking forward to it,' I said.

'It should be a good evening. The production has been widely praised.'

'So I've heard.'

After we'd had coffee in a reception room almost as grand as the Doge's Palace, there was a general shifting and stirring as people prepared to take their leave. I would see some of them the following evening and thought I outdid myself in graciousness, something I'm not usually good at.

A servant appeared at my elbow to tell me that a water taxi was waiting for me at the steps of the *palazzo* to return me to my hotel. Everything had been thought of. When I had disembarked from the taxi and entered the grandiose lobby to get hold of my key, I was handed a note which I took up to my suite. I removed Lena's beautiful dress, changed into my dressing gown, poured myself a very wee dram and sat down to read it.

Twin boys, it said. *All fine.*

Only my brother Hereward could be so succinct about such a momentous event. I felt it was too late to telephone my parents. And Sam wasn't around, or I could have shared the news with him.

I lifted my glass to the ceiling and laughed aloud. 'Here's to you all,' I said.

As I fell asleep, I wondered what archaic names would be bestowed on the poor little lads.

During the night, I woke. My brain churned over the events of the past few weeks. Faces streamed through my head: Sandro, Katy Pasqualin, Sam Willoughby and his girlfriend, the Jago twins, Laura the model, Bianca, Suzy Hartley Heywood and her brother, my parents, my brother and his twins. Connections were still to be made, but with the list of interrelationships which Sandro had given me some time before, I already had all the information I needed to work out the causes behind the sequence of events which seemed to have begun at his dinner party in his uncle's place, though clearly they had been ongoing for years before that.

The Marchese had booked me a suite whose windows looked across the canal to the Palladian splendours of San Giorgio Maggiore, with a giant double bed all to myself. Sipping a cup of tea brought up by room service, I stood at the window and watched the traffic passing up and down the canal. At this time of day it was mostly commercial: vast piles of vinyl piping, plastic-wrapped loads of bricks, fruit and vegetables on their way to the markets, fish and meat in huge see-through boxes. Untended gondolas rocked with the movement of the water.

It was a golden-bright day, the water sparkling, the sky a true Tiepolo cobalt blue. I spent the day walking round the city, stopping in various churches as I passed them. Names rang like bells: Guardi. Giorgione. Bellini. Carpaccio. On and on they sounded in my head. By the evening I was sated. For once I wasn't there for work, just to enjoy a wallow in the whole Venetian ambience. Beneath the calm waters of the lagoon, the heart-stopping beauty, the centuries of civilization, lurked decadence and corruption, generation after generation of cruel deeds and scandalous vice. But what was going to change that? Certainly not me, not today, not ever.

I made a telephone call. Sent an email. Poured a quick medicinal whisky. Then I lingered in the luxurious marble tub, keeping my newly done hair dry – I'd had it done for the second time in two days! – then I shimmied into another of Lena's evening frocks, and I was ready. I planned to wear flatties to walk the relatively short distance to the opera house then duck into a nearby doorway and change into heels.

The Marchesa was waiting for me when I went through the doors of the opera house. A festive atmosphere filled the lobby. Handsome men, gorgeous women, the heady scent of a dozen expensive perfumes, mixed with the more subtle bouquet of cashmere, silk, chiffon and leather.

'Ah,' she said. She tucked my hand into her arm. 'I'm so glad you could come. This is by way of being a truly gala evening.'

'I'm already enjoying it.'

'You must be aware of how grateful we all are for your help in rescuing our beloved Sandro.'

'Well, I—'

'I'm sorry we haven't had time to get better acquainted, Alessandra. As always, I have so many difficulties to overcome and problems to solve, which take up . . .' She patted my hand. 'But not tonight, is that not so?'

'I hope so. Absolutely.' The whites showed all round the irises of her eyes, as though she were a mare about to bolt. Excitement, I guessed. After all, for once this was *her* show, and not her husband's.

As we proceeded towards the stairs, she nodded and smiled, even stopped occasionally to introduce me, without explaining who I was. How many of them even knew that Sandro had been held to ransom, let alone that I had been instrumental in freeing him? Not that I wanted any share of the glory: Joey Preston deserved at least as much of that as I did.

The performance was tear-jerkingly good. An unportly Alfredo with a voice like a god, a Violetta who believably wrung the heart as she moved towards her death from consumption. I was filled to the brim as I followed Allegra – as she had asked me to call her – towards the reception immediately after the final fall of the curtain. Gilt plasterwork, marble pillars, swags of red velvet, paintings, mirrors. It was all so Venetian and over-the-top. I loved it.

Glasses of champagne circulated. Huge trays of hors d'oeuvres were carried round. Conversation was operatic and knowledgeable. I wondered if I could live full-time in Venice but this kind of event – at least ones to which I'd be invited – would be few and far between. The rest of the time my life wouldn't be that different from what it already was. I talked to several interesting people and established some connections which I knew would be useful in the future.

Finally the Marchesa – I really couldn't think of her as Allegra – suggested that it was time to go. More than, I supposed, since nearly everyone else had left, but she had probably had to organize the party and wanted to make sure that all was in order.

Outside, it was chilly and damp, the cobbles slick under our feet. She had insisted on walking me back to the hotel, saying she could get a water taxi from there, so we strolled along the *riva*, close to the wind-chopped waters of the canal. The streets had emptied by now, but voices could still be heard in the distance. It was difficult to walk on the slippery pavements in heels and I was about to ask Allegra to give me an arm to lean on while I got into my flatties when I was suddenly aware of movement behind me, a blur of arms and hands, a glint of light. Something hard luckily missed the back of my head and landed agonizingly on my shoulder. At the same time, the Marchesa put out her hand and pushed hard against me. I only avoided being knocked into the canal by dropping to the ground, howling with pain. I heard the sound of running footsteps, caught a diamond flash as a man rushed past me, heard Allegra cursing.

'Gotcha!'

I'm pretty self-sufficient. I like to think I can take care of myself in most situations, however tricky. But I've never been so glad to hear a familiar voice as I was at the sound of Joey

Preston's shout. Then more footsteps as three or four people emerged from side streets and rushed to help us.

'You're hurting me.' At her most haughty, the Marchesa tried to shake off Joey's restraining hands, but it was no good. He had her in a tight grip, while the others stared at the two of them, murmuring among themselves.

'Couldn't believe my eyes!'

'I swear she was trying to push that other woman into the canal!'

'There was a man with a *weapon* in his hand.'

'. . . attacked that poor girl . . .'

'Isn't that the Marchesa de . . .?'

'Unbelievable.'

'Will you all please leave us alone,' the Marchesa said imperiously. 'There was almost an accident just now. That's all you saw. Luckily this gentleman happened to be right there to help or someone would have gone into the canal.'

'And we all know who,' Joey said grimly.

'I've seen her before,' someone directly behind me muttered. 'At the casino.'

By now, I was on my feet, clutching at my shoulder. Lena's dress was wet and muddy: I hoped it would clean up when I got back to England.

A chap in evening dress approached. 'The police will be here any minute,' he said. He thrust a card into my hand. 'In case you need to get in touch.'

'Thank you.' I had no idea why I might need to contact him. 'How very kind.' Gracious to the end, that was me.

It was much later that Joey and I returned to my suite, after several hours of questioning by the police. In that strange Italian way (or is it just in Venice?) the Marchesa had been allowed to return to her apartment, though clearly guilty of some kind of assault. Fair enough, since apart from my shoulder, there was little to accuse her of. After all, it could have been, as she insisted, an accident. The fact that the skin had already turned a fine shade of purple-blue and I was sure that at least one bone had been fractured, was not of interest.

At the hotel, despite the lateness of the hour, the staff were attentive almost to the point of obsequiousness. But why not? Everyone could do with a spot of obsequious now and then. The reception at the opera house seemed a long time ago so we ordered up an array of cold antipasti and a bottle of Chianti Classico Gran. Perfect.

TWENTY-ONE

'I'm still not sure how it all went down,' Joey said. 'Or why.'
It was three days after our return from Venice, and we had arranged to meet up at a restaurant in Soho which Joey swore produced the best Italian food outside Italy. 'I thought we were keeping our beady eyes fixed on that fossilized mistress. Valentina Thingy.'

'Apart from trying to cling desperately to her lost youth, she had nothing to do with any of it. It was the Marchesa all along,' I said.

'I'm realizing that. But why?'

'I almost feel sorry for her,' I said. 'Her husband is a dictatorial, overbearing bastard. Any self-esteem she might once have had was long ago knocked out of her by his campaign of sneering and belittlement. And when he discovered that she couldn't provide him with an heir . . .' I speared a tiny pastry stuffed with artichoke heart and some kind of creamy cheese. Then speared another. 'Mmm . . . the poor woman. I can't help feeling sorry for her although she's an extortionist, a blackmailer and a murderer.'

'Murderer? You mean Katy Pasqualin?'

'It's obvious when you think about it. Katy had clearly caught the woman removing precious bits and pieces but, since they were from her own *appartamento*, she didn't at first think anything of it. When Sandro mentioned seeing the doge's ring in the pawnshop, Katy was on to it like a terrier on to a rat. *Pay up, or I tell your husband what you've been doing.*'

'So she dropped in on Katy one evening, found her conveniently in the bath and held her under until the girl died. Given that Allegra was more or less Katy's aunt, I'm sure she was able to get hold of a key to let herself in. And if any of her prints were found, well, why not? Because of the family ties, and the fact that the two women were close, she was round there all the time when she was in England.'

'And kidnapping Sandro?'

'I've absolutely no doubt that she will be heavily implicated.'

'And she was in it for the money.'

'That's all she wanted. She herself had lost most of hers at the casino. Not because she was a gambling addict – simply in an effort to win. And if her husband had discovered what she was up to . . .' I shrugged. 'There would have been hell to pay.'

'More than hell, from what you've said.'

'It wasn't just the money, of course. It was the prestige as well. A marchese isn't that high up the aristocratic pecking order, but it does give her quite a bit of kudos, to make up for the humiliations of her home life. And then there was the opera house. From what I was told at the reception, she was one of the most generous sponsors. Where was she getting the money from?'

'My mother is from Milano, and she always goes on about the sleaze and deceit underneath the gold and the glamour of Venice,' Joey said. 'I guess she must have been right.'

'The point about the ransom money was that if the plan had gone right, she would have been able to pocket most of it, after paying off the minions.'

'Seems a bit odd that she would have underworld connections.'

I laughed. 'It took me a while and some phone calls to figure it out. Years ago, there was a bit of a scandal when the Marchese seduced a young Scandinavian *au pair* girl and got her pregnant. There was a hell of a fuss, money changed hands and the girl went back home to Stockholm, Oslo, wherever. Cesare never knew about the pregnancy, but his wife did. She went to the girl's home town and helped her out. Kept an eye on her over the years. And when the kid had grown up and was looking for a job, she found him one in Venice. She probably saw it as a deliciously subtle revenge on her cheating husband. There is indeed an heir who is his own flesh and blood, to carry on the family name. It didn't matter that he doesn't know. In fact, most of the fun comes from the fact that he doesn't, and never will.'

'Very Machiavellian.'

'Agreed. Of course the bald guy – the Norwegian son – would do anything for her, and often did, even if it involved breaking the law, inflicting GBH, perhaps even killing.'

'I take it that the intention was for you to be quietly disposed of that evening after the opera.'

'Of course. And later, she might have come after you. After all, because of us, she lost twenty million euros.' I vividly remembered Sandro saying 'Vengeance is mine!' even if he was wrong.

There were newspapers on a rack on the wall of the restaurant. English and Italian. While the waiter brought us coffee, Joey stood up and brought over a copy of *Corriere della Sera*. The front page was taken up with some tortuous Italian political scandal which I couldn't be bothered to unravel, though Joey was riveted. When he turned to the second and third pages, he went still. 'Oh my God!' he said.

'What?'

'You won't believe this, but she's killed herself . . . or that's what it looks like, anyway. After she got home the other night, according to the housekeeper, she went out again, and this morning they fished her out of the Canale di San Marco. Spotted by a passing *vaporetto* bringing people in to start their day's work.'

'Are you talking about the Marchesa?'

'The very same.'

I said nothing. I recalled the way the whites of her eyes showed; it was obvious that the woman had been in a state of acute nervous tension, probably from knowing that after the performance, she planned to kill me. Despite her murderous plans, I felt slightly sorry for her. I imagine that the possibility of a public enquiry into what had happened that night, even if it hadn't led to any kind of prosecution, would have so undermined her fragile self-esteem, with the cream of Venetian society aware of what she'd tried to do, and the scandal of it all, that she had been persuaded she really had no other option. It seemed to me that her husband was in large measure to blame. But undoubtedly he would immediately become eligible marriage material, the object of avarice and pity. Good luck to the bastard. I forced myself to remember that he had appeared genuinely concerned about Sandro's wellbeing when we were on Burano.

I was tired by the time I got back to Longbury. There were ships anchored on the horizon, lights blazing in the darkness and a pale shaving of moon stood in the sky, surrounded by stars. I parked my car beneath the windows of my flat and sat still for some moments.

I wanted Sam Willoughby. I admitted it. Without him around, my life was thin. Not meaningless, since I had my work, my friends, my family – which now included two new babies. But I had no one to share it all with. No one to eat with or laugh with. No one to give me meaning – or to whom I could give meaning. I was well aware of the tactics he'd been employing over the weeks, to make me reach the conclusion that I needed him. That I loved him.

Tomorrow I would swallow my pride and email him. Ask how he was, whether he was enjoying himself, when he was coming home. Although I doubted it, I might even manage to tell him I missed him. Because I did. I really did.

Finally I climbed out of my car, house keys in hand. A salty little breeze was blowing in off the sea. The stars were very bright. Somewhere nearby a car door slammed. I turned, tensing. And then, miraculously, Sam was there, walking towards me. Bigger than I remembered him. More . . . *assured.* 'Sam,' I said. My limbs were melting.

'I'm just back from New Zealand,' he said. 'I came straight here from the airport.'

'Sam . . .' I said. Tomorrow there'd be questions. They could wait. 'Oh, Sam . . .'

He held me against his chest. 'Sssh,' he said. 'Sssh, my darling.' He pulled me into his arms. His heart was beating like a drum.

As I wrapped my own around him, he put a finger under my chin and tilted my face up to his. He closed his eyes. 'Kiss me, Quick,' he said.

So I did. Yes, I did.